The Darl

Isabelle Nettle

PERIPETEIA PRESS

Published by Peripeteia Press Ltd.

First published January 2021

ISBN: 978-1-913577-99-5

Check out our A-level English Literature website, peripeteia.webs.com

A huge thank you must go to several people. Firstly, to my grandparents, Anne and Colin Marsh, for all the time they spent reading and proofreading chapters again and again. Secondly, to my parents for constantly discussing ideas, talking me out of plot lines that would never have worked, and for putting up with all the time I spent writing. Finally, to Neil Bowen, for reading, editing, publishing, and making it all happen.

The Darkness

Chapter One

The walls were white. As were the floors, the ceilings, and the doors that were evenly spaced along the length of the corridors. White overalls were worn during Working Days and white leisure clothes during Non-Working Days. However, contrary to popular belief, this was not designed to ensure that Revolutionaries and citizens of the Subterrane could be swiftly distinguished between in case of a break-in. It was simply because the iconic colour had become a symbol of the change in lifestyle from that of the Surface.

Each citizen of the Subterrane had up to two 'Non-Working Days' or 'NWDs' per week, during which they would attend a compulsory lecture. These either concerned their specific placement or the Subterrane in general, after which they were occasionally given a duty or short task to complete depending on their rank within their allocated line of work. Then, after a short break, they would proceed either to their assigned Recreational Pod where they would spend the afternoon with other citizens of a similar age and domain, or to previously scheduled monthly medical check-ups.

Eleanor was not entirely certain of how she had ended up at the Zone Six entrance to the Tunnel; most likely she had walked to the West Side Elevators on Level Seventeen, before taking one up to Level Zero. And, although the Tunnel wasn't and had never been out of bounds - in fact, visits to the Tunnel were widely encouraged - she still felt strangely uneasy.

The Tunnel was now the only existing bridge between the Zone Six Subterrane and the Surface, and had consequently played a huge role in the history of the Subterrane.

How the Subterrane had become their home was known in immense detail to all citizens - after all, what would be the point in blurring a past that the majority of them had lived through merely eighteen years ago? Indeed, the Non-Working Day 9 a.m. lectures often outlined the events of those few fateful early hours of 1st January 2047 and how humanity was rescued, thanks to the protection and generosity of the Thirteen Founders:

"At midnight on the 1st January 2047, fireworks had been exploding over the River Thames, cascading a colourful display onto the captivated spectators below. And then, all across the world, a different noise had been heard. At first, it was presumed to be another kind of firework. But, as the distinct sound of gunfire grew more insistent, people began to run and chaos ensued. Then, one person at a time, an intriguing rumour seemed to spread through the panicked crowds, although none knew who it had come from. But it told all those who would listen, that there were underground bunkers not too far away. Thousands of people from all countries across the world eagerly joined the surge of people piling into each of the hidden Tunnels that led to the underground safe houses. After that, each of the Tunnels were sealed for the citizens' own safety. Eighteen years later and it still wasn't safe to leave."

She wandered over to the Tunnel entrance because, although a little anxious, Eleanor hadn't visited it in several years. Looking around, she took in the simple structure of the entrance; a smooth wall-like fortification formed what seemed to be a seamless dead end to the corridor. However Eleanor, like all other citizens, knew the end of the corridor to be a well-hidden, thoroughly sealed door. Then, purely out of curiosity, she absent-mindedly reached out her hand and trailed her fingers along the wall until she reached the sealed end.

It was then that she felt a minuscule gap between the two partitions; it was almost unnoticeable except for when her fingers brushed across it. Frowning slightly, she pushed against the concealed door - expecting nothing to happen - until the wall suddenly seemed to move a little. She would, of course, have to report that later. But, taking a step back, she stared in awe at the small opening that had now formed where the gap had been. Giving the door another, stronger push, she opened it enough to allow herself to slip through and then stopped, suddenly afraid of what she was about to do.

Ever since it had been sealed off, the entrance to the Zone Six Tunnel had never been reopened. Everyone knew that Revolutionaries ran rampant on the surface and that it was for the wellbeing and security of the citizens that the Tunnel had been sealed off in the first place. Being the prime duty of the Thirteen Founders to keep their people safe, closing the exits from the Subterrane had been the only plausible way to ensure that this safety continued.

Eleanor cautiously peered through the opening, almost afraid of what she might see on the other side. But, used to the vivid whiteness of the Subterrane, her eyes could make out nothing in the darkness. She took a deep breath, summed up all of her courage, and was about to steal through the gap when she heard a noise and stopped short. Listening intently, she waited in absolute silence. There it was again - a faint rattle, then a clunking sound coming from above. Springing back from the door in alarm, she shut it as best she could before sprinting back down the deserted corridor to the West Side Elevators. Only as the doors of the central elevator were closing did she dare look back, just in time to see the fingers of a large hand reaching through the gap and pulling the door wide open.

***

Eleanor was not the sort of girl who was often found breaking the rules or in awkward and unfamiliar situations - in fact, she regularly made an effort to avoid such encounters. Which was why she had worked herself up into such a state, going round and round in endless circles inside her head. Should I report it? she thought to herself, wishing she knew what to do. If only there was a procedure for this kind of thing... Yes, I should definitely tell someone about it. Something bad could happen, otherwise. Her mind was momentarily made up, until yet another thought entered it. ...But it's my fault, isn't it? I pushed the door open, so surely I'll get into trouble... That's it! I definitely mustn't tell anyone about it. But what if it was a Revolutionary? And what if they're dangerous! If someone gets hurt it would technically be my fault, so-

"Watch where you're going, Ellie!" a voice exclaimed abruptly, as

Eleanor stepped from the central West Side Elevator and narrowly avoided colliding with a tall, textbook-laden brunette.

"Sorry, Katy," she blurted out apologetically, moving to the side as the girl entered the elevator.

"It's fine - don't worry about it," Katy shook her head reassuringly, but was met with Eleanor's somewhat distracted silence. "Are you feeling okay?"

"I, um, I..." Eleanor considered confiding in Katy, but then thought better of it and merely shrugged. "Yes, I'm fine."

"Are you sure?" Katy persisted whilst scanning her thumb and pressing the button for Level Twelve. "You're looking a bit pale," she added with a frown.

"Really," Eleanor said, stepping back from the elevator. "I'm okay."

The doors closed just in time to cut Katy off before she had the chance to ask anything else.

Upon reaching the door to Recreational Pod 32, Eleanor leant against the wall and allowed herself a few minutes to decide which of her many excuses would be most believable. Maybe no one will ask where I've been or why I'm late, Eleanor thought, pinching her cheeks in an attempt to restore a little colour to them. Or I could say I wasn't feeling well so I went to the Medical Centre. But then they might check... she worried, thoroughly overthinking the situation.

As she stood leaning against the wall, a group emerged from another Recreational Pod - most likely on their way to the Educational Rooms on Level Twelve. After receiving a couple of disapproving looks from a few of them as they spotted her skulking suspiciously by the door, she straightened herself up, regained some composure and hurried inside the blindingly white room; to her relief, no one had even noticed that she was missing.

The fifty Recreational Pods were spread across the entirety of Level Eleven, with a single 'Allocation Office' occupying one of the pods beside the East Side Elevators, that was used for any severe complaints or in case any groups needed altering. Each Pod contained a number of chairs, as well as various beanbags and a large table. Each citizen was assigned to a particular Societal Group with others of similar interests or skills after completing their Placement Exams, just before they turned seventeen. Once placed within a group, a citizen would remain within it for at least the next five years, unless they were transferred to an entirely different line of work due to unsatisfactory performance or being ill-suited to their position.

There were two types of Societal Group. The first was a support-type group for those under full-time employment, giving them a way to maintain their morale and work ethic on Non-Working Days. The second type was a more full-time group for all those who had just completed their Placement Examinations. After completing the testing, each citizen of the Subterrane became a member of a particular Societal Group where they remained for an entire year before continuing with Specialised Education or receiving their official posting within the Society. Members of these full-time groups met six days a week, for anything between three and five hours. Two of these hours were occupied with various tasks or discussions to help the underground complex thrive, in which they would often help out in classrooms, gain experience in different areas of work, or help plan various events and meetings. The remaining time spent with Societal Groups was in the form of a discussion-like meeting, although the content of each session's meeting tended to vary from group to group. For the most part, Group Z617c dedicated most of their time to gossiping about unimportant matters, rather than discussing the fundamental values or whatnot, as well as completing projects and assignments on the few occasions that they were ever allocated any.

Every hour that was taken up by her Societal Group was considered by Eleanor to be a slight waste of time when, instead, she could be helping to improve the way their world worked. Although she was lucky in that most of the members of her Societal Group were extremely chatty, she occasionally found the discussions that took place within the meetings to be rather tedious. And whilst she didn't really mind the education work - although the children could occasionally be a little unruly and wild - she was generally still unable to determine the true purpose and need for the Societal Groups.

Eleanor spent the next hour with the other members of her group discussing the latest issues they were facing; namely that there was a leak in the hydroponics pipeline that had only been discovered that morning, and that there had been two sets of twins born in the previous week which, up until then, was completely unheard of.

"Ellie," the head of the group turned towards her as she made for an empty seat. "Have you had any problems this week? Or have you seen or heard anything interesting?"

Oh God, she thought to herself. He must know - he obviously does. He's just waiting for me to say it first. Surely this is my chance to own up and tell someone what I saw? Maybe I should. But what if I get in trouble for it? It's not like I meant to do it, after all...

Torn between two thoroughly different mindsets, she decided to reply in the most casual manner that she could muster: "Nothing out of the ordinary - or at least I don't think there was."

"Saskia? Anything?" the leader asked, turning his attention away from Eleanor who heaved a quiet sigh of relief.

"Not me personally, but have you heard about the white dye? I overheard someone saying that it might run out altogether in the next couple of years unless we find the means to make more!" Saskia replied dramatically, a mischievous twinkle in her eye as she subtly winked in Eleanor's direction; Saskia loved spreading false rumours.

Saskia was the sort of girl that didn't care what anybody thought of her - the sort of girl that would regularly skip the Anniversary Lectures, and then manage to get away with it, too. The type that often caused trouble, but was too smart to ever get caught or to even be considered a suspect in anything. It was the deciding factor for Eleanor - she was absolutely certain, now: She definitely had the worst taste in choosing friends.

"Yes - I overheard someone saying that this morning," one of the other girls added. Although, since she always claimed to have heard everything first, it was almost certain that she hadn't.

"What?" Another girl exclaimed. "But we can't - the white uniforms are… well, they're us! They're what our whole society is based on!"

And so, the absence of a renewable white dye source became the topic of discussion, for an entire hour. According to Saskia's misinformation, it seemed that in the years before the Evacuation, all the extensive planning that had gone on had not accounted for the volume of white dye needed to maintain their desired unique statement over the years. Consequently, there was an increased possibility that their iconic whiteness might one day soon fade to a dull, more muted grey.

Eleanor was forced to pinch her arm to keep herself from drifting off as they droned on about the highly insignificant matter. But her paranoid logic told her that if she showed a lack of interest in the goings-on of the Subterrane or if she seemed even a little distracted, then someone might suspect her of hiding something. So, by the time they were needed in the Educational Rooms, she had four, deep, half-moon shaped red marks on her forearm from where she had been digging in with her nails.

"I'm telling you," Saskia added as the discussion came to a close, her serious and concerned expression incredibly convincing. "One day soon, we're all going to look like mush."

Chapter Two

"Saskia and Ellie, could you two go to Educational Rooms 1216a and 1216b to help them with their preparation, please?" Dan asked.

"Sure," Saskia nodded.

"Great," he continued. "Lucy and Kate, can you go to Educational Rooms 1206a and 1206b to help them with Maths, English and History?"

"Okay," Kate replied.

"And Hugh, Luca and I will go to Educational Rooms 1212a and 1212b, and then 1213a and 1213b. What time shall we meet back here?" Dan paused to glance around the room, before looking at his watch. "Let's say in two hours," he instructed, confidently fulfilling his newly appointed role as their leader.

"Luca, that's when the big hand reaches the six and the little hand reaches the three," Hugh teased, playfully elbowing the short blonde boy beside him.

"Every single time," Luca said, rolling his eyes in response although he couldn't help but laugh. "I was only late once!"

"I'm pretty sure it was more than that," Lucy chipped in.

"It was not!"

"Is two hours long enough for everyone?" Dan continued, trying to refrain from joining in with their idiotic remarks.

Having received their orders, Saskia and Eleanor began to make for the West Elevators but, seeing that two were currently located all the way down on Level Eighteen and the other four were all on higher levels, they decided that the stairs would be quicker.

"Where were you earlier?" Saskia asked casually as they began the short descent. "I didn't see you at lunch either."

"Oh… It was nothing," Eleanor replied as she racked her brains for a sufficient response that Saskia might find vaguely believable. "I just wasn't hungry so I went back to my Pod for a bit, then lost track of time."

"Right," Saskia nodded her head as though she believed the unconvincing story. "It's just that you don't usually go back to your room during the day."

"I know, but I did today," Eleanor replied briskly, hoping that the conversation would end there.

"Yes, that's what you said. But it's strange, because I could have sworn that I knocked on your door earlier and you weren't there…"

"Oh, I wasn't there for very long," she fumbled. "I went to the Fitness Centre for a bit, after that."

"What a coincidence! I was in one of them for a bit," Saskia played along, although it was clear she knew Eleanor was lying. "Which one were you in?"

Each Residential Level also contained four small 'Fitness Centres' which were located in the far corners of the level. For those in full-time Societal Groups, attending an exercise session in one of the Fitness Centres was a compulsory activity that was to be completed six times throughout the week, at your own leisure and during your own time. For those under full-time employment, one exercise session was to be completed at some point during each Non-Working Day. And for all children between the ages of six and fifteen, visits to the Fitness Centres were undertaken every Monday, Wednesday and Friday within Educational Groups - this was because the Fitness Centres on Level Eighteen were slightly larger than those on other Levels.

"I was in…" Eleanor paused as she decided which to pick - she had at least a seventy five percent chance of choosing one that Saskia hadn't been in. "Centre Two," she said uncertainly.

"That's so weird!" Saskia burst out excitedly. "I was in centre two as well! Although... that's really odd, actually, because I'm sure I didn't see you in there. Unless I'm wrong, of course. Am I?"

"Are you what?"

"Am I wrong?" Saskia repeated.

"Ok - fine," Eleanor admitted: "You got me. Look, I'll tell you where I was, but you have to promise that you won't tell anyone else."

"Why not?"

"Because I don't think I was supposed to be there. You have to promise first, though!"

"Of course I won't tell anyone," Saskia promised, laughing at how nervous Eleanor seemed. "I'm impressed though - who would have thought that good little Ellie would be breaking the rules?"

"Keep your voice down!" Eleanor exclaimed, before dropping her voice to a whisper and adding more urgently: "Someone might hear you."

"Relax. There's no one here. Anyway, go on. Tell me what you were doing!" Saskia pleaded - she never had been one for suspense.

"Fine. So I... I went to see the Tunnel."-

"Why didn't you get me to come with you?"

"Well, it was kind of strange, actually," Eleanor remarked. "I didn't really realise I was going there until I got there."

"What d'you mean?"

"I just... I didn't mean to go there. I kind of just stumbled upon it by accident."

"Weirdo," Saskia said, poking her teasingly before pressing on in anticipation, eager to reach the more thrilling part of her escapade. "And? Then what?"

"What d'you mean, 'then what'?" Eleanor feigned disbelief at Saskia's disappointment, as she made up her mind not to reveal the whole truth, although she was well aware that it was a rather feeble alibi.

"You mean that's it? You only went to the Tunnel - which we're allowed to do anyway, I might add. Seriously? I was expecting something actually exciting," Saskia grumbled, thoroughly disappointed.

"You were really expecting me to have broken the rules that badly? How long have you known me?" Eleanor reminded her playfully as they made their way to their first assigned Educational Room.

"I shouldn't have even let it cross my mind." Saskia rolled her eyes as they reached the door to Educational Room 1216a and grudgingly entered. Unlike Eleanor, Saskia thoroughly detested all educational work, claiming that children were far too messy.

Educational Room 1216a, like all other Educational Rooms on Level Twelve, was rather large - around twice the size of a regular Recreational Pod. Each of the four walls within an Educational Room was decorated with relevant posters and information, such as phonetically sounding words and the simplest sums for nursery rooms, with times tables and commonly misspelt words for slightly older children. For those approaching their Placement Examinations, more complex formulas, linguistic techniques, and key historical dates and decisions lined the walls, along with an ominous poster that said nothing but the date of the upcoming exam in thick black lettering.

Beneath all the posters the walls were, of course, coated in a thick layer of plain yet strikingly bright white paint. The five wide rows of desks, however, were finished in a wood-like plastic with grey metal legs - supposedly similar to those that had existed on the Surface; consequently, they were often referred to as being 'retro'.

"Good afternoon, girls," the class teacher approached them with a broad smile firmly plastered across her lips. "And welcome back - we haven't seen you both for at least a couple of weeks."

"Sorry about that," Saskia apologised sweetly, before reeling off yet another lie. "We really wanted to come last week, but our Group Leader needed us assigned elsewhere. This is such a lovely class too, so we'll try to come more regularly from now on - when we have enough time, of course."

"That would be perfect, girls," the teacher replied gratefully. "Now, as I'm sure you're both aware, they've got their Placement Examinations in two weeks. I thought we could set you two up over there and then they can come up and ask you for help with anything they need or are unsure of. Does that sound alright with you?"

Placement Examinations were taken by all children just before they turned seventeen. They consisted of three tests: Mathematics, English, and History of the Subterrane (which focused on politics, government logistics and how the Subterrane functioned in general). The outcome of the tests would influence and often determine the child's future. If a high grade was achieved in Maths then they would most likely be considered for areas of work concerning technology and machinery. If a high grade was achieved in English then they were most likely to be considered for a teaching role, depending on their performance within their Societal Group work in the subsequent years. Or, they were sometimes considered for a slightly more creative position, such as in the textiles and manufacturing industries. If a high grade was achieved in History of the Subterrane, then it was likely that the child would be considered for a role within the Government, which was also the case if high grades were consistently achieved in all areas of the exams. Any of these could result in a child being selected as the Leader of their Societal Group in the following years.

"Ellie, let's set up a table," Saskia instructed bossily as she moved towards an empty desk.

Struggling slightly, the two girls managed to manoeuvre a table and two chairs to the corner before a small queue of animated and inquisitive-looking children formed a line in front of them.

Just as they settled into their chairs, Eleanor turned to Saskia with a frown. "Wait a minute, did you really go to the Fitness Centre earlier?"

"No," Saskia answered smiling mischievously, confused why Eleanor would even think to ask. "Why would I bother doing that? You really are too easy to read - I didn't even check your room."

"Of course you didn't," Eleanor smiled, shaking her head at her gullibility.

And, returning their concentration to the classroom, they each received their first clients: A tall boy for Saskia and a pale girl with cropped blonde hair for Eleanor.

"What can I help you with?" Eleanor asked, giving the young girl a warm smile.

"When did the building begin for the Tunnel?" the girl asked. "I can't remember."

"Now, just give me a minute," Eleanor began hesitantly. "I think it was... I think it was November - yes, November 2042," she replied. "Anything else?"

"No that's it, thanks," the girl said, before heading back to her desk at the far end of the third row.

"Who's next, then?" Eleanor called over to the children still waiting patiently in front of the table.

"What's the purpose of the Anniversary Speech?" a short yet eager boy asked, stepping forwards.

"I... you know, I had it - I've literally just forgotten," Eleanor wracked her brain in frustration, before turning and prodding Saskia's arm. "Saskia, what's the purpose of the anniversary speech?"

"It's to remind everyone of how grateful we should be that we were saved, so that it serves as a constant reminder to maintain a sense of gratitude and awareness amongst the citizens," she replied fluently; a textbook answer. "Come on Ellie, you know this - it's the easy stuff."

"I know, I just forgot," Eleanor added, shaking her head a little as she faced the boy again. "Sorry about that. Anything else?"

He shook his head and slowly walked away from the table, frantically scribbling her answer down in his worn and slightly scruffy yellow exercise book.

Next in line was a quiet girl who came shuffling up to the desk. She wore thick black glasses, with frames that were slightly too wide and too thick for her pale skin, and study overalls that seemed to hang a little too loosely on her arms.

"What do you need help with?" Eleanor asked, chewing on her thumbnail to overcome her embarrassment from the previous question.

"What happened to all the animals? Like all the pets? Where did they go?"

"That's an... unusual question - no one's ever asked me that before."

There was an awkward pause where the girl stared expectantly at Eleanor who seemed to have forgotten what she was supposed to be doing.

"Right, sorry," Eleanor said, suddenly emerging from her momentary daze. "I think that on the night of the evacuation, all animals that were brought into the Subterrane were taken to an area on Level Four - that's

17

the one dedicated to farming and stuff. I think that's where they've been housed ever since." The girl nodded avidly as Eleanor delivered her answer, then hurried back to her desk to copy it down before she forgot it.

Next came another boy, this time much taller than the first.

"What can I help you with?" Eleanor asked as the boy's face turned a little pink while he struggled to recall his question.

"I... um, oh - I remember!" he exclaimed suddenly. "Why was it necessary for us to leave the Surface?"

Eleanor sighed in relief before delivering the answer that had been drilled into her from an extremely early age; this one she did know.

"There was an imminent threat of war and it seemed extremely likely that it might involve some form of nuclear warfare - at least eventually. As a result, the Thirteen Founders took it upon themselves to evacuate the entire population into underground complexes to prevent the extinction of humanity." The boy nodded in response and wandered over to where a group of his friends stood in the queue. He was immediately ushered away by the class teacher, and slowly plodded back to his seat as he attempted to commit the answer to memory. As he did so, a ginger haired girl hurried over to Eleanor, her arm firmly linked with a friend's.

"How did the Founders know when to be ready for the evacuation?" she asked quietly, seeming to be slightly afraid of both Eleanor and Saskia.

"The Thirteen Founders, you mean?" Eleanor corrected her.

"Yes - sorry, the Thirteen Founders," the girl rectified hastily.

"I... they just knew that it could be needed at any moment and that they needed to be ready for when it was, I guess."

"But how did they know that the right time would come? How did they know that there would definitely be a war at some point?"

"Because no world is ever perfect," she replied. "Even if it might have seemed that the tensions within international relations were decreasing, if the Thirteen Founders hadn't been prepared then the entire human race could have been entirely wiped out without a single warning."

As the girls wandered away from the table, Eleanor couldn't help but wonder if her words were, in actual fact, completely true. No world can ever be perfect - perhaps not even the Founders' manufactured one.

***

An hour later, after completing their question-and-answer sessions in Room 1216a, and their mentoring in Room 1216b, Eleanor and Saskia began to make their way towards the East Side Elevators and then down to Eleanor's Individual Pod on Level Seventeen.

The eight hundred and forty Individual Pods were spread across five Residential Levels within the Subterrane and were allocated by age groups. All rooms for Designated Senior citizens were located on Level Thirteen, as well as a few Pods that were set aside for carers. All those between the ages of fifty-one and sixty-three were allocated a Pod on Level Fourteen; all those between the ages of thirty-eight and fifty were housed on Level Fifteen; all those between the ages of twenty-three and thirty-seven were on Level Sixteen, and all those between sixteen and twenty-two were allocated a Pod on Level Seventeen. Every child under the age of sixteen was allocated a Pod on Level Eighteen, which was also shared with either one or two other children, with teachers' Pods dotted along each corridor and several large nurseries for younger children. Each floor contained three long corridors which stretched between the East and West Side Elevators, with fifty-six Pods on each corridor and a total of one hundred and sixty-eight Pods on each floor, except for Level Eighteen which consisted of fewer but larger Pods.

They were just about to step inside the central elevator when a large group, that they presumed to be Protectors of some sort, emerged from a Recreational Pod and strode past them into the lift, each armed with some kind of weapon.

The Protectors were made up of more elite citizens, most of whom had previously been in the army or police services, although it was also possible to be trained specifically for the role. The purpose of Protectors was, first and foremost, to protect the citizens of the Subterrane in case of any break-ins or intrusions of any kind, but they were also often in charge of crowd control for events such as the Anniversary Lecture and other important announcements that took place throughout the year.

"Sorry girls," one of them began, giving Saskia a strangely friendly smile - almost as though they had met before. "We're going to need these elevators, if you wouldn't mind using the West Side ones."

"Sure," Saskia shrugged, seemingly unfazed by their weapons. "Where are you heading?"

"Sorry - that's classified," the Protector answered with a subtle glance towards Eleanor, as he strode into the elevator on the right-hand side with a handful of the other Protectors.

With the elevators having begun their ascents, Saskia turned to Eleanor in excitement as they crossed Level Eleven to the West Side Elevators. "Where do you think they're going?"

"I've no idea. Maybe they've come from a meeting - or I suppose they might have Societal Groups too. It would make sense," Eleanor acknowledged.

"I guess so... But I want to know where they're going. Why d'you think it's classified?" Saskia was bubbling with the curiosity of an over-excited child.

"I've no idea. I suppose they could have lied," Eleanor answered honestly, unable to conjure up a reason, until she suggested: "Maybe they just wanted the elevator?"

"Or what if they're headed to Level One?" Saskia exclaimed suddenly as they began climbing the stairs. "Imagine if they are!"

"Why? What do you think's on Level One?" Eleanor asked curiously. Strangely, she couldn't remember them ever discussing it before.

Saskia paused for a moment as she thought, cocking her head to the side. Looking over at Eleanor again, she smiled her impish grin.-

"Well, personally, I think that there's a torture chamber up there that you get taken to if you do something terrible or become too dangerous for the Founders to deal with," she began. "Instead of making an example of you and telling others what you've done wrong, you just disappear so that no one even remembers who you are."

"That wouldn't work," Eleanor laughed at Saskia's extraordinarily changeable mood. "People wouldn't just forget who you are!"

"You'd be surprised at how much people are capable of forgetting," Saskia stared into the distance distractedly.

"And what makes you so sure of that?" Eleanor asked, smiling as she nudged Saskia in an attempt to restore her humour.

"I've... I've read stuff about it," she admitted rather distantly.

"Really? You've read stuff about forgetting things? I don't remember anything like that being in the textbooks."

"It wasn't in a textbook."

"I didn't even realise we had any other books," Eleanor laughed. "What was it about?"

"It was... it was ages ago. I can't really remember much," Saskia replied dismissively, clearly not wanting to give away the details.

"Oh okay," Eleanor replied slowly.

They continued to climb the stairs in silence until Saskia finally burst through it, her bubbly attitude completely restored.

"So what do you want to do now? We've got half an hour until dinner."

"I don't mind, really. Up to you," Eleanor replied, still slightly unsure at what their previous conversation had revealed, but not wanting to bring it up again. "We can go to my Pod for a while?"

"Maybe... But, seeing as you said it's up to me, why don't you show me your Tunnel?"

"It's not my Tunnel," Eleanor laughed, then, realising that Saskia was serious, burst out: "What? Are you crazy?"

"We're allowed to, you know. We wouldn't be breaking any rules. Anyway," Saskia teased, "either you come with me, or I go myself. The choice is yours, really."

"Fine," Eleanor replied reluctantly. "But just know that I hate you," she added for consolation, as they stepped into the closest West Side Elevator and Saskia scanned her thumb, then reached out her finger to press the button marked '0'. But, annoyingly, it was impossible for her to stay mad at Saskia for very long.

In just under six seconds they reached Level Zero, with a considerable amount of hyperventilating from Eleanor and a rather excessive amount of laughing from Saskia. As the elevator doors slid open, Saskia wandered out into the vast corridor and ran her eyes over the bare walls, as though studying them intently.

"See? It's not that bad up here!" Saskia laughed as they got out of the elevator. "It's very strange though, isn't it?"

"I guess," Eleanor replied quietly.

"It always freaks me out, a little," Saskia continued studying the corridor almost as though she hadn't heard Eleanor. "The blank walls, the low ceiling and the air's so light up here! It almost makes me dizzy."

"When were you last here?" Eleanor interrupted Saskia's chain of thought.

"It must have been a while ago. I never come here very often - I've probably only ever been a couple of times," she answered quickly before turning away and heading further down the corridor. "Oh my God - look!" she exclaimed in astonishment, as they neared the entrance to the Tunnel. "It's slightly open!"

"That's strange," Eleanor replied unconvincingly, although she had known it would be. "Maybe it's supposed to be like that?"

"Of course it's not," Saskia answered matter-of-factly, turning her focus back towards the door, but not before giving Eleanor a questioning look. "I wonder how it happened - maybe someone broke in!"

"Or maybe the seal just got old over time? It's probably just deteriorated," Eleanor suggested. "It must be - what, almost twenty years old?"

"Well, either way we'll still have to report it," Saskia remarked, unsure why Eleanor didn't share in her enthusiasm.

"But won't they suspect us of opening it?" Eleanor asked, peering closer at the door which seemed to be slightly more ajar than when she had left it.

"Of course not. No one would suspect us," Saskia replied, as though it was obvious.

"But what if... what if someone saw me here earlier?"

"So what if they did? You weren't anywhere near the door!" Saskia attempted to reassure her, whilst doing the exact opposite.

"Yeah, but…"

"The only reason that they would possibly suspect you would be if the security cameras saw you going through the door, or maybe if you were actually touching the door - both of which you weren't," Saskia answered. Then, seeing the expression on Eleanor's face, her eyes widened in disbelief. "Oh my god, you were touching it, Ellie! You do know that we still have to report it, though, don't you?"

"I know," Eleanor admitted.

"Do you want me to do it?"

"No!" Eleanor burst out in fear. "Just… let me do it."

"Okay, if you really want to. But promise me you won't leave it too long," Saskia raised an eyebrow as she waited for the required response.

"Okay. I'll do it soon," Eleanor replied grudgingly.

"Thank you," Saskia said, hugging her as they stepped back into the same elevator. "Can I ask you one more thing about when you came here earlier?" she added in a more hushed tone.

"Of course," Eleanor said, scanning her finger as Saskia pushed the button for Level Nine.

"Did you…" she took a deep breath and lowered her voice to a whisper. "Did you see anyone?"

"Did I see anyone?" Eleanor repeated in confusion. Was it possible that Saskia knew something about the strange figure she had heard coming towards the door? "What do you mean? Who would I have seen?"

Chapter Three

"Attention: This is an automated announcement to inform all citizens that the compulsory Anniversary Speech will be taking place this morning in allocated Lecture Halls. The speeches will commence at 9 a.m. and will continue for two hours, at which point the floor will be open for questions. After the speeches, all citizens will be encouraged to return to their allocated workstations to resume regular afternoon shifts."

Eleanor shoved her way through the surge of people advancing down the corridors, passing the doors to the staircase until she finally broke away from the scrum and began to make her way towards her assigned Lecture Hall - Z6310.

There were four main Lecture Halls in the Zone Six Subterrane, each covering just under a quarter of the floor space of Level Ten. All four halls were identical, each with one large set of heavy white double doors that opened outwards, allowing the bustling crowds easy access to the areas that surrounded the Elevator Blocks. Although, ever since an electrical fault had affected the doors after the Anniversary Lectures three years ago, they were now only ever shut overnight, when there were no citizens present inside them.

"Hey, Ellie!" a voice shouted through the commotion. "Ellie! Over here!"

Eleanor turned and, craning her neck to see over the ever-growing gathering outside the Lecture Hall, caught sight of Saskia waving frantically as she struggled to see over the slow-moving crowd that was making its way along the corridor towards other Lecture Halls.

Saskia and Eleanor had been best friends since they had met at the age of six when Saskia had been transferred to Zone Six. According to Saskia, her parents had fled to the safety of another Subterrane when the Evacuation occurred, several months before she had been born. Consequently, she had been born and raised within the confines and sanctuary of the Zone Five Subterrane, until she was transferred due to over-population. However, being born in any Subterrane had its consequences; parents were not permitted to raise, care for, or to even make themselves known to the child. This was purely to prolong each child's safety and, in doing so, reduce the risk of negative or over impartial treatment, household abuse, and unwarranted familial ties. As a result, Saskia, like Eleanor and so many others born in the Subterrane, had apparently never attempted to meet or even to find her true parents.

The continuance of friendships from before the Evacuation was also highly frowned upon, as they caused you to dwell too much on the past. However, the forging of new friendships like Eleanor and Saskia's was widely encouraged, as they helped the community to look towards a preferable and more unified future.

"You coming to the speech?" Eleanor asked Saskia. "Not bunking off as usual?"

"I decided not to risk it this year - they seem to be tightening up on attendance," Saskia replied with an extremely obvious grimace. "I heard that there was someone who got in masses of trouble for just skipping their NWD lecture recently! I suppose I sort of understand that because they're important, but the fact that we have to listen to someone ranting on every year about the same dull events again and again…"

"It's not that dull." Eleanor automatically attempted to defend the Thirteen Founders and nudged Saskia as she pretended to yawn widely. "It's our history - it's important that we know it!"

"But after nine years of listening to the same tedious lecture, I'm sure I must have it memorised by now."

"Careful no one hears you," Eleanor glanced warily at those closest to them.

"It's fine - no one's going to pay attention to what we're saying, silly," Saskia scolded.

"One day someone will, and then you'll wish you'd listened to me. Anyway, you haven't been to it nine times - you've skipped it twice."

"Alright, but even after seven times it's still dull," Saskia rolled her eyes and smirked. "Anyway, no one would ever report us. Come on - let's see if the doors are open yet. I want seats this time - we had to stand at the back last time I came because you were so late," she added in an attempt to guilt-trip Eleanor.

Saskia dragged her to the ID Recognition Lens on the wall where they both scanned their thumbprints, before heading through the open door and into the huge Lecture Hall.

The two of them made their way over to an almost empty row at the back. Far enough back to allow their imminent lack of concentration to go unnoticed and just near enough to the doors so that they could sneak out quickly once the speech was over.

As they sat down, the speaker made his way over to the lectern with a small wad of papers, which he then proceeded to sift through. He was both taller and younger than the seemingly ancient leader who had led their lectures for the past few years. He was perhaps in his late forties or early fifties, and had an air about him that seemed to command attention; almost every citizen in the Hall had their eyes fixed on him.

"He's new, isn't he?" Eleanor pointed out as she squinted towards him.

"I'm not sure. I don't think so," Saskia replied.

"Really? I'm sure I've never seen him around before."

"Maybe he's just always done the speech in one of the other halls," she suggested, glancing at him momentarily.

"I suppose so," Eleanor shrugged.-

An uncomfortable silence settled between them.

Inconspicuously she glanced sideways at Saskia to see if something was wrong due to her rare silence, but found no noticeable change mirrored in her expression.

"Oh god, I hope it's over quickly," Saskia eventually uttered, her lack of enthusiasm attracting a few unimpressed glances from those sitting within earshot.

"I doubt it will be," Eleanor muttered back, sounding equally as bored. "It never is."

Chapter Four

"The seventh of July, 2042. This crucial day was when the fate of the world as we knew it was decided once and for all. Precisely at midday, those who later became known as The Thirteen Founders gathered at a conference room within the British Branch of the International Preservation Society, to begin discussing the uncertain possibility of our future on the Earth. This society was not well known - generally, you were only aware of it if you were either an existing member or if you had been approached about joining it. It was comprised of the most influential individuals who had reached the very height of their occupation; scientists, politicians, architects, top quality constructors and a few others. The society met yearly, in various locations across the globe and was always directed by one of the members from the hosting country. In the case of 2042, it was hosted in London by the only British representative. It was not simply a conference of science or politics, because the three scientists and two politicians present among them were greatly outnumbered: It was a conference concerning the morality, ethics and possible outcomes of the many changes that were occurring across the globe.

"This monumental meeting was organised in response to two particularly significant events. The first was the Intentional Flooding that occurred in February, 2039. This had recently been undertaken to prevent the capital from being submerged, due to the significant increases in temperature which had caused sea levels to begin to rise. The second event was the dramatically heightened tensions between the USA and the Russian Federation, which risked the outbreak of a war that the United Kingdom would most likely find itself caught in the middle of.

"The great vision of the Thirteen Founders saw the project rescuing the majority of the population from the possible end to civilisation, through means of rehousing into permanent shelters. These would shield those within from any flying shrapnel that resulted from any explosions or attacks that occurred above ground. This would be done to create a new culture, a new world and consequently a new way of life. This way of life would follow the leadership and direction of the Thirteen Founders and would explore a world in which all individuals were equal. This meant that every citizen would work the same number of hours per week and with just as much effort as any other citizen of that same age, as opposed to working as much or as little as necessary, according to social status or wealth. To create the accommodation for this new way of life, large passageways needed to be built connecting the Earth's surface with the potential underground spaces. The 'Tunnels', as they were to be called, would later be sealed off from the surface, in the interest of safety for the population that now resides within this underground world that we call home." The speaker paused momentarily to cast his gaze across the mostly enthusiastic audience as they hung on his every word.-

"It was decided that there would be a total of sixty-seven Tunnels positioned in different locations around the globe, unbeknown to the public. This was done so that, when the time came, a Tunnel was accessible and near enough to anyone and everyone, whilst also being far enough out of the way so that the public had been entirely unaware of them until it became necessary for the planned evacuation to be set in motion. To execute this enterprise without creating a prior sense of panic and suspicion, they had to be constructed without disrupting day-to-day life, whilst keeping the knowledge of the project to as few people as possible. They needed to descend far enough underground to link up with the underground dwelling, either by a series of stairs or a large slope. However, if it was chosen to use a slope, it needed to have a steep enough gradient so that those travelling along it would reach the underground network without being forced to walk for miles before reaching Level Zero.

"The original proposition stated that the civilisation would be formed of large communal pods on various levels underground. The levels would be connected by several Elevators that would operate on facial recognition and ID cards, as well as staircases which would also require facial recognition or ID cards to open the doors. This idea was later expanded so that several Underground settlements existed, creating an intricate network with large and extremely fast Elevators connecting all countries and regions - known now as Zones. However, this latter idea was eventually abandoned as it proved too complicated and intricate a task to achieve safely and effectively, without greatly exceeding the original budget.

"It was decided that each zone would consist of 20 levels underground, each one more secure than the one above and each having a different purpose and use. And I am very pleased to inform you that, once again, each department has continued to achieve numerous feats this year. For example, our Food Technology sector has increased its output volume of soy milk produced from 1,700,000 litres to 1,850,000 litres per year. Our Medical department has found a simple cure to the common cold and has improved the efficiency and effectiveness of seventeen other cures, as well as having found an easy remedy for arthritis. And our Textiles Industry has also found a successful way of recycling clothing and materials effectively, with next to no waste."

The speaker looked up and cast his eyes around the watchful room. "And now we come to the story of our founding: At 12:05 on New Year's Eve 2047, whilst fireworks were still detonating over the River Thames, a series of gunshots were suddenly heard all across England, after which all power was immediately cut off all over the country and panic ensued. Word then began to spread about a series of underground bunkers, which instigated a mad rush to each entry point of the Tunnels. Once everyone was safely inside a Tunnel, they were all simultaneously sealed off for the safety, security and wellbeing of the citizens, while the Revolutionaries continued to fire shots on the Surface. This same process was repeated numerous times all across the globe until every non-Revolutionary was ensured to be in a place of safety. For the following weeks, all who inquired as to when they were able to leave were informed that Revolutionaries were running rampant above them, and consequently that it was not yet safe to return to the Surface.

"Months soon turned into years and memories of life on the Earth's surface were gradually fading into a more and more distant echo of the past. Those with mobile devices had soon found no use for them, due to the lack of charging sockets and therefore a lack of power in these devices. As a result, with no devices and no connection to the Surface, it slowly became a thing of the past - and remains so today. This new lifestyle and way of life paved the way for an alternative society which brought about the great culture that we are a part of today.

"And now to conclude, let us refresh our memories of our fundamental values," the speaker said. "Who can give me the first? You?" He pointed to a tall girl in the second row who was pointlessly attempting to sink lower in her seat, desperate not to be picked.

"R-react?" she answered quietly.

"A little louder, perhaps?" he prompted rather cruelly.

"React," she repeated, then breathed a sigh of relief as he turned his attention back to the rest of the audience. It wasn't that she hadn't known the answer - in fact, it would be more of a challenge to not know the answers, for they had been constantly drilled into them since before their first birthday. It was simply that with such large numbers attending each lecture, the embarrassment at the possibility of momentarily forgetting the answer in front of so many other citizens was unthinkable.

"Quite right," the speaker continued. "The Thirteen Founders' reaction to the various events that were occurring around the world - both environmental and political - allowed them to devise a plan to save the human race from extinction. What was the second?" he pointed to a woman at the end of the front row.

"Revise," she answered flawlessly with a know-it-all expression, before giving the definition too. "The process of studying the prior failings of the world on the Surface, which was undertaken by the Founders as they planned the construction of the Subterrane and outlined what life would be like within it."

"Very nicely put," the speaker replied with a nod, clearly impressed.

"You on the fifth row, what was the third?"

"I, um... I," the boy stuttered, terrified that he had been called on. "Re-re... re-"

"You, next to him," the speaker interrupted, gesturing to the boy beside him. "Can you help him out?"

"Reshaping the way of life that had proved unsuccessful for many years on the Surface."

"Good," the speaker said, before pointing to someone in the middle. "The fourth?"

"Renewing previous lifestyles with a new and improved way of living."

"And finally, you at the back," he pointed to Saskia who subtly sighed in annoyance, although Eleanor noted that she didn't actually seem too bothered.

"Restore," she answered, then waited for him to open his mouth to speak before cutting him off and continuing with her answer. "Restoring the order and normality of a regular and ordinary life, that each citizen of the Subterrane deserves."

"Nicely put," the speaker answered, subtly raising an eyebrow at her - but not so much that anyone would notice.

"Before we finish for today, I'd like to open the floor for questions." The speaker glanced around the room, then reluctantly selected one of the few hands that had popped up: "The girl in the fourth row?"

A girl from the audience lowered her arm as she was selected and rose from her seat. "Who began the project in the first place?" she called from the audience. "I mean, who came up with the idea of building the Tunnels and the Subterrane?"

"As I hope you would all have been previously aware of from the Doctrine of the Founders, the Tunnels were created as part of a project to improve the economic and environmental impact that we make as people. It was first mentioned as part of a private conference, around four and a half years before the first of January 2047 - on the seventh of July 2042."

"But I heard that there are fourteen signatures on the Doctrine of the Founders? How come we only have thirteen now? Did the fourteenth come up with the idea but then back out or was there some other reason?"

"I assure you that it was a culmination of ideas from several people. The fourteenth made the decision to step away from the project because they had lost faith in its core values. However, the remaining thirteen all later formed our highly influential Thirteen Founders."

"But did the fourteenth make it to a Subterrane?"

"I believe they did - Zone Three or Four, I think. Any other questions? Yes, you?"

A woman in her early twenties stood. "A significant number of rumours have been circulating, saying that the overall amount of white dye needed was underestimated and that now there's a shortage of it. Is this true? What's going to be done about it?"

"I have heard these rumours myself, in passing - thank you for addressing the matter." The speaker glanced up to the back of the hall where Eleanor and Saskia were sat, with what Eleanor interpreted as a rather knowing look.

There's no way he could know Saskia started that rumour, she reassured herself. That would be almost impossible - no one else knows who made it up!

"However," the speaker continued, "I am pleased to inform each and every one of you that these rumours have been vastly exaggerated. In fact, as I mentioned earlier, our Textiles Industry has just recently found an exceptional method of recycling clothing entirely. I assure you that we are experiencing no such problems in that department. Anyone else?"

A boy whom Eleanor recognised from the Technology & Development Department raised his hand and stood once he was selected.

"Our ventilation system obviously runs universally through the subterrane, but the air that it circulates must be from the Surface. You mentioned the 2039 Deliberate Flooding Act, but what happens if there is another flood? Being a kind of natural disaster, it's not subject to the presence or impact that humans may have made on the Surface." He paused momentarily before clarifying his question. "What I'm trying to ask, is what happens if there is a flood that compromises the source of our oxygen? I heard somewhere that our ventilation system filters the air for any traces of radiation or other debris, but what if water somehow gets into our ventilation network?"

Ventilation consistently came up at every Anniversary Speech, usually asked by those with more academically inclined positions.

"I can assure you that our ventilation is sourced from an extremely secure location that would go entirely unaffected by any other flooding, should it ever occur. Likewise, our filtration system would also experience no difficulties whatsoever," he replied concisely. "Let's have two or three more questions. Any volunteers?"

The quivering hand of a young boy in the second row was singled out, and he stood up hurriedly, gulping. He looked no older than twelve or thirteen and, taking in the vast crowd of spectators around him, it became clear that this was only perhaps his third or fourth time at an Anniversary Speech. Certainly, it seemed to be his first time asking a question.

Up until the age of eight, children were not required to attend the Anniversary Speeches. Instead, they would spend the day learning about the variety of events that took place on the 20th January 2047, and how the night of the evacuation unfolded in general. Consequently, when the children witnessed their first lecture, their innocence on matters that seemed so trivial to others was almost refreshing.

"W-why don't children live with their parents?" he stuttered shakily. The separation of biological parents and children was one of the education topics covered in detail at the age of twelve. "I know that it's discouraged, but is there any particular reason for it?"

"That's an excellent question, young man," the speaker smiled in a friendly manner at the boy, before turning his focus back to the entirety of the audience. "Now, this one requires a slightly more in-depth answer. Most children form very strong emotional bonds and attachments within their families; with brothers, sisters, parents, grandparents. However, whilst these are very positive experiences for children to undergo, surprisingly they can have an extremely negative impact on the society around them. The main reason is that parents will always put their children first - and rightly so. This is because, no matter how destructive it might be for those around them, a child is always what matters the most to any parent. However, if there are no longer any emotional ties between citizens, then no one is any more important than anyone else and we consequently have a much stronger society as a result. Of course, in some cases it remains obvious who the biological parents are due to inherited traits, birthmarks and hereditary conditions. However, whilst the parents may always hold a slightly sputtering candle for their child, with no investment in them - be it emotional or financial - the parents remain quite indifferent and therefore detached from the child in question."

"Thank you, sir," the boy said, before sitting down heaving a huge sigh of relief.

The speaker smiled a little at the boy's bravery, before repeating his incessant question for a final time: "Any more questions?"

Eleanor thought back to the strange events of the previous day. What had been on the other side of the door? Almost wishing she had stayed to find out, she considered the options of what it could have been; a Revolutionary, a citizen who had found the door open and had ventured to the Surface - which was very unlikely, or a regular person. She considered the latter option long and hard: Was there any chance that there were any regular people still on the Surface? What if someone had been left behind, or just hadn't made it to the Tunnel in time? What if someone had been asleep when the alarms went off? Or if they were deaf? Or if they had been listening to music loudly? Eleanor had been told that things such as music had once been commonplace.

Surely if that had been the case, they could have been locked out of the Subterrane? The Founders considered everyone who remained on the Surface to be a Revolutionary, but what if someone was just in the wrong place at the wrong time? What would a regular person on the Surface even be like?

Eleanor raised her arm tentatively.

"At the back - yes, what's your question?" the speaker called to her.

"Sorry, this might be really stupid, or the answer might be really obvious… but anyway I was wondering, who exactly lives on the Surface? Because someone has to. Surely not everyone was able to make it to the Tunnels before they were sealed? And I doubt that even if there was a war, as was extremely probable before the evacuation to the Subterrane I, well, I doubt that every single person that didn't make it down here was killed in the war? I mean, if you think about it logically, surely it's impossible?"

Her question was met with an awkward silence as the audience anxiously awaited a response. No one breathed. No one moved. Then, as those around her began to become a little restless in their seats, straining to turn around and see who had asked such an impertinent question, the Leader attempted to regain his composure.

"At 12:05 on New Year's Eve, 2047, after gunshots had been heard, the Tunnels were made available to anyone and everyone." He cleared his throat loudly - it was obvious to Eleanor how carefully he was choosing his words now. "I'm well aware that the vastness of the Thirteen Founders' worldwide influence must seem implausible and, quite frankly, unimaginable. But, rest assured that everyone made it to the Tunnels in time, other than the Revolutionaries who were not permitted entrance - although some did try. Only a few still remain on the Surface. Any other questi-"

"-so we know that for definite?" Eleanor interrupted.

"Ellie, leave it," Saskia hissed forcefully.-

"How do you distinguish between a citizen - or future citizen, at least, and a Revolutionary? How do you know that one of the Revolutionaries you wouldn't let in actually wasn't a Revolutionary at all - just someone trying to get to safety?"

"As I stated earlier, and as is mentioned in the Doctrine of the Founders, the Tunnels were an available sanctuary for any citizen. The sole reason that several Individual Pods still remain empty is that the sheer numbers of Revolutionaries were, I believe, slightly underestimated. Although we also expected a growth in the population of our community in the coming years."

"But how do we know that no one else is out there if we're all sealed underground?" Eleanor persevered.

"Well, I suppose we... we can't be entirely sure, but there's no need to worry about anyone getting through the Tunnels," he added hastily as a low murmur coursed through the audience. "I assure you that the Tunnel is sealed very securely."

"So technically there could still be life outside of the Subterrane, then?" Eleanor pressed on, uninterested in how secure he considered the Tunnel entrance to be.

"That's very unlikely," he added adamantly. "The amount of detectable warfare above ground has been gradually decreasing, suggesting that there can't be many Revolutionaries left above ground."

"Couldn't they just have made peace? Or reached an agreement to ensure they don't wipe themselves out?"

"Well... I-I suppose so," he answered.

"So who's up there? Who else is left?"

"Only Revolutionaries live outside of the Tunnels," the speaker repeated once again, becoming visibly irritated.

"But you just said yourself that there might be life up there! And how do we know that there's no one who didn't make it to the Tunnel that night, for one reason or another - perhaps they were too scared, or they were injured. Or maybe they just couldn't get there in time and only reached the door after it was sealed? How could we possibly know? For definite?"

"We... we just do. As stated in the Doctrine of the Founders, anyone who remained and now resides on the Surface is considered to be a Revolutionary in the eyes of the Founders, and is therefore our enemy. That will be all for today," the Leader concluded forcefully, as he eyed Eleanor with a cautionary stare before his gaze flitted to Saskia momentarily. He rushed out of the side door of the Lecture Hall just as it dissolved into a buzz of gossip and unanswered questions.

Chapter Five

Saskia grabbed Eleanor's arm and rushed her from the Lecture Hall. Dragging her down a flight of stairs, she pushed her into one of the few entirely soundproof Recreational Pods on Level Eleven. Saskia hastily shut the door behind them and only let go of Eleanor's arm once she was sure that it was firmly locked.

"What the hell was that about?" Saskia yelled.

"What do you mean? I was only asking him questions."

"You know exactly what I mean. Asking how our light is powered is a question - how our water gets around the Subterrane is a question! You know very well that those are the sort of things you're supposed to ask," Saskia exclaimed. "You could get in masses of trouble for this - it could blow up hugely! Do you know what could happen now? They could call you in for a meeting or you could... you could get sent to another zone or something."

"I really don't think-"

"No. Obviously you don't," Saskia replied angrily. "I probably don't know anything more than you do about the procedure for this kind of thing, but I heard that someone got sent away once. It can happen - I'm sure of it!"

"Relax - all I did was ask how we know that no one lives on the Surface! It was only a question - what's the worst that could happen?" Eleanor was unsure why Saskia had worked herself up into such a frenzy.

"I don't know what could happen - that's the problem. And neither do you! But you're just not supposed to ask that! How do you not get it? Now they'll have decided that you might be dangerous or something, so they'll probably look into you and who you are. Don't you think they'll find it a little odd that you were the one that opened the Tunnel - or saw it when it was open at least?"

Eleanor rolled her eyes and sighed; Saskia was overreacting way too much.

"You did tell someone, right?" Saskia paused for a response, but received none. "Oh my God, you didn't tell anyone! How could you?" she yelled in outrage. "I trusted you to fix this! You could have just reported it and that would've been that. But no - of course, you had to ask stupid questions and make a total idiot of that speaker. What's wrong with you?" Saskia was frantic now.

"You didn't report it either, remember?" Eleanor shot back.

"That's because you promised me you would!"

Completely taken aback, Eleanor said nothing as she struggled to find the right words to apologise properly; strangely, she realised that they'd never had a real argument like this before.

"I… I didn't realise it was such a big deal to you," she finally mumbled weakly. "I'm really sorry."

Saskia turned away, fiddling with the tassel on her bracelet.

"There's a reason why I was so reluctant to report it," Eleanor began. "When I went to see the Tunnel, I heard something. It was a faint noise some way above me, but not far - at least, not far enough for my liking. The moment I heard it, I knew it obviously wasn't safe to stay there, so I immediately pushed the door to, as best as I could, and ran back to the elevators. But as I was stepping into one, I looked back and saw that it had swung ajar. Of course, I was too afraid to go back - I was longing for the elevator doors to close so I could feel safe again. But just as they did so, I saw four fingers reach through the gap and close around the edge of the door. That's why I was late for our Societal Group and that's why I was reluctant to tell you where I'd been. I know this is all my fault and I truly am sorry that I've somehow involved you in this mess, but I was too scared to let anyone know that…" she paused, then took a breath as she summed up the courage to say the words aloud. "I was too scared to tell them that I was the one to open the Tunnel and that I... that I let someone in."

Saskia finally turned around to face Eleanor and studied her face, eyes wide with fear.

"Don't you realise what you've done?"

Chapter Six

Having hidden herself away in her Individual Pod for most of the day following the incident at the Anniversary Speech, Eleanor rose from her desk with a start as a cautious knock sounded at the door. Hurrying to press the door release, she was surprised to find Saskia standing before her.

"Are you coming to see the produce?" Saskia asked. And, although Eleanor knew she would never admit it, she could tell that Saskia seemed a little regretful of her earlier outburst.

"I… wasn't really planning on it," Eleanor began uncertainly.

Saskia's face fell. "Oh, okay. I guess I'll… I'll just see you later, then." She turned away reluctantly and began to traipse slowly back down the corridor.

"Saskia, wait," Eleanor called out a moment later. "Alright, I'll come with you."

"You will?" Saskia repeated, spinning around to face her excitedly.

"Yes," Eleanor stepped into the corridor and allowed the door of her Pod to swing shut behind her.

They made their way towards the East Side Elevators in awkward silence, occasionally taking turns to glance sideways at each other. The evening festivities that took place every year typically commenced just after 1900 hours. And, since it was already twenty-five minutes past the hour, most of the East Side Elevators were vacant. They stepped inside one and began to ascend.

Subtly glancing out of the corner of her eye, Eleanor surveyed Saskia's expression, then quickly looked away as she caught her staring. Heat immediately rushed to Eleanor's cheeks, tinting them with a deep pink. Is it hot in the elevator? Eleanor wondered to herself, although she was sure it must be. Promptly she pulled one of her three monthly-distributed hair bobbles from her wrist and hurried to tie her hair back.

Saskia turned to face her.

"Listen, I'm sorry," she began. "I shouldn't have got so worked up earlier, and I-"

"Saskia," Eleanor stopped her mid-sentence. "It should be me apologising. I was in the wrong and, as you said, I'd promised to report it. You had every right to get upset."

Saskia nodded in response as the doors opened onto Level Five and they walked out into the gradually emptying corridor. As others claimed their elevator to head down to the Food Halls on Level Nine, they each attempted to convince themselves that the tension between them had dissolved.

As they reached the doorway that led to the lab, Eleanor was immediately struck by the level of noise gradually crescendoing to a climax as the doors slid open before them; hundreds of citizens were making their way along the meandering path that wound through the centre of Hydroponic Lab 4. A surge of cool air immediately flooded into the corridor, enveloping them with the sweet, rich aroma of the plants.

Level Five was wider and longer than any other level within the Subterrane, measuring almost double that of the residential levels. The ever-growing demand for food needed a considerable number of workers and a substantial amount of space available. Consequently, the Hydroponic Laboratories consisted of eight main spaces, each housing different types of produce.

The first housed various vegetables such as beans, spinach, celery, peppers and avocados, all of which were simple to grow hydroponically, whilst also housing a number of Chilli pepper plants and a small herb garden. Labs 2 and 3 also dealt with vegetables, although only ones that either needed constant care and attention or more space to grow - onions, carrots, mushrooms, broccoli and lettuce. Lab 4 was devoted to the cultivation of fruits - mainly berries, such as raspberries, blueberries, grapes, and tomatoes, but also a small number of other fruits - mainly strawberries and watermelons. The smallest of the laboratories, Lab 5, was more commonly known as the 'Citrus Orchard' and contained an array of trees with brightly coloured produce; oranges, lemons, limes and grapefruits, whilst the lab also had a wide border of chia seeds along each of its edges.-

Lab 6 was the largest of all, appearing to be more of a plantation than a laboratory. Its floor was carpeted in row upon endless row of rice plants that were harvested every sixty-eight days. Lab 7 contained only five varieties of plants, three of which were used in the production of tea, and were the sole source of caffeine for the citizens. As well as these, the lab housed a large number of olive trees used in the making of olive oil, and soybean plants which were used in the making of milk, butter and occasionally for yoghurt. The final laboratory - Lab 8 - contained no live plants. Instead it was used to store and dry out various fruits, vegetables, leaves and herbs, before they underwent various processes. These included the extraction of citric acid from the fruit grown within Lab 5, the drying and shredding of plant leaves from Lab 7, the making of olive oil from the olive trees grown in Lab 7 and the drying, crushing and powdering of various herbs and spices.

The entirety of Level Five was off-limits to all citizens of the Subterrane, other than those who worked there. However, the only exception to this rule was on the day of the Anniversary Speech. On this particular day, between 1900 and 2100 hours, all citizens were permitted to visit either Laboratory 4 or 5 to see for themselves the success that the year had brought. And, as they walked through the lab along the prescribed central path, citizens were permitted to pick a few of the fruits that were growing within reach. This meant that every citizen was able to experience the work put in by the Technicians from both the Hydroponics and Cultivation departments, as well as to truly appreciate just how lucky they were to have such an incredible array of agriculture.

Eleanor and Saskia stood in the doorway, surveying the lab in awe. Dozens of overall-clad Pollination Technicians were carefully treading between the fragile plants, transferring pollen from one delicate flower to the next with thin brushes and gentle movements. Gradually they worked their way along the rows of various plants that stretched lengthwise from the double doors, and towered above them from the multiple shelves soaring upwards to the very roof of the laboratory. Metres of raspberries, blueberries, blackberries and cucumbers were stacked to the ceiling; twice as many of strawberries and tomatoes, and a quarter as many of watermelons, cantaloupes, goji berries and chia seeds, each taking up half the length of an entire row. A wooden pergola, which had been both constructed and sourced before the Evacuation, arched above the entire length of the circular path and bridged the gap between the towering rows of shelves. It was adorned with plump, ripe, purple and green hanging grapes, both of which they were temporarily permitted to pick.

Descending the short set of steps, Eleanor and Saskia began to follow the path through the spectacular laboratory. Pausing momentarily, Eleanor stooped down and, reaching behind a bright green leaf, plucked a bright red strawberry from an otherwise uninhabited plant and placed it in her mouth, savouring each sensation from the sweet juice. Saskia laughed as Eleanor pulled a face at her, and crouched to pull one from a neighbouring plant for herself. They continued under the canopy of grapes, occasionally pausing to marvel at a perfectly formed fruit or intricately patterned leaf.

"We should probably be getting to the Food Halls now," Saskia sighed, reluctant to leave the paradise of the lab. "There aren't many people left here."

"I suppose," Eleanor agreed unwillingly, deciding it would be wiser not to argue with Saskia whilst their friendship was only being held together by a thread.

They followed the path as it looped back on itself, this time bordering the left-hand side of the lab where they walked beside the watermelons and cantaloupes - although they were obviously not permitted to pick them.

Finally leaving through the same set of doors, they hurried back towards the East Side Elevators and pressed the call button.

"They're all quite a way away," Saskia complained, after seeing that each elevator was at least a couple of floors above or below.

"People are probably still going to the Food Halls from their Pods," Eleanor replied. "Let's walk down - we don't want to be late."

Saskia nodded and they began the four-level ascent.

As they opened the door to Food Hall Six, the first thing that hit Eleanor was the smell. An overwhelming aroma filled the air, one that she recognised only too well as that of the Subterrane's traditional cuisine.

Each of the four, long, originally-sourced wooden tables were weighed down with trays of glistening cutlery and glasses, stretching down the length of the hall. The seats of the central two tables were packed with citizens, all attempting to shout over the clamour, and the outer benches had only a few spare spaces on each side of the tables. Saskia pointed out a couple of spaces next to a group of their friends, at the end furthest from the door and the two of them hurried down the hall to slot themselves in on the far right.

"Katy!" Saskia exclaimed. "I couldn't find you at the speech this morning. Where were you?"

"I've been reassigned - so has Bella," she answered with a slight shrug. "Something about uneven numbers. We're in LH4 now."

"I guess that would make sense since - it was so packed last year," Saskia replied. "Do you remember? We had to stand at the back through the whole thing."

"Have you been to see the labs yet?" Katy asked, directing the question to Eleanor so that she wouldn't feel excluded from the conversation.

"We've just been - have you?" Eleanor answered.

"Yes," Katy replied. "I went with Bella. We would have come to get you, but we thought you'd probably be going together."

"Have they made any of the announcements yet?"

"Not yet," Katy replied, glancing at the large clock that hung above the doorway. "They only began letting people in at 1945 hours, so the speeches should begin at around 2000 hours."

"So how long have we got?"

"Only a few minutes, I think. I'd get some food before they start, if I were you."

Saskia and Eleanor hurried up to the food counter built into the wall and surveyed the traditional Anniversary Meal options that were typically much more enjoyable than regular meals.

Having loaded up their plates, they eagerly headed back to their table, where they were joined by a few more of their friends.

"Ellie!" a voice called from across the table, as she settled herself down on the bench. "Nice debate this morning."

She glanced up to see who it was and rolled her eyes, resisting the temptation to laugh with him.

"No, really," Ryan continued, nudging his friend on his right. "We enjoyed it - it was the most exciting thing that's happened round here since the founding."

"Yes it was quite the scandal," his friend added teasingly.

"You shouldn't say things like that," Katy warned as he mimicked the stereotypical uppity tone of the Founders.

"I'm kidding, Katy," he grinned. "But in all seriousness, Ellie, that probably wasn't the smartest question you could have asked."

"Yes, I'm well aware of that," Eleanor replied, keen to move onto a different subject. "But thanks for the concern," she added as she poured herself a drink from the jug on their table.

"Do you guys ever wonder what it would be like if we still lived on the Surface?" Bella piped in rather randomly.

"Not really," Saskia replied.

"It's just because, well, before we were born, our parents would have expected all of us to grow up on the Surface - at normal schools with normal friends. They'd expect us to live with them and to do everything with them. Who knows if we would have even met!"

"Imagine if we hadn't," Johnny said, inviting himself to join the conversation. "That would just be weird."

"I can't even imagine it," Katy frowned as she looked up from her food.

"Then it's just as well that we're all here, isn't it?" Saskia gave Katy a warm smile.

A bell-like chime rang through the large hall, instantaneously quieting the citizens as they all turned to face the far end of the hall.

At the very end of it, a smaller table was positioned at right angles to the four larger tables. Sitting in the centre were a man and a woman - two representatives from the Thirteen Founders - and sitting on either side of them were several members of the Government. The woman, who was gently tapping her glass with the blunt edge of a knife, looked to the other for direction. The man nodded and they both stood simultaneously; the submissive congregation followed.

"What an impressive year we've had," the woman began, before giving a disapproving look to a small group as they entered the hall and scurried down to seats at the opposite end. "And I hope you have all taken the opportunity to see for yourselves what our incredible Hydroponics and Cultivation Technicians have managed to achieve this year - or if you haven't already, that you will have done so by the end of the day. We have really had a tremendous year. Our hydroponics teams have provided us with masses of produce - more than in any other year. We have seen our Genetics Technicians overcoming tremendous hurdles; namely the engineering and adapting of particular fruits so that they are able to produce the maximum quantities of food possible. Our Hydro-Technicians have succeeded in reaching optimum temperatures and humidities for each and every one of our vegetable crops, therefore enabling each to function most efficiently. As well as this, they have finally managed to eliminate the various needs of seasonal crops, allowing them to be grown all year round in the same location with only slightly altered conditions. Our Plantation Operatives have been victorious in achieving their annual target, once again, and have increased their output produce by just under half. They have also managed to decrease the concentration of minerals required for each species of plant by a quarter. This was, of course, aided by our superb Genetics Technicians, who also deserve significant recognition for helping achieve this remarkable feat."

The Founder turned to the other beside her.

"We would also like to take this moment to acknowledge some phenomenal achievements in other areas," the second Founder began, his voice booming through the hall.

"Isn't he the one from our speech?" Eleanor whispered to Saskia, squinting in an attempt to see him better. "Yes, I'm sure it is!"

Saskia shrugged. "It looks like him."

"How come he's here?" Eleanor wondered aloud. "I didn't realise he was a Founder - I just thought he was a Leader or something."

"Shush, Eleanor," Saskia hissed. "Just pay attention!"

Huffing, Eleanor turned her attention back to the two Founders.

"Just two days ago, our Food Technology sector announced that they have increased their output volume of soy milk by 150,000 litres per annum. Our Medical department recently revealed that they have found a simple cure to the common cold, and have improved the effectiveness of several other cures, as well as having found a remedy for arthritis. Our Textiles Industry has also disclosed that they have found an effective way of recycling clothing with absolutely no waste, whilst maintaining the qualities of the fabrics."

An animated rumble of applause pulsed through the Hall.

"Let's raise our glasses to our terrific Industry Workers!" He lifted his glass and touched it to the other Founder's.

Glasses clinked, swilled and were drained all too quickly.

"What do you think they drink?" Eleanor asked randomly, turning to Katy who was sitting on her left.

"How would I know?" Katy said, looking up from her food.

"I just mean that, well, look at their glasses."

"What about them?" Katy seemed unsure as to what she was getting at.

"It just doesn't look like anything we ever get to drink," Eleanor shrugged. "I mean, it's purple, for one thing."

"I heard that every citizen used to receive a glass of wine on Anniversaries," Bella interjected in an excited whisper. This was a piece of their history that only someone as intelligent as her would ever bother to remember.

"Wine?" Katy set her fork down. "What's that?"

"It's made from grapes - they press them and then do something else to them I think," Bella replied. "We looked at it briefly at the start of the Special Ed course, I think, but I can't really remember the whole process."

"And everyone used to get a glass?" Eleanor asked in surprise, pushing her plate away so she could lean on the table.

"Well, I think so, but only if they were over the age of fifteen or something. But yes. Everyone who was old enough got one."

"But was it different from grape juice?" Eleanor asked.

"Yes, I think it had to be made a while before it was going to be drunk - maybe even years before. I remember being told that it had to sit for a while. There was a special word for it - formation? No... um, fo-fermentation? Yes, that's it! Fermentation."

"And it would still be safe to drink?"

"I presume so."

"How do you know all about it?" Eleanor eyed her friend curiously.

"We were talking through the different processes that transform food into other things - like turning fruit into juice. The instructor mentioned wine and I got talking to her about it afterwards, because I'd never heard of it before." Bella was one of the smart ones who had been selected for Specialised Education in Biology.

"So do you think the Founders still get wine? There's only thirteen of them, after all," Eleanor pointed out.

"Well I don't know, but I wouldn't think so," Bella replied, pushing her food around her plate as she thought. "I don't think we make wine anymore. The way my instructor was talking about it, it sounded like it was years since it had been made."

"I bet they do," Eleanor continued. "We still grow grapes, and no one would notice if there was a shortage of them because it wouldn't be a significant enough amount, just a small amount each year."

"They wouldn't lie to us," Bella answered before picking at her food once more. "So I don't think they'd make it anymore."

"Really?"

"Well, I suppose the only way they theoretically could still have it, if I'm right about us not having a wine industry anymore, would be if we still have wine in storage or something."

"Katy?" Eleanor turned to face her. "What do you think?"

"Don't look at me. How would I know?" Katy hastily returned her focus to the plate of food before her, hoping to avoid any more questions on the matter.

"Saskia? How about you?" Eleanor asked, hoping at least one person would agree with her.

"I've no idea," Saskia retorted, rolling her eyes as if she was bored of Eleanor's endless questions. "How do you even get such ideas in your head in the first place?"

Chapter Seven

Eleanor and Saskia left Food Hall Six a little earlier than the others - at just after 2130 hours - and proceeded to wait for one of the East side Elevators.

"So what did you think of this year?" Eleanor asked, almost sarcastically. "As bad as last year?"

"I thought…" Saskia seemed to catch sight of something behind Eleanor, and an expression almost of annoyance flickered across her face. "It was alright. Could have been better, could have been worse - the same as always, really." She straightened up awkwardly and clenched her jaw, just as Eleanor noticed the shadow of a figure approaching.

"Girls, how have you enjoyed the day?" the Founder from their Food Hall asked, smiling almost too amicably.

Saskia looked away pointedly, leaving Eleanor to answer as politely as she could.

"It's been a very pleasant occasion, thank you," Eleanor replied, heedful of the fact that she had been arguing with him only that morning.

"Excellent. And you?" he turned to Saskia and cocked an eyebrow expectantly.

"It was terrific," she answered sardonically, giving him a cold stare.

"Good to hear," he answered, just as sarcastic. "Saskia, can I have a quick word?"

"Alright," Saskia replied as Eleanor stood there awkwardly, wondering how he knew Saskia's name.

There was a rather uncomfortable silence as they both stood watching her.

"Alone," the Founder prompted.

"Oh, of course!" Eleanor realised, heat rushing to her cheeks. "I'll see you tomorrow," she smiled at Saskia.

Hurriedly, she made for the stairs and closed the door behind her.

Crouching down, she pressed her ear to the slight gap between the floor and the foot of the door - one of the very few, yet for the most part unnoticeable design flaws of the Subterrane - and listened intently as she attempted to decipher their conversation.

"What was that earlier?" the Founder asked Saskia angrily.

"I don't know. I tried to stop her but she wouldn't listen. Just forget about it."

"It's easy enough to turn a blind eye to her opening a door that was technically already open, but to overlook such an unruly public display - that really is a rather tall order."

"Oh come on - don't give me that," Saskia retorted. "You know full well she's never reported me for all the things I've done!"

"But even if she had it wouldn't matter - that's the problem. I can defend you in everything and give you the benefit of the doubt in whatever you do; you've got immunity. But unfortunately I just don't have the authority to grant that of her as well."

"But why not? If you don't have the authority then who does? Couldn't you just say it was me?"

"Not now that there are hundreds of witnesses to say otherwise."

"What if I... what if I gave up my stupid immunity? I could stay out of trouble - it can't be too hard."

"How selfless of you," Eleanor could hear a slight hint of mockery in his voice. "She would be proud."

"Don't talk about her like that - she's not dead," Saskia shot back. "She might as well be, though..." she trailed off sulkily.

"It was her choice, remember."

"But why couldn't I have stayed with her? I don't seem to remember getting a choice."

"How many times have we been over this? We thought this place would be so much better for you. People would kill for a place in a society like this - you've constantly been encouraged to socialise with others your own age and you learnt vital skills from a very young age. It was a once in a lifetime sort of opportunity for you - you know that."

"So I couldn't have lived a reasonably decent life with her? Is that what you're saying? I only get to see her once a year!"

"You know very well that's because it's not safe. If someone saw you…"

"You literally have a door that leads up to the house!"

"Alright, enough of this," the Founder ordered. "But what am I going to do with your friend? If she so much as suspects that there might be something up there, then-"

"-well if she does then it's your fault."

"How is it my fault?"

"She went up to Level Zero, the other day."

"Yes, I know. And?"

"And she saw you."

"Saw me what?"

"Coming in through the door."

"What? But how?"

"What were you even doing? Why couldn't you have just gone from Level One?"

"I was checking if you could still get through from there," he replied. "Besides, it's so much nicer if I actually show up at the front door once in a while, as opposed to just appearing inside the house."

"Well, congratulations," Saskia replied. "I hope you had great fun doing it."

"I did, thank you," he shot back.

"This isn't a game! She saw you!"

"Then why doesn't she recognise me or confront me, or something? And how come I didn't see her?"

"Because she only saw your hand so she doesn't know it was you - but she knows she saw something. Well, someone. And she said that she heard something else through the door, and from what she described I think it must have been the lift," Saskia added.

"That doesn't mean she thinks there's anyone up there that isn't dangerous."

Eleanor frowned and pressed her ear closer to the door, listening intently.

"No, it doesn't," Saskia agreed. "But why were you using the lift?"

"Why not?"

"Because they're not safe, remember?" Saskia retorted. "They're the only reason you were allowed to buy the station in the first place."

"Look," he began. "The lifts work fine, and she won't have suspected anything - she'll probably just dismiss it like a bad dream or something."

"But the fact that she saw your hand closing around the edge of the door would suggest that there's life up there. If it was me, I'd think there was," she added.

"Well, I didn't see her at all."

"That's because the elevator went down just as you opened the door," Saskia said despairingly. "Luckily for you, she didn't see your face so she doesn't know it was you. Next time you might not be so lucky."

"Well then, you had better make sure that there won't be a next time. And make sure she doesn't tell anyone else what she saw."

"She won't," Saskia assured him. "But if she does, I'll let you know. I don't hate you quite enough to keep you entirely in the dark about it."

"But if she-"

"-and as if you'd actually trust me to do that anyway."

Eleanor stood and backed away from the door in a daze, trying to process all that she'd heard. Did that mean something was up there? What did Saskia know? Why would it be dangerous for her to tell anyone? Did Saskia know what was on Level One?

"You remember what tomorrow is, don't you?" the Founder continued.

"Kind of hard to forget when you keep reminding me."

"Well, all I'm going to say is that I hope you're ready," he replied. "They won't go easy on the training - not even for you."

"Yes, I think you might have mentioned that just once or twice before," Saskia muttered, sounding bored.

What was tomorrow? Eleanor thought. What training?

Suddenly realising that the footsteps of a rather vexed Saskia were approaching the door, she hastily scrambled down the stairs. Several steps above her, the door opened a fraction, but just as she reached the landing below, she realised that she couldn't hear Saskia's tread on the stairs. Eleanor paused and held her breath in an attempt to catch the last remarks of the conversation. Listening intently, she could just make out the Founder calling Saskia over to him again.

"Just one last thing," he began, before lowering his voice to a hushed whisper.

Eleanor cursed herself in annoyance as she struggled in vain to eavesdrop on the remainder of their conversation. But she was finally forced to acknowledge that, at least from her current spot further down the stairs, she could make out nothing of what they were saying.

Chapter Eight

Eleanor woke with a start as an ear-splitting noise pierced the darkness of her dimly lit Pod. Sitting up in a daze, she drowsily shielded her eyes as a bright alarm began to flash and the cursed as she recalled what it meant: Intruder drill. Although the Founders always promised that each biennial drill would be quick, containing and accounting for just over a thousand citizens within twelve Emergency Pods was not an easy task and had never yet been completed in under seven hours. Eleanor was absolutely certain that today's drill would be no different.

Her room was a standard-issue Individual Pod that contained only an average-sized single bed, a chair with a rather uncomfortable woven seat and upright back, and a simple metal table which, when nudged, made a hideous screeching sound that echoed around the dingy room. During the day, each Individual Pod was lit by a bright, white bulb in a small cage of thin metal wiring. However, during the night the Pod was lit only by the muted light of a feeble, automatic lamp which stood on top of the desk, beneath two metal shelves.

What a waste of time, she thought grudgingly as she gathered the clothes that she had carelessly dumped on her chair the previous evening. However, as she scrambled into them, she couldn't help but wonder why there had been such a delay between the door being opened and the alarm going off - or perhaps it really was just a regular drill and had nothing whatsoever to do with yesterday's events.

She walked over to the door of her Pod, and after pressing the Release Lock button, was immediately overwhelmed by the uproar which flooded in from the corridor as her door slid open. Stepping from the safety of her Pod, she was soon swallowed up by the heaving crowd of panicked citizens, jostling each other down the corridor as they struggled towards the Emergency Pods.

The Emergency Pods were a series of twelve large rooms with the highest security in the whole of the Subterrane, and were located among the Government meeting rooms on Level Nineteen. The Pods, as well as the rest of Level Nineteen, were permanently and unequivocally out of bounds to all citizens who held no seat in the government, except in a case of absolute emergency when they were needed to house the citizens for reasons of a threatening nature, such as in the event of a break-in. This was due to Level Nineteen predominantly being where the vital meetings of the Thirteen Founders took place. Each of the Pods was equipped to accommodate up to one hundred citizens, complete with chairs, tables and a large food supply. However, it was a well-known fact among all citizens that the supplies were capable of lasting for only up to five days, if a Pod was at maximum capacity.

As Eleanor was swept along by the heaving crowds, a sudden thought occurred to her: If everyone else is heading down to Level Nineteen, then surely no one would notice if I just had a look at what was through the door?

The conversation between Saskia and the Founder had far too much potential to go uninvestigated. Ever since she had heard them, the Founder's words had continued to echo around her head tauntingly: "If she so much as suspects that there might be something up there...". After all, amidst the chaos of a drill, who would be paying enough attention to notice that one of the elevators was on Level Zero? And, although it was mandatory to scan your thumbprint on the ID Recognition Lens once you were in an Emergency Pod, it was never entirely accurate as there was always someone who forgot and consequently went unaccounted for without any significant repercussions. Eleanor was determined, now: She was going to see what was through the door.

She unsuccessfully attempted to wrestle her way towards the edge of the corridor where the shoving seemed to be slightly less brutal, until she was finally able to seize her moment and launch herself towards the East Elevators. Keeping close to the shut doors of the central elevator, she paused in an alcove to plan her route. She faltered for a minute, unsure whether she should press for the elevator or re-join the floods of people that were pushing towards the stairs. Then, from far above her, she heard the faint rumbling of one of the elevators as it descended from one of the higher floors. Looking around to ensure that no one was watching her particularly closely, quickly she pressed the call button and waited anxiously as the dial of the lift slowly turned in an anti-clockwise motion. Several excruciatingly long seconds later, the doors prised themselves apart and out stepped a tall girl rather awkwardly ushering an elderly woman through the doors of the elevator - most likely the girl had only recently been assigned the position of a carer to the more elderly members residing on Level Thirteen.

Those nearby looked disapprovingly towards the elevator, before continuing towards the staircase; the use of elevators was discouraged during drills and other emergencies, as they were susceptible to being intercepted by any Revolutionary that may have triggered the alarm. However, in some cases, the use of elevators was wholly unavoidable, such as for some of the more elderly citizens who would simply find it impossible to descend a whole six floors of stairs.

"This'll do, won't it?" the girl spoke soothingly as she guided the older woman out of the elevator. Eleanor noticed that the woman was sporting a neatly printed white band around her wrist, which displayed her full name in block capitals - obviously she was beginning to experience symptoms similar to that of dementia.

"But we pressed the button for Level Nineteen," the woman complained, frowning.

"I know we did, but we can walk downstairs from here," the girl replied, leading the woman into the crowd before they disappeared from sight.

As soon as the elevator was vacated by the mismatched pair, Eleanor lurched forwards and slipped through the doors just mere moments before they closed. Taking a deep breath, she held out a shaky hand, pushed the button marked '0' and gripped the rail as the elevator began to ascend, the air gradually becoming a little thinner with each Level she passed.

On arriving at Level Zero, Eleanor waited impatiently for the doors to open. But as the seconds ticked by, she immediately sensed that something was wrong. Suddenly beginning to panic, she hammered on the glass elevator doors (which in hindsight probably wasn't the finest of her limited options) before attempting to prise them apart, succeeding only in breaking one of her nails. As she began to despair at her stupidity, she leant her forehead against the cool glass side of the elevator; there was no way she could talk her way out of being stuck in an elevator on Level Zero.

The ominous depths of the elevator shaft loomed far below her, shrouded in the clinically harsh lighting that beat down from fluorescent strip-lights that illuminated each Level. Until then, Eleanor had never considered what it might be like to have a fear of heights; now she understood. Sticking close to the edge of the elevator, she inched her way around the perimeter and attempted to prise the doors apart. Suddenly, her foot slipped across the glass floor and, in an attempt to steady herself as she regained her balance, she reached out and pressed her hand against the elevator wall. Entirely by accident, her elbow hit the door release button which slid the doors open in one swift movement, sending her tumbling into the deserted corridor.

Typical, she thought, with a shake of her head. Why didn't I think of that sooner?

Stepping from the East Elevator in relief, she took the faintly familiar passage on her right; one of the few which were slightly curved. Moving quickly down the unusual winding passageway she finally reached a vast concrete chamber filled with several metal benches that looked a little old and out of place. Gazing up in awe at the dome of the underground cavern, she found it hard to believe that she'd ever been in there as a child. She could faintly recall a large room on Level Zero in which her Educational Group was first told about the history of the Subterrane, but she was unsure which of the large spaces it had been in. It was in one of these rooms, too, that she and a very excited Saskia had first been told of the Tunnels, before being led along a short corridor to be shown the infamous doorway to the Surface.

Flinching as her footsteps echoed around the empty space, she crossed and selected one of the two other winding corridors to investigate. Following it further, turning this way and that, she eventually reached a sharp turn. She took her time, convinced that there would be someone - a Protector, perhaps - lying in wait for her just past the next bend. She held her breath as she peeked around the corner; all clear. It was only then that she truly realised where she had ended up. And, although it had been the target of her entire escapade, she was still slightly taken aback to find herself standing opposite the West Elevator, just ten paces from the entrance to the Tunnel.

Continuing towards it, she surveyed the door uncertainly, as the memory of her untimely discovery of it came flooding back from a few days prior. Could she really do it this time? Turning her focus to the unsealed gap that still remained, she shifted her weight from one foot to the other debating whether or not she should leave the safety and security of the Subterrane. Yet, as she did so, she could just make out a minute sliver of darkness from the other side of the door, silently taunting her. Edging towards it in eager yet nervous anticipation, she reached out her hand and, grasping the edge of the solid metal door, she pulled it towards herself.

She carefully considered what she was about to do one last time: Surely no one would notice if she was only gone for a few hours. After all, if anyone noticed she could just say that she had been in a different Emergency Pod and forgot to scan her fingerprint when she entered - although she doubted they'd really believe her if she said that...

Eventually making up her mind, she approached the door and stepped through into the blackness, closing it behind her. She gasped in shock as the darkness enveloped her, almost suffocating her. Scrunching up her face, she rubbed her eyes as she waited for the pulsating brightness of the Subterrane to fade away. Finally, she opened her eyes and attempted to squint through the murkiness; she could see nothing.

Remaining completely motionless, she waited in the shadows as her eyes gradually adjusted to the darkness after a lifetime of light. After a few minutes, she managed to make out from a scrap of light emitted from the doorframe behind her, that she was standing at the base of a coiled set of stairs winding upwards.

As she tentatively reached into the darkness, she grasped hold of the rickety railing and stretched out her right foot to find the first stair. Anxiously, she ascended the spiral one step at a time, until she arrived at a tall, narrow doorway with a dull metal handle. She pressed down on the handle, jiggling and jostling the door as much as she dared, until finally it gave way and she emerged onto a long platform. As she peered along the derelict stretch, she took in the earthy, dust-filled scent of her surroundings. She could just make out a small drop down to a set of tracks that were bordered by the platform, and then wound around the corner and out of sight. Both the platform and the tracks were littered with peculiar strips of yellow paper, on which a few words were printed uniformly. She quickly pocketed one and returned her gaze to the remainder of the strange space.

Through the gloom, she could just discern the outline of a large sign that clearly read 'WAY OUT'. It pointed towards what appeared to be a dank and dusty passageway. Walking towards it, she paused to study a poster on her right that read, in faded ink:

Madame Tussaud's
The London Planetarium
Open all day, including Sundays

Eleanor smiled at the ancient relic and wondered to herself what a planetarium might have been. She had, of course, heard of planets from friends of hers who had been selected to study physics in Specialised Education, although she was still unsure of what they actually were.

Specialised Education was the continuation of education for a few select children, in the study of any mainstream science of their own choice. A child was usually chosen following either outstanding achievement in

Placement Examinations, or a good understanding and keen interest in any specific scientific area. The outcome of these specialised courses would undoubtedly result in them receiving either a coveted placement within the Medical Research and Development Centre, or a position within a domain of the Hydroponics Laboratories.

As Eleanor entered the corridor, she noticed that it was lined with an array of shiny tiles that appeared to be in a mixture of pale colours and dark, richer shades. A staircase wound upwards from the end of the corridor, with a thin handrail running up the centre and dividing it in two, while another trailed along each wall. Walking up the right-hand side, she smiled to herself as she realised that she was, in actual fact, going to walk on the Surface - something that, as far as she knew, no citizen of the Subterrane had done in over eighteen years.

But then it dawned on her that she would also see the Sun. Like the seemingly mythological Planets, the sun was something that she had only ever heard rumours about. And even then, these vague accounts came solely and infrequently from the older generations within the Subterrane, of which there was only a small number who could remember the Surface well. She wondered what the sun might feel like - one particular person who had described it to her had said that it was like a 'warm breeze seeping over your skin'. But, not knowing what a breeze felt like either, the explanation was rather meaningless.

As the intricate staircase came to an end, she stepped out onto a grand, coloured terrazzo floor and walked beneath the beamed ceiling to the centre of the room. The corner of the ceiling appeared to be allowing light in through a small crack, and the slightly warped surrounding area which had once been coated in a cream sheen of paint was now speckled with black spots of mould.

Gazing around in awe, she took in the lobby area with its original wooden ticket office and phone booths. A glass screen glinted from within the centre of the wooden, panelled office front and contrasted against the uniform emerald green tile squares that adorned the wall farthest from her. Following three larger steps down, she glanced backwards and noticed a large sign in antique writing that read: 'TICKETS & TRAINS'.

If the sign points to the platform, the way out must be this direction, she reassured herself, trying not to think about how dark it was. What if the Surface is this dark, too? What if it really is all destroyed? She forced the idea out of her head and continued through the large hallway.

Continuing further with her exploration, she passed under a finely ornamented arched corridor and, emerging from the other end, looked back and spotted yet another sign that pointed in the direction she had come from. Squinting, she could just make out the words: 'ENTRANCE TO BOOKING HALL'. She paused for a moment before deciding that, since she was passing the signs in reverse order, she was hopefully en route for the exit. Striding over to the next doorway, she proceeded through it and immediately noticed a concertina-like sheet of metal lodged in the wall on her right. Edging closer to whatever it was, she noticed a small, inconspicuous handle. Yanking it back, she jumped as a shrill cry of metal-on-metal echoed through the silence, revealing what seemed to be an original elevator-style artefact. She remained perfectly still, praying that no one had heard the noise. When there was no response, she finally forced herself to relax.

This must have been the noise I heard when I first opened the door, she realised; finally everything was beginning to fit into place. The strange rattling sound must have been this elevator door being closed manually, and the whirring was the sound of the elevator descending to Level Zero. I suppose using an elevator would make the journey down to the Subterrane much less confusing.

Eleanor pressed on past the old elevator, eager to see where she would end up, and eventually found herself in front of another large sheet of mesh - this time stretched between the walls and locked with a large padlock.

Perhaps this was the Thirteen Founders' attempt at sealing the entrance to the Tunnel, she thought to herself, somewhat unsurprised at their lack of effort.

However, the side of the iron grating had been bent a little way away from the wall, revealing a sizeable gap that was just large enough to slip through. So, crouching down, she wormed her way through the small opening until she was able to stand again. Continuing along the never-ending corridor, she heard a faint noise - a slight mumbling that grew stronger with every step she took. She rounded the final corner with a new spring in her step and at last, saw her first inconceivable sliver of sunlight as it crept through a crack in the great, hefty door that stood between her and the undiscovered outdoors.

She bent down, truly mesmerised as she watched the light caressing the dust and leaves that coated the floor in a thin carpet of years of neglect. The bright light threatened to blur her vision, but she refused to look away as she drank in the surreal glow of the pale and gentle ray. She cautiously inched her hand forwards, letting the pale sunlight sink into her skin as she soaked up the unfamiliar warmth.

Straightening up, she endeavoured to find the source of the sunlight, carefully tracing it to a small gap between panels in the large wooden door up ahead, that seemed to be shedding its rust-coloured paint. One last hurdle stood between her and the Surface so, determined not to give up after coming this far, she took a deep breath and began shoving the heavy door.

After a tremendous struggle on Eleanor's part, it suddenly gave, sending her tumbling to the ground in a heap. Then, immediately realising where she was, her first response was to look up.

The sky was like nothing she'd ever imagined before; a delicate, pale blue canvas streaked with shades of white radiated a warm glow, like golden honey. Keeping her eyes transfixed on the wide stretch of blue above, she slowly stood up and spun around, desperate to take in every single detail of the captivating scene as it slowly glided over her. A breeze caught in her hair, lacing it with a musty, fume-filled scent. As she finally lowered her gaze, she began to survey the strange new world around her.

She was standing at the side of an empty road. A group of young children stood at the far end of it, yelling as they aimlessly kicked around a battered old ball decorated in an alternating pattern of black and white pentagons. A boy caught sight of her suddenly, then stopped and gasped; the others quickly followed suit and watched with a mixture of fear and curiosity. Remaining completely motionless, they stared at her as though they were unsure of what to think.

"Look at her," one jeered in a booming whisper. "She's so pale."

Eleanor couldn't help but agree that compared to some of them, at least, she seemed positively ghost-like. But surely that couldn't be from the lack of sunlight? After all, the lighting in the Subterrane had been altered to ensure that there were no negative repercussions from the lack of natural light.

"Do you think there's something wrong with her?" another whispered.

"And what's with her clothes? What's she even doing there? I didn't see her coming up the road either - it's like she just appeared from nowhere."

"Who is she? I've never seen her round here before," the first added.

"Yeah, me neither," a third added apprehensively.

"I think we should go," the first decided, clearly trying to be the responsible member of the group.

The children darted around the corner as fast as they could, desperate to get away from her. Deciding to ignore the encounter, Eleanor crossed the quiet road and studied the exterior of the tall building in front of her. White concrete blocks streaked with at least fifty years worth of filth were edged with black borders that framed dark and grubby windows. A CCTV camera hung limply from the facade, its lens having been long-since smashed, opposite which a battered streetlamp stood, its shattered bulb no longer giving off any light.

Continuing down the street, Eleanor curiously observed the grand old houses with their crimson fences, their ornate fronts and their multitudes of long, dark windows. To her right rose a tall building with a worn sign that she couldn't quite decipher; on her left, she passed a large construction site and peered eagerly through a gap in the wooden barrier to stare at the demolition that was taking place below. Monstrous vehicles ferried barriers, beams and equipment to and fro across the site, in the centre of which a colossal structure was gradually heading skywards.

Taking a right turn, she passed an exquisite sandstone building adorned with a large, worn crest above the central window. She continued past a series of arches that stood below an elegant palace-like building, where she marvelled at a seemingly endless procession of magnificent sycamore trees that reached high above her head. As she laid her right hand on the trunk of the first, she watched as a single leaf fell towards her and, holding out her left palm, she watched as it landed in it, glowing a faint caramel as the sunlight caught it. Delicately reaching towards it, she gently traced her finger along the narrow veins of the nimble leaf - a pale amber fading to a deep vermillion. And after carefully tucking it into her back pocket, she continued walking along the pavement until she reached a stone flight of stairs on her right. Ascending them hastily, she finally reached the top and found herself standing on a magnificent bridge. Running along it until she reached the centre, she leant over the railings and watched as an inky blue barge appeared from beneath where she stood and gracefully cruised across the river to moor behind two shorter boats at the opposite bank. The air was so sweet, so fresh, the light so dazzling! Only then did she let the reality of where she was truly sink in.

Soon after, she continued her exploration, winding her way through a small park area and around a large building until she found herself standing on the opposite bank to the Tunnel, which was lined with a similarly long archway of flourishing trees. Continuing down the sidewalk for a while, she passed several hideous, grey buildings and paused to peer in through the glass doors of an empty, yet equally ugly building. A strange brass statue was positioned near an elegant sculpture of a dancer, and an empty food cart. Eventually, she found herself passing under a bridge with slanting walkways crisscrossing far above her head. And, as she walked through the gloomy shadows of the underpass, the faint buzz of life slowly began to grow.

Chapter Nine

As Eleanor emerged from beneath the bridge, she was immediately taken aback. Instead of a panic-stricken population that was gradually wiping itself out, she saw a bustling crowd in front of her. And, in the supposedly dreary world in which nothing could or would ever survive, she saw a spectacular thriving market. Hundreds of charming wooden stalls lined the square, each flaunting their garish wares in a multitude of colours. Everywhere she looked, fairy lights and lamps were flickering in an array of hues. The chatter of the crowd was overwhelming, with stallholders fighting to be heard above the racket of their competitors. Peculiar smells swarmed towards her from all directions, drawing her in and overwhelming her senses entirely.

Eleanor looked around herself in a daze, trying to find something familiar - something to reassure her that everything wasn't quite as alien as it suddenly seemed to be. She spun around faster and faster, scanning the market stalls and the skyscrapers that towered above. Her breathing began to grow heavier and she became more panicked by the second. She continued looking about, desperate to find something she might recognise from the numerous stories and things she'd been told about the Surface. As she did so, she was suddenly hit with an immense feeling of nausea. Her vision started to blur and her ears began to ring as her trembling palms prickled with sweat. Nothing was as she had expected - had everything she'd been told about the Surface been a lie?

She stumbled backwards until she bumped into a low wall which she clung to dearly. Remaining with her eyes clenched tightly shut for several long and distressing minutes, she waited for the dizziness to subside and her racing heartbeat to begin to slow. It was only then that Eleanor began to realise the true severity that came with the critical decision she had made. What am I doing here? She asked herself. Where even is 'here'? I'm completely lost in the middle of a strange world that I know nothing about - a week ago I didn't even think it existed! What if she couldn't find her way back? She'd be stuck there forever!

Finally, she convinced herself to open her eyes. As soon as she had done so, she leapt up and stepped away from the wall which, to her horror, seemed to be the only thing keeping her from falling into a wide stretch of water far below.

She returned her gaze once more to the market. There were two possible choices of what she could do next, both with the same end result which, to her at least, was inevitable and entirely unavoidable. Either, she could retrace her steps to the Tunnel and join the queues of citizens most likely still waiting to enter an Emergency Pod, where she could claim she had been too tired to find her way down to Level Nineteen or that she had got lost on the way there. Or, she could spend the day learning about the Surface before returning to the Subterrane in the late afternoon, hoping that no one had realised she was missing - although Saskia was almost certain to have noticed her absence.

There was no question as to which option would be the correct one in the eyes of the Founders. However, it wasn't the thought of what the Founders would think of her if she chose the wrong option - at least in their minds - that caused Eleanor to hesitate. What would she think of herself if she gave up and went back after coming so far? After all, she was already here: She had managed to venture from the confines of the Subterrane, and she had somehow managed to navigate her way through a world that was entirely foreign.

What harm will it do to have a quick look? It's only a few hours, anyway. No one will even know I'm gone.

Taking a deep breath, she slipped into the crowds of people milling around the stalls and smiled to herself at the quaint market that seemed to stretch on for miles.

Intrigued, Eleanor approached the first stall in her path and reached out her hand to feel a thin blue piece of fabric. She rubbed it between her fingers, gasping at the velvety touch; she was certain that she had never seen anything remotely similar to it in the Subterrane. And just as she trailed her fingers over it, she jumped. Someone on the other side of the stall suddenly began to move.

The young woman who stood opposite her was dressed in a jazzily patterned top, a style unfamiliar to Eleanor, with tight blue trousers that Eleanor thought looked a little odd, accompanied by a puffy black coat. A black hat studded with beads sat atop her ruffled dark curls and she was chewing something with a rather bored expression. Deciding that the woman looked harmless enough, apprehensively Eleanor faced her.

"Anything caught your eye?" the woman asked leaning on the stall and propping herself up with her right elbow. "Are you looking to buy?"

"I - no, no thanks," Eleanor replied, a little hesitant of what it meant to actually buy something.

"If you're sure," the woman shrugged, continuing to watch Eleanor as she wandered around the stall.

Each item on display seemed so finely detailed, so exquisitely crafted, that Eleanor wanted to reach out and touch them.

Gazing at a tray full of translucent round objects, she wondered what the curious things might be. She reached her hand towards the delicate pieces, then suddenly stopped herself, not wanting to attract any attention. Stepping away reluctantly, she turned and stared around the market, unsure of where she should head for next.

"Are you alright?" the woman asked her, seeing that Eleanor was a little disorientated.

"I'm fine, thanks," she replied.

"Do you know where you're going? Or need a hand getting anywhere?"

"Um… no, I'm alright," Eleanor reiterated and began to back away, becoming slightly suspicious of the stallholder's nosiness.

There could still be revolutionaries up here, she reminded herself. Just because the Founders were wrong about what the Surface would be like doesn't mean they're necessarily wrong about everything.

She continued down another row of stalls. The first few were weighed down with bowls of various types of juice-packed fruits - most of which Eleanor recognised, as well as a few that she couldn't identify.

The next sizzled with strange smells and omitted a steamy sort of warmth from a large black pan in which rice was being cooked. She peered a little closer, wondering what the ruggedly cut cubes of food within the strange mixture were.

"Alright there?" the young man running the stall asked her.

"What's the…" she squinted at the sign beside the large pan, attempting to decipher what it read. "the …that?"

"Would you like to try it?"

"I, um… alright," she answered, chewing on her thumbnail.

The man took a cardboard pot and spooned a very small amount of the contents of the pan into it. Taking a little wooden fork from a pile beside the pots, he handed both to her and waited eagerly for her response.

Dubiously Eleanor took the pot from him and surveyed its contents, poking and pushing the food around with the fork - it looked nothing like anything they had ever had in the Subterrane. She was mere moments away from handing it back to him in disgust, when she reminded herself that this might be her only chance to experience what things were really like on the Surface. She lifted the fork to her mouth, chewed hesitantly and swallowed.

"What did you think?"

"It was… it's good," she said, surprised. "What is it?"

"Paella," he replied, looking at her expectantly as though that should mean something to her.

"What's that?" she asked uncertainly.

"Well, it's just rice - obviously, and vegetables, chicken and chorizo," he said.

"Rice, vegetables and what?"

"Chicken and chorizo."

"And what's that?" Eleanor was fairly certain she had never even heard of either of them.

The man smiled at her briefly and ignored the question, presuming that she was joking.

"Do you want more?" he asked, clearly pleased that she had liked it.

"If that's alright," she said, nodding eagerly.

"How much d'you want?"

"I-"

"Or how much d'you wanna spend?"

"Spend?" she asked with a frown.

"Yeah. How much d'you wanna pay for it?"

"Oh, I didn't realise I had to… 'spend' on it," Eleanor said, unsure if that was the correct way of saying it. "I haven't got any money."

"Then what are you doing at a market?" the man asked.

"I'm just looking around," she said.

"And you really haven't any money with you at all?" He was looking at her more closely now.

"No, sorry," she said apologetically then, as another customer approached the stall, she added: "I'd better get going."

"Wait a second," he called her back over as she began to walk away. "Give me your pot."

She handed it back and he refilled it.

"There you go," he said, passing it back to her.

"Thanks."

"Enjoy the market," he said, giving her a wave.

She continued past the array of food stalls - one selling something called curry smelt particularly good, as did another that was selling freshly baked bread. The left-hand side of the next pathway was filled with what Eleanor expected would be known as Flower Stalls. Having only ever seen flowers on plants such as strawberries - where they were necessary to produce the fruit - the idea of flowers being grown purely for an ornamental purpose was rather strange. Nevertheless, she happily marvelled at the spectacular array of colours, sizes and shapes before her.

The right-hand side of the pathway consisted of various one-off stalls that sold odds-and-ends; stray pieces of jewellery, shoes, hats, photo frames and crockery. Eleanor wandered past jumbled stalls displaying rusty antiques and mismatched items, occasionally pausing to trace her fingers along the intricate details of various mismatched objects.

A sudden movement on her left caught her eye. She turned and did a double take as a flash of white moved between two stalls. She froze and watched in panic as the figure dressed in white slowly turned in her direction. Standing on her tiptoes, she heaved a deep sigh of relief as she saw that the figure's white jumper was printed with some kind of pattern on the front.

She shook away her paranoia, until another thought suddenly hit her: What if there were cameras watching the door? Why didn't I think to check? Even if there weren't cameras, what if a Protector followed me up here? What if there were some sort of spies on the Surface?

Forcing herself to calm down and dismiss the ridiculous idea, Eleanor turned onto the next row and hurried off towards another gaudy stall that caught her eye. An impressive array of coloured spices was lined up across the counter - deep oranges, striking reds and vibrant yellows.

"Are you buying?" an elderly woman sidled up to her.

"Just looking, thanks," Eleanor replied, reaching her hand out to pick up one of the smallest jars that contained dainty, blood-red strands of something labelled Saffron.

Just before she could select the jar, the woman thrust out her arm, took it from her and leant across the counter to pick up a brown paper bag. Placing the pot inside, the woman turned back to her.

"Anything else you might fancy?" the woman asked. "Paprika? Carda-mon? Star anise, perhaps?"

"No, thank you. I-"

"Or some ceramic pots?" she continued relentlessly. "I have some lovely patterned bowls perfect for jewellery or spice mixes. Or perhaps you would like an incense burner and some sticks? I have great reviews for them from all of my customers." She reached across the table and pulled a few thin sticks with a dark brown coating from an upright, coloured pot.

"How many would you like? Seven? Eight? I think eight makes a very tasteful set," she added, counting out eight and slipping them into the bag with the spice jar.

"No, I really can't-"

"-and I'll do you a great deal: Just three pounds for the incense sticks and twelve for the synthetic saffron," the woman said, holding out her left hand expectantly, while her right clutched the now bulging bag.

"I'm sorry, but I really can't buy this," Eleanor said nervously.

"Of course you can - it is the best deal I can possibly do for you!"

"I really can't buy it," Eleanor repeated, fearing she sounded rather desperate.

"You don't like them?" the woman was growing angrier by the second. "They aren't good enough for you - not quite up to your standards? Is it that?"

"No!" Eleanor exclaimed, frantically attempting to get a word in edge-ways. "I just don't have any money."

"Oh… I see," the woman seemed a little surprised.

Eleanor breathed a sigh of relief as the woman's hassling ceased.

"How about I reserve your order while you go and get your money?"

"No, thank you," Eleanor said, beginning to back away.

"I can wait here for you?" the woman suggested.

"I haven't any money nearby," Eleanor told her.

"I can reserve your items until tomorrow?" the woman shouted after her as Eleanor scurried away as fast as she possibly could.

Afraid that the experience might repeat itself at another stall, she scanned the area for somewhere away from the hubbub of the market, where she would be able to sit in peace for a while. Spotting a bench that overlooked the river she headed over to it, feeling thoroughly down-hearted at being alone in such an unfamiliar world.

Perhaps I should have convinced Saskia to come with me. Or maybe I shouldn't have come in the first place…

And as she sat down, she began to feel her first-ever pang of home-sickness for the Subterrane.

Chapter Ten

"Hey, you mind if I sit here?" came a voice to Eleanor's left, as a girl looked up from something that rested neatly in her hand to wait for her response.

"Sure," Eleanor replied, shuffling along the bench to make room.

The girl was tall with dark-ish hair that she flicked behind her shoulders absent-mindedly, and a skin tone that Eleanor noticed was significantly darker than her own. She was dressed in such a multitude of colours that Eleanor's eyes began to water slightly and her head began to ache - although that could easily have been due to how bright the sun seemed or because of how much purer the oxygen was on the Surface. As she sat down, the girl appeared distracted by a small shiny object resting in her hand that gave off strange images and lights.

Eleanor craned her neck awkwardly in an attempt to see what was displayed on the dark object.

"Can I help you?" the girl asked, turning towards Eleanor as she sensed her staring.

"No! I-I… sorry," Eleanor replied meekly, blushing.

They sat awkwardly for a while, until the girl finally broke their silence.

"You from 'round here?" the girl began, dragging her gaze away from the luminous object which she then slipped into her pocket.

Eleanor remained silent, unsure of what to answer.

"I'm only asking because I've never seen you here before. I'm here most days, pretty much - my mum owns a stall and so me and my sisters help out when we can. Although I'm not sure how much help we really are..." She trailed off, expecting a reaction from Eleanor, but got none.

Eleanor glanced over again, apprehensively surveying the strangely friendly girl.

"Anyway," the girl continued, looking back at Eleanor. "As I was saying; I always notice the people that are regulars here - and most people that come here are. Except for tourists, obviously, but it's not

really the right time of year for them. What I'm trying to say is that I've never seen you here before. Where you from?"

Again, Eleanor said nothing. What's a tourist? She thought to herself. She had no idea what a regular might be, and didn't even have a clue where she was.

"Come on, you've got to say something at some point!" the girl continued relentlessly. "Okay, how about your name? Alright, I'll go first: I'm Abbie... although my mum insists on calling me Abigail, for some reason. Honestly, what is it with parents and nicknames?" she gave Eleanor a look as to signify that it was definitely her turn to say something, this time.

"I'm Ellie," she began cautiously. "I'm from... an area near here," she continued, reassuring herself with the fact that it wasn't technically a lie - she just hadn't mentioned the exact details of her home.

"Where? Although I might not know it, of course," Abbie pressed on.

"It's... it's across the river," Eleanor glanced away, before hastily adding: "You wouldn't know it, I don't think. Not many people do."

"Oh," Abbie replied.

"So where are you from?" Eleanor asked.

"Me?" Abbie smiled at Eleanor and shifted a little on the bench. "I live just near here with my parents and my sisters - they're both younger than me, though. They're with my mum on our stall at the moment," she said. "Do you want to meet them?"

"Meet them? But I've only just met you." Eleanor was unsure why Abbie was being quite so friendly. She was, after all, an absolute stranger.

"Oh, you don't have to," Abbie said, with a little shrug. "It was only an idea."

"No - I didn't mean that I don't want to," Eleanor attempted to rectify her reply. "I just meant that, well, I wasn't expecting anyone to be this friendly, I guess."

Abbie beamed in response. "Well I know you said you're from near here, but you seem like you don't know the area very well," she replied, as though it was the simplest thing in the world. "If I didn't know my way around somewhere, then I'd want someone to chat to me and, well, just make me feel a bit more welcome."

"Well, thank you. You really have," Eleanor assured her. "So, which way to your stall?"

Seemingly unable to contain her excitement, Abbie grabbed hold of Eleanor's arm, hauled her into the thick of the market and dragged her through the crowds. But just before they reached the stall, Abbie stopped suddenly.

"Listen, there's a couple of things you should know about my family before you meet them," she began. "So, first things first, my mum owns a fabric stall - she sell's other stuff as well, but she works there basically non-stop. The second thing is that, although she's always really busy, she loves having us bring friends round so she can pamper them. Believe you me, she'll try and make you stay as long as possible."

"Surely that's a good thing?"

"It usually is, but I'm just giving you a heads up," Abbie answered. "My dad's your more… regular dad, I'd say - he won't be home though, cause he's out working. He's a police officer - my mum's not too keen on it, but he loves it. And his station's only just across the Thames, which is really handy for us. Oh, and then there's my sisters, Veronica and Becca. Ronni - that's Veronica, by the way - she's… well, she's thirteen and she's always a bit grumpy, to be honest. And she loves arguments, so probably best to steer clear of her unless I'm there, because she's never yet won one against me. Becca's eight and she's really smart - definitely smarter than Ronni, and probably smarter than me as well. She's very funny, but she can be a bit, I don't know, dismissive with people she doesn't know. But just ignore her if she says anything or does anything that, well, she shouldn't."

"I'm beginning to think I don't want to meet your family…" Eleanor nudged Abbie teasingly.

"They sound much worse than they really are," Abbie smiled. "What's your family like?"

"Oh, um… kind of average, I guess, for where I'm from," she answered awkwardly, as she glanced behind them, before changing the subject. "So where did you say the stall was?"

"This way," Abbie led her down a row of assorted stalls, each entirely different from the next. Then, as Eleanor looked over her shoulder again, Abbie asked: "Are you alright?"

Someone was following them - or a car was, at least. Eleanor was sure of it. She couldn't help noticing how it moved forwards whenever they did and pulled in at the side of the road every time they paused at a stall.

"Yes, I just… it's nothing. Don't worry."

Perhaps she was just being paranoid. Nevertheless, she glanced back one last time. And it was still there. Is it even following us? she thought anxiously. Maybe I'm just imagining things. Besides, the driver's wearing black, so he can't be from the Subterrane. And if he wasn't, how would he know who she was or where she was from?

They stopped in the middle of the row, where Abbie darted between two stalls and led the way towards the back entrance of the stall. Eleanor watched as Abbie opened the door and then disappeared down what appeared to be a ladder fixed to the wall. Intrigued, Eleanor followed her down, before catching her first glimpse of the inside.

The area beneath the stall closely resembled a den. Rugs, drapes and materials of various sizes and colours were fixed to the ceiling and hung across each wall. A sturdy length of string was fastened to the sides, criss-crossing all the way to the wooden stall, across which more swathes of fabric were draped.

As soon as they entered, the buzz from outside seemed to dissolve into nothing as though it was caught in the fabrics. A pleasantly warming aroma - that of spices mingled with the musty scent of old furniture - filled the room and, as Eleanor stifled a sneeze, Abbie began making her way through the jumble.

"Ronni! Mum! Where are you?" Abbie called out, ducking behind a rug and tugging Eleanor through with her. They wound their way through the muddle of things; miscellaneous lamps stood on the floor, low stools and colourful pots stood in rows along the floor and on miniature tables, which were also dotted with various mugs and other china and enamel ornaments.

"Mum's with a customer," a voice called from behind one of the many patterned rolls of material, that sounded vaguely similar to Abbie's. "She said to wait a sec."

"I've got a friend I want you to meet," Abbie yelled, making her way towards the source of the shout.

"Another one?" Eleanor could hear the exasperation in the girl's voice.

"Yes, 'another one'," Abbie replied, sounding irritated by her sister's tone.

"Anyone I know?"

"Probably not," Abbie answered as they emerged through another curtain and found themselves standing before Abbie's sister. She was a little shorter than Abbie, although not by much, and had frizzy dark brown hair identical to her sister's.

"This is Ellie," Abbie announced proudly, gesturing in Eleanor's direction. "Ellie, this is Veronica."

"Hi Veronica," Eleanor answered rather awkwardly.

"Don't call me Veronica," the girl burst out rather rudely, glaring at a smirking Abbie before correcting herself and smiling civilly at Eleanor. "It's Ronni, thanks."

Just then, an older woman tossed a curtain open and bustled through to join their little gathering.

"Mum, Ellie. Ellie, mum," Abbie introduced quickly. "Ellie's my friend - we just met."

"Lovely to meet you, dear," Abbie's mum replied warmly. "I'm Rosalind. Are-"

"You just met?" Ronni interrupted. "When you said she was a new friend, I thought that you'd at least know her a bit. Who even is she?"

Abbie rolled her eyes and was about to continue explaining how they'd met when Ronni continued with her outburst.

"Seriously, though? You thought you'd just bring a total stranger here? How long have you even known her for? Knowing you it'll be, what, fifteen minutes?"

"Shut up, Ronni," Abbie shot back at her. "She's not a stranger - she's my friend."

"A friend that you've only just met," Ronni reminded her.

"Veronica, don't be rude," her mum scalded. "She's your sister's guest."

"But mum, have you even seen what she's wearing?" Ronni persevered.

"You're going to judge her on what she's wearing, now?" Abbie retaliated. "You've got about the fashion sense of a teaspoon!"

"Look who's talking," Ronni rolled her eyes. "At least I don't look like a paint factory exploded!"

"Stop bickering, girls!" their mum interrupted, giving Eleanor an apologetic look. "Ronni, go and mind the counter while I apologise to your sister's friend for you."

With one last glare at Abbie, Ronni flounced off.

"You don't need to apologise," Eleanor began. "I totally understand why she doesn't want a stranger in your house - well, your stall."

"Even so, she knows better than to say things like that," their mum frowned. "Was it Ellie, dear? Yes, well, we'd love for you to stay for lunch, if you'd like?"

"Really?" Eleanor asked excitedly. "I-I don't really know if I can." She looked over to Abbie, eager to stay, yet not wanting to intrude if she wasn't welcome.

"Of course you should stay," Abbie replied. "It'll give you a chance to see what the Heim family is really like - I bet your family's much better behaved than ours!"

"The Heim family?" Eleanor repeated. "What do you mean?"

"It's our surname," Abbie explained. "What's yours? I never asked."

"Desdemona."

"Seriously?" Abbie replied. "I'd kill for a surname like that."

"Don't be silly, Abigail," her mum chipped in. "Anyway, that's settled, Ellie. Lunch will be ready in about twenty minutes."

"That sounds great," Eleanor replied, feeling rather overwhelmed by the kindness and hospitality of the family. "Thank you - it means a lot."

"Well, you haven't tried it yet," Abbie's mum joked back, although it was clear that she was delighted at Eleanor's enthusiasm. "Let's hope it lives up to expectations!"

"'Course it will, mum," Abbie smiled.

"Thank you, sweetheart. Now, you two run along and I'll call you when I need you to set the table. Oh, and try and find Becca if you can! She's been hiding under the tables all morning and I haven't seen her since I made her do the washing up after breakfast."

"Ah, I can imagine she wasn't too happy about that."

"To put it lightly," her mum replied. "Just keep an eye out for her, will you?"

"We'll find her mum," Abbie said.

"Thank you, Abigail."

As soon as Abbie's mum had disappeared, a figure popped out from underneath one of the many tables. She also looked like a much younger version of Ronni, and was holding tightly onto the ear of a rather worn-looking, fluffy toy rabbit.

"Abbie, who's that?" the short girl pointed at Eleanor.

"Don't point it's rude," Abbie scolded, ruffling the girl's hair as she blew a raspberry. "This is my friend Ellie," Abbie continued. "Ellie, meet my youngest sister, Becca."

"I'm not that much younger than Ronni," the girl said, frowning.

"I'm afraid you are, Becca," Abbie replied, laughing. "Ronni's still five years older than you."

"But you said that last week, and I've grown up more since then!"

"Yes, but so has Ronni, annoyingly."

"But I've really matured over the past week, and Ronni definitely hasn't!"

"Well you're right about that, but I'm afraid that still doesn't make you older than her."

Eleanor smiled at the funny little girl before her and was about to say something when Becca continued with her endless questions; she was extremely talkative for an eight-year-old.

"So why's Ellie here?"

"Because we just met and I thought it would be nice if she came over for lunch."

"But why?"

"Because she's my friend."

"But why?"

"Because I think she's nice."

"But why?"

"I think that's enough why's for one day, don't you?" Abbie said to Eleanor, putting a finger to her sister's lips.

A few moments later, Becca had managed to wriggle her way out of her sister's grasp.

"Come and play, Abbie," she begged excitedly. She began tugging on Abbie's arm and jigging about on the spot.

"Not now, Becca."

"But when, then?"

"Another time," Abbie said, this time a little more firmly.

"You always say that," Becca whined. "You never come and play anymore."

"That's because I-" Abbie broke off as Becca gave a little pout, folded her arms across her chest and turned away from them, holding her head high in indignation.

"Do you mind, Ellie?" Abbie mouthed silently to Eleanor, who smiled and shook her head in response. "Fine, Becca."

"Really?" Becca spun around ecstatically.

"Yes, but only until mum needs me."

"Alright," Becca nodded eagerly. "Ellie, come and see my things!"

Taking hold of Eleanor's hand, she dragged her through the winding maze until they reached a large wooden chest adorned with a collage of sticky labels that read: REBECCA'S STUF - DO NOT TUTCH.

After flicking back the little catch, Becca lifted the lid and began rummaging through the contents of it, occasionally pausing to show Eleanor a few items. The chest contained what appeared to be a jumble of very crumpled clothes, most of which were dresses. One at a time, Becca tossed them onto the floor with an exasperated "definitely not" or "not today, I don't think", until she finally seemed to have found one that she liked.

Handing the item to Abbie, she seemed to suddenly adopt a much younger personality, and said: "You put this on and you can be the princess. I'll be the evil witch, okay?" Then, turning to Eleanor, asked: "Do you want to join in?"

"I'll just watch, I think," Eleanor said, as Abbie struggled to pull the child-sized dress over her hips.

"Becca, I don't think this is going to fit."

"It definitely will," Becca insisted adamantly.

And so, Abbie began trying to pull the dress over her head, still with no luck.

"Becca, I really don't think it's going to fit me," Abbie repeated.

"It will, Abbie. I just know it will."

This time, Becca joined in the struggle by attempting to twist the dress around Abbie, which only succeeded in tangling the long dress sleeves.

"You know, Abbie, I don't think it's going to fit you," Becca decided sensibly, as though the thought had just occurred to her.

"Right, if you say so," Abbie nodded, forcing herself not to laugh.

"Let's try with me being the princess and you being the evil sorceress, Abbie," Becca said, happily scrambling into the dainty princess dress that fitted her perfectly.

As soon as she had done so, Abbie got into character and fixed her sister with a menacing stare. "I, the evil Abbie of... the distant realm of witches, summon you, Princess Becca of..." Abbie paused.

"Bubbletown," Becca whispered to her, deadly serious.

"Princess Becca of Bubbletown," Abbie repeated with a giggle. "I summon you to return to my realm with me for a duel to the death!"

"But Abbie," Becca whispered anxiously. "I don't have a wand…"

"See?" Abbie continued flawlessly without breaking character once. "You, princess, are no match for me!"

"Abbie, stop!" Becca exclaimed, backing away. "You're scaring me. I-I don't think I want to play anymore," she added, running past them and diving under a table. Eleanor crouched down and watched as Becca hastily crawled deeper and deeper into the tangle of desks and chairs.

Abbie got up and turned back to Eleanor.

"She's so funny sometimes," she laughed with a shrug.

"Will she be alright?"

"Yes, she'll snap out of it in no time," Abbie replied as she tossed the clothes back into the chest, before they began making their way back through the maze of furniture and other bizarre objects.

"Abbie! Ellie!" The voice of Abbie's mum came from the other side of the labyrinth. "Come and set the table, girls!"

"Coming mum!" Abbie shouted back.

Eleanor took a few steps down the path on their left which she was sure they had come from.

"It's this way," Abbie laughed, walking off in the other direction.

"But I'm sure we came this way earlier!" Eleanor retorted as she ran to catch up.

"Afraid not."

"How do you know your way around here so well? I would get lost after just five minutes walking around on my own!"

"You get used to it," Abbie shrugged. "But at least I know not to let you loose in here any time soon."

"Probably best not," Eleanor laughed.

"Come on," Abbie hurried down the path a little faster. "Mum'll be wondering where we are."

They rounded a corner and passed a row of cabinets, lampshades and a few wardrobes decorated with various doodles that just so happened to be at Becca's height. Then, they reached a thick purple curtain hung across an arch-like entrance.

"It's to keep all the cooking smells away from all the furniture," Abbie explained as she saw Eleanor's confused expression. And, without warning, she slipped through the curtain and out of sight. A few moments later, she poked her head back through the gap to see what was keeping Eleanor. "Aren't you coming?"

Eleanor nodded eagerly and, intrigued to see what awaited her on the other side, disappeared through the curtain to join Abbie.

Chapter Eleven

The first thing that hit her about the room she now found herself in was its size. It wasn't that it was particularly large - in fact, it was almost cramped. However, for the limited space available, it was made to look absolutely huge. On either side of the curtained entrance was a wooden counter, which stood atop a set of cupboards and beneath several shelves stacked with crockery, vases and various bowls. A small sink was set into the counter on the right-hand side of the entrance, crowded by a variety of other bowls and utensils. On the left hand side, Abbie's mum was chopping something on a large wooden board.

In the centre of the room was a large wooden table that seemed to be very well used and had five chairs of various shapes and sizes dotted haphazardly around it. At the far end of the room, several coloured throws hung across the end wall, making the underground room seem much brighter than it really was. And, tucked behind them, Eleanor could just make out a large, colourful mural that stretched across the entirety of the wall.

"Would you mind setting the table, girls?" Abbie's mum asked as Eleanor gazed about the room in awe.

Abbie immediately headed over to the counter, opened a drawer and took out a handful of cutlery. She began placing it neatly around the table, while Eleanor stood watching awkwardly, wishing she had asked for something to occupy herself with.

"Pop these on the table would you, Ellie?" Abbie's mum asked, handing her a stack of plates.

"Of course," Eleanor replied, taking them to where Abbie stood.

"Ellie, anything you can't eat that I should know about?" Abbie's mum asked.

"Not that I can think of," Eleanor replied uncertainly.

"You're not veggie or vegan or anything, are you?"

"What's a veggie?" Eleanor whispered to Abbie.

"It means you don't eat meat. Do you?"

"Oh, um, I don't think so," she replied, thinking it was probably the safest option since she didn't even know what meat was.

"Ellie says she's veggie," Abbie called to her mum.

"Okay, no problem."

"Where's Ronni?" Abbie asked, looking over at her mum.

"She's minding the stall - I told her to be on her best behaviour. Else she knows her pocket money's out the window."

"But she terrifies the customers," Abbie said. "You should have asked me."

"I know, sweetheart, but I thought it was unfair since you had a friend with you. Becca's still a bit too bossy to manage the stall just yet," Abbie's mum said. "Speaking of Becca, did you manage to find her?"

"Sort of, but I think I might have scared her away again."

"What happened this time?" her mum laughed.

"I was the witch," Abbie said, as though it happened regularly.

"I see," her mum replied with a knowing look. "She is silly, isn't she? I'll just give her a shout when it's ready."

"Ellie, can you grab those glasses from up there?" Abbie asked as she took a large bowl from a cupboard and passed it to her mum.

Eleanor took the glasses from the shelf and placed them on the counter.

"Would you mind filling them as well?" Abbie asked as she began ferrying various things to and fro.

"Girls, don't worry about doing that. I'll finish up here," Abbie's mum said. "Abigail, why don't you get Ronni to come down and then you can also show Ellie the stall, if you like - close it up while you're there."

"Alright," Abbie replied. " Come on Ellie - this way." She made her way past the table, walking towards the wall opposite the curtains they had come through.

"Where are we going?" Eleanor asked.

"To the stall."

"But surely it's that way," Eleanor said, motioning to the curtains behind them.

"Well, you'd think it was. But actually…" Abbie reached for the rug furthest on the right and pulled it back to reveal a small alcove. About the size of a small fireplace, it had a rusty and rather rickety-looking ladder fixed to the wall.

First Abbie and then Eleanor climbed the short ladder before emerging through a trap door behind a wooden counter that spanned the perimeter of the small, rectangular stall.

"Ronni, mum says lunch is nearly ready," Abbie said. "She needs you to help."

"Well, you can tell mum I'm busy," Ronni replied grumpily.

"Busy doing what exactly?" Abbie began provocatively, with a mischievous smirk at Eleanor. "Being rude to the customers? Scaring them all away?"

"Oh shut up, Abbie," Ronni snapped. "I need to close up, at least. Tell mum I'll be down in a few minutes."

"She asked me to close up."

"Of course she did," Ronni said, rolling her eyes at Abbie as she hopped onto the first rung of the ladder and hurried down it.

"Do all the stalls here have rooms beneath them?" Eleanor asked, beginning to think that living underground might not be as rare as she had thought it would be.

"No, there's only one other I think," Abbie explained. "Besides, there wouldn't be enough room for everyone to have one the size of ours!"

"So how come you have it, then?"

"Well, it was originally a storeroom - kind of still is, I guess," Abbie began. "Dad managed to buy it when someone was selling it off. Thought it'd be good being able to store all the furniture near to the stall. Mum used to have to take orders of what people wanted, and then we'd have to drag them across London every time there was an order."

"But surely if it joined up to your stall it should have been yours anyway?"

"Well it didn't join up, originally," Abbie said. "But after he'd bought it, dad was convinced that it was beneath our stall, so he drilled down and luckily it did."

"Imagine if it hadn't," Eleanor laughed.

"Fifteen centimetres closer to the front of the stall and he'd have missed - mum would have been livid!"

"So he put the ladder up as well?"

"Yeah. And he fitted the trapdoor; he's our handyman," Abbie said with a laugh.

"What d'you mean?" Eleanor asked. "What's a handyman?"

"Oh, it means he fixes stuff around the house - and the stall, I suppose. And he does things like…" Abbie paused to look for an example around the stall. "…like putting up these shelves under the counter."

"And putting the ladder and the trapdoor in?"

"Exactly," Abbie said. "Can you switch all these lights off while I fasten the covers down?"

"Sure."

"The switch is over there," Abbie said as she grabbed a key hanging from the underside of the counter then lifted part of the counter, allowing her to step outside of the stall. One side at a time she reached above the stalls display and pulled down the tarpaulin covering, before unlocking a padlock then re-locking it once the metal hoop at the corner of the tarpaulin was safely inside.

Once the stall was completely locked up, the two of them headed back down the ladder to the kitchen, where they found Becca and Ronni in the middle of an intense argument.

"Let's just wait here for a minute," Abbie whispered, crouching behind two chairs that were laden with blankets, and looked as though they might once have been a den.

"What's that?" Eleanor whispered, pointing at the mural as she crouched beside Abbie.

"We did it when I was about three or four - just after Ronni was born," Abbie explained, smiling at the memory. "Well, I say we, but my gran did most of it. She was looking after me while my mum was still in hospital, so we did it together. It's just a bit of fun, really."

The scene was of various houses - obviously designed and drawn by a child - with each one in a multitude of colours, and all drastically different sizes. The buildings had been divided up into dozens of smaller shapes, each one decorated with a different pattern, and painted with vibrant, clashing colours. Above the houses, the sky had been painted in similar patterns to the houses, but was made up of larger shapes and painted solely in shades of blue. The only ordinary part of the mural was the large clouds, which had been made to look as fluffy as possible and used only one shade of bright, white paint.

"It's amazing!" Eleanor whispered, thoroughly impressed. "You should have it on display, not hidden away."

"Thanks," Abbie smiled. "We used to, but Becca always seemed to think that the only reason it was on display was because she was little. She was always telling us how she was too old for it, but she didn't seem to re-alise that it was actually more for me than her."

"Abbie, is that you?" her mum called, as Abbie knocked a blanket off one of the chairs.

"Yes, sorry," she said, standing up and heading over to the table to watch the argument. And, despite the fact that Becca was five years younger than Ronni, she nevertheless seemed to be winning.

"Oh Becca, I do wish you were as quiet as other eight-year-olds some-times," her mum said despairingly as she motioned to the two empty seats and filled Eleanor and Abbie's plates.

"But every other eight-year-old I know is just dull and they're no fun at all. At school, no one ever says anything interesting and I-"

"Oh shush, Becca." her mum said.

"But mum, it wasn't me - Ronni started it!" Becca exclaimed.

"I didn't even say anything!" Ronni retorted adamantly.

"Well, you started it earlier."

"I didn't. It was Becca!" Ronni exclaimed.

"You're such an awful liar. You always blame everything on me."

"I do not."

"Do too."

"Well if I do it's only because you did start it."

"See! You admit it."

"That's not what I said. Becca - you're always making things up! You're such a baby."

"Am not."

"You are too."

"That's enough girls," their mum interrupted. "I want you both to apologise to each other."

"Only if she does it first," Becca muttered back.

"I'm not saying it first because it wasn't my fault," Ronni retorted irritatedly.

"But it was!" Becca exclaimed.

"Girls! I expect better from both of you - especially when we have a guest. And you should know better, Veronica. You're five years older than your sister, for heaven's sake."

"Fine," Ronni replied moodily. "I'm sorry for arguing Becca."

"I don't believe you," Becca replied, cocking an eyebrow.

"Well at least I said it," Ronni said angrily.

"Maybe this time you could try to say it like you mean it."

"Shut up, Becca," Ronni fumed. "Stop being so difficult."

"I'm not being difficult. You're the difficult one."

"Becca, she's right you know," Abbie chipped in. "It's your turn to apologise."

"Abbie, can you just leave this to me, please," Becca said dismissively.

"Becca, come on," Abbie said. "Just apologise to Ronni. It's not that hard."

"Why should I?"

"Because she did and regardless of whether she meant it or not, she still did it." Abbie raised an eyebrow at her sister. "And quite frankly that's more than I can say of you. I thought you were more grown-up than this."

"I am grown up, but-"

"Then apologise," Abbie said sternly.

"Alright," Becca muttered, finally defeated. "I'm sorry Ronni."

"What was that you said?" Ronni said, smirking. "I didn't quite hear you."

"I said I-"

"Speak up," Ronni said smugly.

"I said I'm sorry, Ronni, and I'm not going to say it again," Becca said.

"Are you two quite finished yet?" their mum asked, but was met with silence.

"I can carry on, if you like," Becca replied, her usual bubbliness restored. "I could talk all day - I bet I could. Did I ever tell you that I tried to once at school? I made it all the way to break time before my teacher threatened to send me home if I didn't stop, and I thought that would be boring since there would be no one to argue with at home because Abbie would probably be out and Ronni's awful at arguing." Becca paused to take a deep breath.

"Becca, I have no doubt that you would be able to talk all day, but let's leave that for another time, shall we?"

"I really wouldn't mind doing it today. I-"

"Well I think the rest of us might," Abbie interrupted.

"Exactly. Why don't we just have some peace and quiet now?" her mum suggested.

"Boring," Becca grumbled in a sing-song manner, swinging her legs under the table and earning a glare from Ronni as she accidentally kicked her chair. "So can I go now?"

"No, Rebecca, you can't. You can wait quietly until everyone has finished."

"But they've hardly even started yet!"

"Then it looks like you're going to be here for a while," her mum replied.

Becca sighed and leant her head on the table, as though sitting both still and quiet were the hardest things in the world for her to do.

"Where did you say you were from, Ellie?" Abbie's mum asked, hastily switching topics.

"It's-"

"I thought we weren't talking!" Becca exclaimed.

"No idiot, you're not talking," Ronni explained to her.

"I am not an idiot," Becca said. "I'm cleverer than you'll ever be!"

"Becca! Be quiet," her mum ordered sternly.

"This is so unfair," Becca slouched in her seat.

"Sorry, you were saying Ellie?"

"I live just across the river," Eleanor answered. "Although I doubt that you'd have heard of it."

"Right, and what do your parents do?"

"My parents?"

"Yes - or perhaps I should have asked if you live with your parents, first."

"I... don't live with my parents," Eleanor said slowly, trying to think of a reason she could give.

"So are you on a gap year?" Abbie interrupted.

"A gap year?" Eleanor repeated, unsure what that was. "I, um, yes."

"I wish I was taking a gap year," Abbie replied.

Eleanor smiled, trying to pretend she knew what they were talking about.

"Mum, Ronni kicked me!"

It seemed that two minutes was the limit for Becca behaving.

"Oh, Becca," her mum sighed despairingly. "Does your foot need amputating?"

"I don't think so, but I could be wrong. After all, I'm not a doctor."

"Well unless you're absolutely sure that it needs to be cut off, I don't really want to know about it every time Ronni kicks you."

Becca frowned and glared at Ronni, who stuck her tongue out.

"Ronni, I saw that," her mum said, winking at Becca.

Then, both Becca and Ronni suddenly dissolved into fits of childish giggles as their mum tutted to herself. It seemed almost as though they'd never had an argument; like they'd always been the best of friends. But even with all the petty squabbling and the name-calling, Eleanor finally realised what it must be like to have a family. And, for the first time ever, she felt as though she might have been deprived of one of the best parts of life.

***

"There'd better be a very good reason why I was disturbed." The Founder didn't look at all impressed as he stepped from the elevator to join the two Protectors waiting for him.

"Sir, we've got a problem."

"Can't you sort it out yourselves?"

"I'm afraid not."

"Well what is it, then?" He crossed his arms in annoyance.

"Someone's missing, sir." The first Protector anxiously studied his face for a reaction.

"Then take another register!"

"We already have, sir," the other Protector said.

"Who is it?"

The first Protector looked down at his clipboard. "Eleanor Desdemona."

It seemed the Founder couldn't help but laugh. "Have you checked she's not in another Pod?"

The Protectors nodded. "We've double checked them all, but there's still no sign of her."

"Should we send someone up to look for her? On her residential level, maybe?"

The Founder paused. "Yes, I think you should."

"Who should-"

"But not to her residential level," he interrupted.

"Where would you like us to look, then?"

"Well, you see, a few days ago, a slight… malfunction occurred with the door to the Surface."

One of the Protectors frowned. "But surely that means-"

"That the door is open? Yes," the Founder finished.

"You can't mean that she…" It was almost unimaginable.

"I imagine that Miss Desdemona found out that the door was open, and decided to have a little explore."

The Protectors stood listening, their eyes wide in disbelief.

"I'll double check the security footage and contact our… well, someone who just might be able to help. In the meantime, I want someone waiting near the entrance for when she comes back in."

"On… on which side?" the first Protector stuttered.

"The other side. As soon as she returns, inform me immediately."

Chapter Twelve

"Are you sure you won't stay longer?" Abbie's mum asked as she walked to the back door with them.

"Thank you so much, but I think I should be getting back, now," Eleanor replied gratefully.

"Surely you could stay for just another hour or so?" Abbie's mum suggested. "We'd all love it if you did."

"Really, I can't," Eleanor shook her head. "I should be getting home."

"Abbie!" came a shout as Ronni came thundering through the kitchen and raced towards them. "Abbie, where did you put the key? I told you I should have closed up - I bet you've lost it."

"Um, no… it's on the hook," Abbie told her. "You know, the hook that it's supposed to be on?"

"It is?" Ronni said, looking a little embarrassed. "Where's the hook?"

"Under the counter, like it always is."

"Which counter?"

"Really, Ronni?" Abbie said. "Have you never opened the stall before?"

"Mum always gives me the key," she mumbled.

"Well, go and look for it," Abbie said, and Ronni traipsed off in the direction of the kitchen once more.

"Right, well I should probably see to that," their mum said regretfully, then smiled warmly. "I hope we'll be seeing you again soon - any friend of Abbie's is always very welcome here."

"Thank you," Eleanor said.

Abbie's mum bustled off towards the kitchen. Once she was out of sight, Eleanor turned back to her new friend. "Do you mind showing me the way through the market? I think I can probably find my way back from that bench where we started."

"Sure, it's this way," Abbie led Eleanor towards the way out.

"Thanks," Eleanor said, as they finally came to the top of the ladder and emerged through the back entrance.

"So what did you think of our market, then?" Abbie asked as they began their walk back past the array of stalls.

"It's... it's different," Eleanor settled for. "It was nice meeting your family, though."

"Different how?"

"Well, it's vibrant, colourful and so lively - I guess I'm just not used to that."

"Really?" Abbie replied with a frown.

"Yeah," Eleanor shrugged. "It's kind of just the... the culture of where I'm from."

"The culture? How?"

"Oh, um, well we only use a limited range of colours, really," she said carefully.

"But why would you limit colour?" Abbie seemed unable to grasp the concept.

"It's just because it's cheaper."

"Oh, right," Abbie nodded. "Also, I meant to ask you earlier but, why are you actually here here? Only because you said you're not from here, and I've never seen you here before and you don't seem like you're here to buy anything."

"So what am I doing here?" Eleanor repeated for clarification.

Abbie nodded.

Eleanor mulled over the rather unexpected question. She could have made up some far fetched story but wasn't sure how much good it would do in the long run. After all, it might do some good to have an ally on the Surface. And so, she chose to give an answer that was as close to the truth as she dared.

"I'm not sure," she admitted honestly.

"How come?"

"I came here looking for… well, answers, sort of. I wanted to see what it would be like for myself."

"Answers for what?" Abbie prompted.

"Just… general stuff," she replied quickly.

"Alright, then. And did you find whatever answers you wanted?"

"I think so, but I'm not sure how they help."-

"I see… wait, actually I don't. I've no idea what you're talking about," Abbie frowned, an expression of confusion on her face.

"Sorry, it's just that I was… I was looking for answers about this place, really, and I-"

"The market?" Abbie sounded even more puzzled.

"Well no, but I-"

"Look, I'm guessing that you're trying to hide something, and I get it - I do. I'm the first person to try and conceal something - I've got two sisters after all, so I've become something of an expert at it. But I've also become rather good at detecting secrets too, so if you want me to help with something, then you need to tell me what's going on. You can trust me - I promise I won't tell anyone."

Studying Abbie's face to see if she was being genuine, Eleanor blocked out the little voice of her inner conscience that was thoroughly disagreeing with what she was about to do. And, finally giving in, she began to relay every single detail of her past to Abbie.

***

"So you're telling me that you've never been outside before?" Abbie asked in amazement, having sat patiently listening to Eleanor for the past half hour.

"That's right," Eleanor couldn't help feeling awkward and slightly embarrassed.

"And you're not kidding? You promise?"

"Of course!"

"Alright. Either you're telling the truth or you're insane."

"Well, I'm definitely not insane - although that's probably just what an insane person would say anyway..." Eleanor smiled.

Abbie still didn't seem totally convinced. "And you've never been outside before? Not even once?"

"No, never."

"But... how does that even work?" Abbie asked. "Aren't there any repercussions now that you're up here? Do you feel okay? Is it weird? Are you-"

"It's not too bad," Eleanor cut in. "The main difference is that the air just feels much lighter and... it seems thinner, almost. The smells are weird too - there's virtually nothing with any scent in the Subterrane, whereas the different smells here are so intense. And it's hot so up here, as well."

"Doesn't the light hurt your eyes?"

"A bit," she admitted. "I'm used to it being bright, but I'm just not quite used to it being this harsh - it's a very different kind of brightness."

"I still don't get how your... world works. I mean, it just doesn't make sense - why would anyone believe that there was nothing up here whatsoever? I just... how could anyone believe that? I would never... it's such a... a violation! I would never believe something like that unless there was actual proof."

"I guess it lasted for so long that everyone forgot. Well, not forgot, exactly, but I expect they just figured that there had to be nothing left. They'd react like you, because surely no one would trap people down there unless it was true."

"But why would someone pretend that something terrible had happened, when nothing had changed since they'd left?"

"I think they must have thought there was some kind of threat when they first evacuated everyone - or that there was going to be, at least," Eleanor replied.

"But there hasn't been any kind of danger like that for years, now. They've just... indoctrinated everyone completely."

They sat in silence as they tried to find a legitimate reason as to why Eleanor, along with the rest of the citizens of the Subterrane, had been kept in the Subterrane for so long. But the truth was, that a lie of such magnitude as that would never be justifiable.

"So when they first went down there, everyone just suddenly became equal? How would that even work? Surely some people wouldn't be happy about that."

"Kind of," Eleanor shrugged. "Some people became Sub-Leaders, or something - mostly politicians, lawyers and other people like that. They don't really do that much, though."

"I guess they would want to feel important."

"Exactly," Eleanor nodded.

"So what now?" Abbie asked. "Are you going to go back?"

"I'm not sure," she answered. "I don't really want to, since I know the truth about it all now, but I think I probably should."

"What? Why would you go back?"

"It's not that I want to, particularly. But if no one knows that nothing's changed up here and that it's all just one great fabricated story, then they could be trapped for years. It could be decades before anyone else figures it out! If you think about it, there's a chance that someone might have found the way out before me - who knows how long the door had been open before I saw it? If I'm right about that, the only reason that no one knows about it is because anyone that did make it up here never came back to tell us; they found an opportunity, took it and disappeared. If anyone had ever come back, then we could have been liberated years ago. I guess people might have tried to in the past, but even if they did, they were obviously unsuccessful," Eleanor trailed off, suddenly realising how much she was waffling on. "Sorry, that was..."

"No, it's fine," Abbie smiled back in response. "But you'll stay for a little while before you go back, won't you? After all, we have only just met."

"Well, I suppose I could. But what would we do?" Eleanor asked dubiously.

Abbie shrugged. "How about I show you London?"

***

The call hadn't surprised him in the least. In fact, it had come a good half-hour later than he had expected. Of course, he had already known who the girl in question was, having spotted her at the market from his car. Although it would have been hard to miss her, with that pale complexion and the rather lost look on her face. That, and all the white she was wearing - another instant giveaway. Which was why he'd had the sense to track her whereabouts from the moment he set eyes on her. And, although he'd been told that she hadn't become a threat, yet, he couldn't help but check the gun tucked into his coat pocket and wonder when he might need to use it.

Chapter Thirteen

"Where are we going?" Eleanor called, trailing behind Abbie who was already dashing ahead.-

"Come on - we're nearly there," Abbie coaxed.

"Nearly where?"

"Ellie, seriously it's not far!"

"Can't you tell me first?"

Abbie ignored Eleanor and led her along the riverside until they stood before a huge wooden, circular building.

"What is it?" Eleanor asked as she stared up at it with a frown.

"It's called the Globe Theatre. I'm pretty sure it's a copy of a similar one somewhere else," Abbie explained.

"What's it for?"

"It's a theatre. Didn't I say that?"

"Yes, but what's a theatre?"

"What's a theatre?" Abbie repeated.

Eleanor shrugged. "We don't have them."

"And you don't even know what one is?"

"No. I've never heard of them."

"Seriously? Well someone down there must remember them," Abbie commented. "Especially with a surname like yours."

"What do you mean? Why?"

"Sorry, I'll explain," Abbie began again. "You said that names are chosen from a larger selection, and each one is picked out by part of your government, right?"

"Yes. They're all names that have been approved for our use." Eleanor didn't quite understand what Abbie was getting at.

"And surnames too?"

"Yes."

"Well, this theatre is where the plays written by the most celebrated playwright who ever lived are performed."

"Alright, but what does that have to do with me?" Eleanor shrugged and looked back out over the river.

"It's not you, it's your name - your surname, actually."

"But how?"

"Well, in one of these particularly famous plays called Othello, one of the central characters is Desdemona. She basically goes against her family's wishes and marries for love, but then she gets killed and it all gets a bit messy at the end. I only know about it because they've just finished doing it here - mum and I went. My point is that someone in your world must know Shakespeare. You don't just come up with a name like that. Besides, it's a pretty rare name now, I'd imagine."

"Really? Why?"

"It's kind of got bad connotations, now - because of the play."

"Oh, well let's hope the Founders weren't trying to tempt fate," Eleanor laughed, smiling at Abbie as they continued walking.

"You see that?" Abbie said, pointing across the river. "The huge dome over there? That's St Paul's Cathedral."

"St Who's?" Eleanor furrowed her brow, trying to understand how someone could own something quite so large.

"St... well, it's named after a Saint," Abbie clarified.

"What's a saint?" Eleanor was still confused.

"Sorry, I keep forgetting."

"It's fine," Eleanor shrugged, realising how difficult it must be for Abbie when she knew next to nothing about her world.

"How to describe a saint..." Abbie murmured to herself before turning her attention back to Eleanor. "A saint is like a holy person - if you believe in all that stuff, at least. Otherwise, he's just some random lucky guy that got a huge cathedral named after him."

"So, do you?"

"Do I what?"

"Think he's holy?"

"Me? No way," Abbie said, shaking her head. "Hardly anyone believes things like that, nowadays."

"Why not?"

"I'm not really sure, actually," Abbie admitted. "It was probably, well, I guess it was probably because all these bad things were happening - like all the flooding we had, and then you lot disappearing. All these bad things began outnumbering the good things that happened, and after that people kind of just... lost faith, I guess you could say."

"Oh."

"I never really understood it all, anyway."

"Understood what?"

"Religion and stuff - that's what I was saying isn't very popular any-more. I suppose you don't have that either," Abbie reminded herself. "It's basically when you believe in a higher power that controls everything that happens, although I don't get why you'd want to believe everything was all up to someone else. If I do something, I want it to be because of me - not because of someone up there who has power over me," Abbie motioned towards the sky.

"But why would there be someone up there?" Eleanor asked in bewilderment, glancing upwards. "How could someone live in the sky?"

"Because..." Abbie trailed off. "It wouldn't necessarily be a person like us. It was more that it was just something for people to believe in."

"Right," Eleanor frowned, totally lost and eager to change the subject to something that she wasn't clueless about. "So where next?"

Abbie bit her lip in thought, then her face lit up as an idea suddenly popped into her head.

"I've got just the thing!"

"What is it?" Eleanor asked eagerly.

"Actually it's quite close to something else, too," Abbie added pensively.

"Can you tell me?" Eleanor asked, displeased at being kept in the dark.

"I can't yet - it'll ruin the surprise. But you'll love it - trust me!"

"Alright," Eleanor replied reluctantly, then waited a moment before saying: "Can't you just give me a hint?"

"No."

"Please? Just a tiny hint?"

"Ellie, I said no!"

They walked a little way along the embankment in silence before Abbie began chattering away once more.

"I was thinking that I should've taken you to see one of the old palaces round here. The only thing is that I've had to take Becca so many times that I just find them so dull, now," she said. "I'll admit that they're incredible, though. Perhaps if you ever come back again I'll take you to see one."

"What's a palace?" Eleanor asked.

"Sorry, my fault again," Abbie replied. "Palaces are where our royal family used to live. And before you ask, a royal family is a family that's descended from previous kings and queens. It meant that whoever was the eldest member of the same bloodline became the country's monarch. And then the monarch was the country's head of state and it meant that they were also head of the government, I think. It's all a bit complicated to explain."

On 9th March 2053, after six solid months of complaints, protests and demonstrations, the English Monarchy had finally been abolished. Less than two months later, the United Kingdom had been divided into four separate countries: England, Scotland, Ireland and Wales - all with similar, re-invented government systems.

"So the monarch and their family live in palaces?"

"They used to," Abbie explained. "But we don't have a royal family anymore. We have someone called a Chancellor who's in charge of the government, but they're elected by our government every four years."

It had been decided that, after the names of several influential members of parliament were put forward, a new head of state - known as a

Chancellor - would be voted for by all members, over the course of six days.

"What's the point in that?"

"It makes the government a democracy because everyone over a certain age votes on who they think should be in the government, according to which party they support or what they want the country to become. It just means that everyone has a say in what goes on. Don't worry if you don't get it - it's actually a very complicated system to explain," Abbie assured her, laughing at how confused Eleanor looked.

Consequently, every very four years since then, each established member of the House of Commons had the opportunity to put their name forward and potentially be voted into the position of Chancellor. Then, in May, the same six day procedure would occur until one candidate had received over 58% of all votes.

"Well, at least the Subterrane isn't as confusing as that," Eleanor replied, amazed at how something that should have been so simple could be quite as complicated as Abbie had made it sound.

Eleanor carefully followed Abbie across a busy road - narrowly avoiding being hit by a dark car with tinted windows - until they finally made their way down an alleyway that led onto a much longer street, Abbie once again attempting to tell Eleanor the plot of Othello.

"How much further?" Eleanor interrupted, whining like a child.

"Not far," Abbie replied. "It's just that building up ahead."

"We're going in there? It looks a bit odd."

"Just wait until you're inside," Abbie said. "Then you'll think it's odd - but if you don't like it in there then just say and we can go."

"Alright," Eleanor replied as they were about to enter a covered passageway, before she suddenly ducked and looked upwards warily. "What's that noise?" she asked fearfully, but saw that the skies were empty, save for a few distant passenger planes that she had spotted on her way to the market. "I've heard that before."

"Really?" Abbie asked. "Are you sure?"

"Definitely," Eleanor nodded.

"What did you think it was - the last time you heard it?" she asked.

"I'd always thought it was explosions or planes or something from the war up here, but… it obviously can't be, can it?"

"Explosions?" Abbie remarked, casting her a quizzical look.-

"You can hear it from Level Zero, so we were always told that's what it was," Eleanor replied. "What is it really?"

"It's, well, I won't be able to explain it very well out here," Abbie said, 'so just wait a few minutes and then I'll show you."

They both remained silent until they reached the other end of the walkway and emerged into a large open space, across which stretched some strange kind of barrier.

"Wait here." Abbie headed over to a wall where she briefly tapped on a peculiarly bright panel that was set into it. She returned a few moments later with two pink slips of paper and handed one to Eleanor.

"What is it?"

"A ticket."

"What's it for?"

"You'll see," Abbie answered coyly.

Following closely at Abbie's heel, Eleanor watched intently as she inserted the intriguing ticket into the barrier, which then swallowed it up before spitting it out from a different opening. Abbie then retrieved the ticket, stepped through the barrier and the doors closed behind her.

"What should I do? I'm locked out!" Eleanor exclaimed.

"Just put your ticket in," Abbie laughed. She didn't seem to understand quite how strange and distressing the experience was for Eleanor.

Eleanor did so very carefully, so that the barrier didn't devour her fingers along with the ticket, and then snatched it back as soon as it reappeared through the second opening and darted through the barrier doors.

"You're doing well," Abbie coaxed. "Now, the next part might be a bit much…"

"Why?" Eleanor asked, thinking that it couldn't possibly get any worse.

"Come and see," Abbie said, leading her over towards the far side of the room.

Eleanor stopped abruptly and stared, mesmerised, at the sight before her. A long set of stairs led into the depths of the strange building. Only they weren't quite stairs. Instead, each step slowly peeled away from the floor on which she stood, before descending in an orderly manner at a gently slanted angle, and finally melting into the ground that loomed far beneath them, just in sight.

"Are you ready?" Abbie asked, jolting Eleanor from her trance.

"For what?"

"To go down, obviously."

"We go down... that?" Eleanor repeated, partly amazed and partly terrified. "Is it safe?"

"If it's safe enough for everyone else, then I'm sure it's safe for us." Abbie pointed to the people who, Eleanor noticed, were dotted all the way down the right hand side of the staircase. "Think of it as... a lift, but with stairs."

"A lift with stairs..." Eleanor repeated, unconvinced.

"Do you want to go back? I don't mind if you do," Abbie assured her.

"No. But you go first," Eleanor said quickly, nervous at the prospect. Edging backwards, she glanced back at the station entrance, and did a double take. A figure stood in the shadows, his face hidden from view. But she was sure she had seen him somewhere else.

"We don't have to if you don't want to," Abbie told her, noticing her distraction. "It's completely up to you - I don't mind."

"No, I-I'm fine," Eleanor said. And, with a reassuring nod from Abbie, they stepped onto the escalator together.

After finally disembarking from the dizzying contraption, Abbie led the way down the winding passageways that grew noisier with every step they took, until they eventually emerged onto a booming platform.

"So first we're going to get a tube - it's just an underground train, really," Abbie chattered away. "Do you even know what a train is?"

Eleanor shook her head.

"Ok, well you'll see in a minute. Anyway, we're currently at a station called Southwark Barrier - it used to be known as London Barrier or something like that. It might have been London Bridge, actually..." she trailed off thoughtfully. "Anyway, we're going to take a tube to another station that's called Canada Water, and from there, we'll cross the Thames at the Quay Barrier and go to the Woodland Glasshouse. Sound any good?"

"Yes - other than the fact that I have no idea what half those things are," Eleanor replied.

"Well," Abbie began, then paused as the tube thundered up to the platform. After guiding Eleanor safely through its double doors, she continued: "They're like big bridges that are used to prevent flooding within London."

"Why would there be flooding?"

"There was some here around thirty, thirty-five years ago. That was before your Evacuation wasn't it?" Abbie recalled.

By February of 2039, significant rises in temperature had caused the polar ice caps to melt completely, which had consequently caused the sea levels to rise. When the sea level readings from 2039 were compared to those taken in 2022, the results showed that the English borders had shrunk by almost 5.38 square kilometres over the course of only seventeen years. As the sea levels increased, so did the water levels of the River Thames, thereby putting the Nation's capital and thus the entire English economy at risk.

"You might want to hold on, by the way," she added, motioning to the handrail as the train jerked forwards and Eleanor let out a little yelp of fear. "Anyway, they had to flood some coastal areas to stop London from flooding - it's why my family moved here."

An executive decision was then made by the English Government to intentionally flood what was to be known as the 'Borderlands'. This intentional flooding would contribute to the reduction of sea levels worldwide, by a small but necessary amount. The one drawback was the increase of population density across most parts of England, as a result of coastal inhabitants moving more inland. Nevertheless, it was an insignificant sacrifice that was made to increase the sustainability of the country.

"My parents used to live further South but it freaked my mum out, so my dad decided they should move to London for safety."

To further ensure the preservation of London and, thereby, England, numerous flood barriers were built along the length of the River Thames to prevent torrents of water gradually creeping upstream. This also guaranteed that, in case any particular barrier was unable to contain the sheer quantity of water constantly building up against it, the capital would remain impermeable to flooding.

"So, let me tell you my theory." Abbie continued. The tube was thundering along the tracks at what seemed like lightning speed to Eleanor, yet Abbie seemed completely unfazed by the speed. "So you mentioned that there are certain vibrations that you can feel from your Ground Floor Level or whatever you call it. And I can kind of see why bombings and explosions from the above ground would be a pretty believable explanation - unless you know otherwise, of course. But you and I both know that that's not the case. I've got a feeling that your underground world is located beneath a train or tube station - probably similar to the one we've just come through, except that yours is empty. At any kind of public station, there's almost always at least one or two members of the public going somewhere, so someone would probably have noticed if you came through a door in the wall. My guess is that you've been living beneath a derelict station. Obviously it has to be one that trains still run through, but I think there's quite a few like that."

"So the trains cause the vibrations that we hear?"

"I think so," Abbie confirmed. "That's the noise you recognised when we were outside - it's what gave me the idea, actually."

"So this train might have even gone over the Subterrane?" she asked in excitement.

"It could have done," Abbie nodded.

"That's... well, I never expected that."

"I bet," Abbie smiled then, as the tube's brakes squeaked, she added: "Look - we're here."

After chaperoning Eleanor off the tube and up another escalator, Abbie managed to coax her through the station exit - this time without Eleanor becoming too flustered in the process.

Abbie pointed across the river at what appeared to be a spectacular curve of glass bent towards the sky, covering the whole of the vast building beneath it.

"That's where we're going."

Chapter Fourteen

The Woodland Glasshouse was situated on a small Island - one of the many that had been the result of a series of meanders that had run through the city. On one side of the island ran the river, and on the other side was a small, partially dried-up oxbow lake.

Gradually they neared the building, marvelling at the great dome that rose high above them. It was surrounded by a neat grassy border dotted with brightly coloured wildflowers.

"So what exactly is this place?" Eleanor asked as they approached the entrance.

"It's called the Woodland Glasshouse. There used to be a park here before that, so they just built it up a bit, I think," Abbie explained. "It's a preservation centre, which means it houses any endangered species of plant that would otherwise have died out. I'm guessing you don't have much interaction with plants, so I thought this might be fun for you to see." She pushed the door open and guided Eleanor towards the registration desk.

"Go straight on in, girls," the receptionist called out, waving them towards another set of doors. "We're not very busy today."

"Thanks," Abbie replied and led the way inside.

As soon as they entered the extensive space, they gazed upwards in awe. The glass dome gleamed in the brilliant sunshine, projecting its warmth inside.

"I haven't been here in over a year," Abbie commented. "We used to come here loads, but Becca finds it a bit boring so we haven't recently."

"It's incredible!" Eleanor was struggling to tear her eyes away from the intricately panelled roof.

"Where do you want to start?" Abbie asked, seemingly eager to look around.

"Over there?" Eleanor suggested, pointing to the right.

"Okay. Which area is that?" she wondered aloud, before running back to the entrance, grabbing a guide, and hurrying back. "Apparently it's the Marine sector, so it's for plants that used to grow by the sea - they try to replicate the habitats so they grow better," she explained, pointing towards a small stream-like stretch of water then, referring back to her guide, she read out a passage about the plants. "It says: 'The Marine Sector of the Woodland Glasshouse is home to many of the country's most prized coastal plants, a significant amount of which exist nowhere else in the world. The Channel Stream consists of a short circuit that recycles the same twenty-five gallons of water, originally infused with 160 grams of sodium chloride, and topped up with an extra 4 grams every five weeks. Our Botanists regularly take clippings and store them in our underground freezer storage space in case any particular plant is, for some reason, unable to grow within the Glasshouse.' That's quite clever, I guess."

"What's that?" Eleanor pointed to a flower with a periwinkle blue head and spiny leaves.

Abbie peered closer to the plant and flipped over its label to read what it said. "It says it's a sea holly. 'Previously found on sandy shores and dunes, this flower was once a common sight all across the English and Welsh coasts. Although the leaves bear some resemblance to that of the universal Christmas plant, the two are not related. Originally the Sea Holly bloomed between July and September, but due to the slight increase in the temperature of our current climate, its blooming season has been extended and is now between May and October.'"

"It looks a bit odd," Eleanor remarked.

"Yes, it does a bit," Abbie agreed. "Do you know what regular holly looks like?"

"No."

"Perhaps we didn't need to come here - we could have just walked past a flowerbed," Abbie joked, although Eleanor wasn't quite sure what she meant by it. "What's that one?" she asked, as another caught her eye.

Eleanor crouched down to read the label. "It says it's a sea campion," she began as she glanced over the information. "Why are there two names on the label?"

"It's an old way of categorising them, I think," Abbie explained. "One's an English name, and one's Latin - my dad told me about it once, but un-surprisingly I lost interest in it pretty quickly."

"It says they're occasionally found on the English coast in north-west England and western Scotland," Eleanor read. "And they typically used to bloom between June and August, but now flowers between May and Sep-tember."

They continued through the Marine Sector, occasionally pausing to see what a particularly eye-catching plant was called. They passed marshy plants, rock plants, water lilies, and a wide variety of orchids, grasses and blossoms.

"I would have suggested that we look around this whole place, but it would probably take us days! We should probably get going if you want to see some other parts of London," Abbie said. "But we can stay here if you want, though. Up to you."

"No, let's go somewhere else," Eleanor agreed. "I want to try and see as much of London as I possibly can in one day."

"Alright. I know exactly where we should go next," Abbie said, as she enthusiastically led the way to the exit, Eleanor following closely at her heels.

"Where?" Eleanor asked, struggling to keep up with Abbie's quick pace.

"Wait and see," Abbie replied.

They crossed at the Dockland Barrier and followed the slightly eroded perimeter of it until they reached the famed Peninsula Bridge, which was swarming with tourists.

"I knew it would be busy at this time of day," Abbie admitted.

"What's so special about this bridge?" Eleanor asked, unable to see what the fuss was about. "It looks the same as all the others."

"It's not the bridge that's special. It's what's on the other side of the barrier," Abbie replied. "Can you see that huge building up ahead?"

Eleanor craned her neck in an attempt to spot it: "Yes, I can see it. What is it?"

"It's a huge arena."

"But what's so special about it? Aren't there any others?"

"There are, but it's the most popular one. And it's prime time for getting last-minute tickets now," Abbie explained. "It's also quite well-known because the island it's on is called Peninsula Island. Do you know what a peninsula is?"

"No," Eleanor admitted, shaking her head.

"Well," Abbie tilted her head to the side. "A peninsula is a stretch of land that's almost entirely surrounded by water, but not completely."

"But I thought you said it was an island?"

"Exactly," Abbie stated contradictorily. "See, it used to be a peninsula, but then the course of the river changed and it became an island. And since they had to name the island something, I think someone thought it would be amusing. The story's a bit anticlimactic, but it's done its fair share of recruiting tourists."

"What's that noise?" Eleanor asked suddenly.

"What noise?"

"In the background. What is it?" Eleanor looked around in an attempt to locate the source of the strange noise.

"You mean the music?" Abbie frowned.

"Is that what it is?"

"You mean you don't have music?" Abbie asked, staring at Eleanor in disbelief.

"No," Eleanor shook her head. "I'm sure I've heard it mentioned before, but I've never really understood what it is."

"But how can you possibly eradicate music?" Abbie wondered aloud. "Surely that's next to impossible! Music can travel purely by word of mouth."

"It must have been discouraged, then. No one in the Subterrane would have wanted to do anything to offend the Founders, after everything they had supposedly saved us from. If they had said they wanted to stop music, it could easily have been done."

"I suppose," Abbie still didn't sound convinced.

"What's over there?" Eleanor pointed towards the south-facing railing, where crowds of people were jostling to get the best view across the river.

"Oh, you'll like this," Abbie laughed. "So the area directly across the river from here is off-limits to everyone - that's why there's no bridge to it from here. But it's rumoured that it's owned by the English Space Agency."

"What's the English Space?" Eleanor asked, misunderstanding the question.

"Oh, um…" Abbie paused to gather her thoughts. "Well, do you know that we live on a planet?"

"Kind of, yeah."

"Right. And our planet - Earth - it orbits the sun. Got it?"

"Yeah."

"And there are seven other planets like ours that also orbit our sun. Still following so far?"

"I think so," Eleanor answered, frowning a little as she tried to concentrate.

"Well, our planet, our sun and the other seven planets form our Solar System. And our Solar System is amongst other Solar Systems and Galaxies within Space. So basically we live in Space."

"So what does the area across the river have to do with… Space?"

"Well, none of us knows, really," Abbie admitted. "It's all just speculation. And don't get me wrong - the theories might be right, but it could easily just be a military base or something. Although, according to the rumours, at least, they're building a Space Station there and - bear in mind this is something someone came up with a few weeks ago - apparently they're building some kind of shuttle that will take people up there."

"Up to space?"

"Exactly."

"But what would you do up there?"

"Nothing, I imagine. Think about it though… Just floating around up there." Abbie gazed up towards the sky longingly before snapping out of it. "Come on, we should probably get going."

"Where now?" Eleanor asked.

"Well-"

"Actually, how long have I been gone?"

Abbie glanced at her watch.

"It's just gone two," she answered. "Should we go back? We can if you want; I don't mind. We can go past a few things on the way as well, if you like?"

"We should probably start heading back that way," Eleanor agreed. "Someone might notice if I'm gone for too long."

"Alright. This way's quickest."

Abbie led the way back over Peninsula Barrier and then, instead of crossing back to the island where the Woodland Glasshouse stood, she led Eleanor along the river.

"We're taking a different route back," she explained as they followed the curve of the dried-up river. "There's a couple more places I want you to see before you have to go. You see that one just up there?"

"The big building?"

"Yes. It's not actually very interesting, but it's the police station that my dad works at," she explained. "I'd take you inside to meet him, but he doesn't like me going in while he's working."

"What does he do there?"

"He… well, he does a lot of supervising and policing events, I think." She shrugged, as though she wasn't entirely sure.

"What's that building over there?" Eleanor pointed further inland to a large, regal, walled building with white towers.

"That's the Tower of London," Abbie said. "It's one of the oldest buildings in London - or some of it is, at least. It's where the crown jewels are kept - there's a few art galleries too."

"What are crown jewels?"

"Oh, you'd love them!" Abbie began excitedly. "They're - do you know what jewels are?"

"No..."

"Okay, well, they're - they almost look like coloured pieces of glass," she began. "The only difference is that they're naturally that colour, or sometimes they're clear but then they get cut into particular shapes. They're basically these really beautiful, expensive stones and crystals."

"I think I might have seen a couple of people with things like that."

"Yes, I wouldn't be surprised if you probably have," Abbie said. "By the way, I wanted to ask you a couple more things about your world. Do you mind?"

"Of course not. You can ask anything."

"Okay, so you live underground, right?" she began.

"Yes..."

"You said it goes down really deep, but how does it work with getting oxygen around it all?"

"There's a ventilation system that apparently comes from an area on the Surface, and then it circulates the oxygen around the entire Subterrane."

"Alright, fair enough," Abbie nodded. "But how do you make food?"

"Hydroponics," Eleanor answered swiftly. "We have an entirely plant-based diet except for a few vitamins that we have tablets for."

"But where do you get the plants from?"

"There's eight huge labs full of hydroponically grown plants."

"What are hydroponics?"

"Oh, it's where plants and crops are grown without soil, only using only water. We change the temperature and humidity of each lab according to what it houses and what the plants require."

"So everything is made from plants?" Abbie asked.

"Yeah - some stuff takes more work, but one way or another it's all originally from plants."

"What takes more work?"

"Well, milk and yoghurt cause you have to make it from the soybeans and stuff, and then tea leaves, because they have to be picked and then dried and then shredded a bit," she added.

"You grow tea leaves?"

"We only get a specific caffeine allowance each day, but yeah. Someone told me that they thought about having a coffee plantation at one point, but it was going to be too much hassle."

"I can imagine. But where does all the water come from?"

"I think it originally came from the Thames and now it's just filtered and recycled over and over - but I'm not entirely sure about that one," she admitted.

"I guess that makes sense," Abbie looked out over the water. "What do you do with the rubbish?"

"We don't have any. Everything we use can either be recycled or re-used."

"Seriously?"

"Yeah," Eleanor nodded.

"That's pretty impressive," Abbie said. "Has it always been like that?"

"For as long as I can remember."

"I suppose that's one thing in their favour," Abbie admitted, before continuing with her questioning. "Where does the sewage go?"

Eleanor paused.

"I'm not completely sure," she answered honestly. "I think it's sent to sewage works via a few large pipes that are connected to all the different washrooms. There's six washrooms on each residential floor, so I'd guess there's one or two pipes with clean water and another couple for the used water. I'd have to check that, though."

"I suppose that works," Abbie replied. "See, I've been expecting there to be something - anything, that someone should have picked up on, by now. A tiny flaw in a plan that admittedly seems to be very well thought through."

"And? Is there?"

"See, that's just it. There's nothing," Abbie answered. "As far as I can tell, it's a flawless plan."

Chapter Fifteen

"This is it," Eleanor said, a hint of pride in her voice as they stood outside the abandoned station.

"It's in there?" Abbie replied, sounding utterly bewildered. "It's well hidden - I'll give you that."

"It is, isn't it?" Eleanor replied, smiling proudly.

"I was right, though. It's an old station."

"Piccadilly R-L-Y," Eleanor read the tiled lettering off the station front.

"I can't remember what it had to do with Piccadilly, but I think it's actually called Aldwych Station. It must have closed, what... a hundred years ago? Maybe more. We used to have a house a few roads over. Actually, I wonder if it was because of your evacuation..." she added as an afterthought.

"What do you mean?"

"Well," Abbie began. "A while ago this company found all these empty private houses and blocks of flats - they were still full of furniture and everything, but completely deserted. And because they technically weren't owned by any council or housing agents, they kind of rented them under the radar - a bit like on the black market or something. We rented one for a while, so I used to pass this station every day with my mum on the way to the market. I never would have suspected that there was anything more to it than being an old derelict station, mind you."

"What's a black market?"

"Sorry, I guess you don't have them. It's like… I guess it's kind of an illegal way of trading. They used to be quite common, but not so much nowadays."

"And that's how you got your house?" Eleanor frowned.

"Yeah," Abbie answered, a hint of a smile playing upon her lips. "My dad knew a guy who knew a guy…"

Eleanor laughed, then added: "I think I should probably be getting back now."

"Can't I see inside?"

"I'm not sure that's such a good idea," Eleanor said apologetically.

"Please?" Abbie begged. "I won't tell anyone about it - I only want to see what's there."

"Well, I… I suppose it probably won't do any harm," Eleanor conceded far too easily although, in truth, she was only too happy to show her.

After wrenching the doors open, they moved along the musty hallway, Abbie complaining wholeheartedly as she sneezed at the dust.

"Maybe I should go back," she began.

"We're nearly there. Just a little further and I promise it'll be worth it!" Eleanor coaxed Abbie towards the lobby. "Sorry, it's a bit dark in here. Maybe we should have brought a light…"

Automatically, Abbie reached into her pocket, retrieved her phone and switched on the torch. And, as she shone it around herself as they entered the old ticket hall, she found herself at a loss for words. She gazed around at the ageing signs and worn handrails, carefully stepping over the slightly uneven flooring.

"It's incredible!" she admitted.

A few rays of sunlight were filtering through a crack in the corner of the ceiling, before being swallowed up by the darkness of the hallway. After the grand entrance hall, there were countless gates and endless corridors to be traversed before they would reach their destination.

Finally reaching the platform, Eleanor led the way to the very end with Abbie following. Eleanor reached out her hand and began prising the door open. Once she had done, she stepped down onto the first step and turned to check Abbie was watching.

"You see that?" Eleanor pointed to a small chink of light pouring onto the lower steps from a minuscule opening in the wall opposite the foot of the stairs. "That's the doorway I told you about."

"Can I come through with you?"

"Sorry, but no - definitely not. They can't know that I left in the first place, and if they see you it'll be pretty obvious," Eleanor refused to budge on the matter.

"So is this goodbye for forever? Or just for a while?" Abbie said.

"I don't know," Eleanor admitted as she glanced warily towards the door. "I hope it's not for too long. Look, I really should be getting back - it feels like I've been gone for way too long. Do you think you can find your way out?"

"I'll be fine," Abbie said, before adding: "It was really good getting to know you."

"You too," Eleanor said with a smile, before she began descending the steps. "And thank you, thank you so much for today," she called to Abbie and glanced back. Finally turning away, she reached the illuminated entrance and slipped through into the light behind it.

★★★

"Ellie! I've been looking everywhere for you - where have you been? We need to talk," a voice called from the opposite end of the long, narrow corridor as Eleanor stepped from one of the West Elevators.

"Saskia! Quick - come in here. I need to tell you about something," Eleanor replied as Saskia rushed over to her. The two of them hurried into an empty Fitness Centre, where Eleanor led the way over to two stools in the corner and faced Saskia with a wide grin.

"You'll never guess where I've just been!"

"Alright, you go first," Saskia said impatiently.

"Promise you won't tell anyone?"

"Of course I won't," she replied, looking around distractedly. "Where have you been?"

"Out," Eleanor stated proudly.

"What do you mean 'out'?" Saskia's expression suddenly darkened.

"I went up to the Surface," Eleanor replied with a broad smile.

"But... but the door can't still be open - that's impossible," Saskia said.

"Well, it's not impossible because I did it."

"Did anyone see you?" Saskia pressed anxiously.

Eleanor shook her head. "No one saw me leaving or coming back - trust me. But Saskia, you wouldn't believe what it was like! It's so beautiful, and the sun, it - it's like this gorgeous golden hue," she gushed. "And these huge trees line the streets, and then they have these little market stalls swarming with customers. And the people up there! They're nothing like we've been told. They're not Revolutionaries at all - they're just like us."

Saskia looked up from the floor suddenly, seemingly afraid of what Eleanor was telling her. "You spoke to them?"

"Of course I did. What did you expect me to do?" Eleanor frowned as she tried to understand Saskia's disbelief. Still, it was odd how she hadn't seemed surprised that people were living on the Surface. Immediately she banished the thought from her head. I'm not about to start suspecting my best friend, now.

"I wasn't going to go up there and ignore everyone!" she continued. "I wanted to learn as much about the Surface as I could."

"Okay, look, here's what you're going to do," Saskia took a deep breath. "You can't tell anyone about going up there - ever. You have to forget about everything that happened and everything that you saw. Got it?"

"I don't get why you think it's such a problem!" Eleanor exclaimed. "What's the matter with you today? Yesterday you were all up for an adventure but now you've suddenly become so serious."

Saskia looked away momentarily, before continuing: "Ellie, listen to me. Things have... they've changed since yesterday. You could get in serious trouble for this."

"And I wouldn't have got in trouble for it yesterday?" Eleanor rolled her eyes.

"No, well yes, but you… you just don't understand," Saskia continued. She seemed exasperated by Eleanor's inability to comply with the simplest rules. "If-"

She broke off suddenly as the door to the Fitness Centre opened and in walked a small group of friends. "Let's go," she instructed quickly, hopping off her stool and making her way over to the door, Eleanor trailing behind.

As soon as they were in the empty corridor Saskia turned back to Eleanor: "Listen, if you were-"

"If I was what?" Eleanor hissed. "If I was you? If I was friends with a Founder like you are?"

Saskia frowned, taken aback. "What are you talking about?"

"I heard you," Eleanor answered. "Having your chat yesterday. What makes you good enough to be exempt from everything? What makes you special enough to have a Founder that always gets you out of trouble?"

"Keep your voice down," Saskia said in a forceful whisper. "And it's not like that - you've no idea what that was about!"

"You told me that you didn't know him!"

"No, I never said that. You just didn't ask me if I did," Saskia answered quickly.

"Well, you should have told me, at least," Eleanor retorted angrily.

"Fine," Saskia raised her eyebrows. "I'm sorry I didn't tell you that I knew him."

"Who is he?"

"He's…" she paused. "Okay, you have to promise never to tell anyone."

Eleanor nodded.

"You promise?"

"Yes! I promise."

"Alright, well he's…" she paused. "He was an old friend of my mum."

"Your mum?"

"Yes," Saskia admitted, looking away sheepishly.

"Wait, what? Your mum?" Eleanor repeated in astonishment. "You knew your mum?"

"Yes."

"But… But how?"

"Look, no one else knows - no one can know."

"Why not?"

"Because they just can't."

"But then where is she now? How come I've never seen you together?"

"She isn't here," Saskia said quietly. "I didn't grow up in this zone, remember? Anyway, the Founder was always just someone who I'd heard my mum mention a couple of times."

"What do you mean?"

"I didn't grow up here."

"Yes, I know - you were transferred from Zone Five or something when you were younger, weren't you?"

"Something like that," Saskia said dismissively. "It was just after I turned six - but children weren't separated from their parents, there. Anyway, my mum was… she was in contact with this friend of hers, and they decided that it would be better for me to come here. He pulled a few strings, and here I am."

"But why?" Eleanor asked in disbelief. "Why wouldn't she want you to stay with her?"

"She did, but here… it gave you a much better start in life. Every job actually means something and plays a key part. They thought it would be better."

"Better than Zone Five? But I thought they were all basically the same."

"What?" Saskia frowned, before realising what she had just said. "Oh - yes, they're mostly the same," she finished quickly.

They sat in silence for a few moments as Eleanor thought over what Saskia had told her.

"What was the thing that you wanted to tell me earlier?" Eleanor asked quietly.

"Someone - the Founder - he's asked me to, well, I'm going to be… actually, never mind," she said shaking her head.

"Are you sure? It sounded important."

"It doesn't matter," Saskia replied.

"You can tell me," Eleanor said. "I don't mind."

"It's nothing," Saskia repeated, dissolving back into the silence. "Did you… find anything interesting out about the Surface?" she asked a few moments later.

"Lots," Eleanor nodded excitedly. "Like… um, oh! My friend was telling me about my surname."

"Desdemona?"

"Yes," Eleanor nodded.

"Why? What's so special about it?" Saskia asked.

"Apparently it's the name of a character from a famous play," Eleanor said. "But, apparently, they die at the end, so now the name's quite rare. I was saying that I hope the Founders weren't trying to tempt fate."

"Not while I'm around," Saskia assured her with a smile.

Eleanor laughed, their earlier argument almost forgotten.

"Now come on," Saskia began. "What was it like up there?"

"You really want to know?" Eleanor said, thrilled at Saskia's enthusiasm.

"Tell me everything."

Chapter Sixteen

"Ellie, before we go, I want you to promise me that you won't go back up there," Saskia said.

"Why do I have to promise you that?"

"Because I'm asking you to," Saskia pleaded. "Because you're my friend and I want to be able to trust you."

"You already know you can trust me," Eleanor said. "Or do the last eleven years not count for anything?"

"Ellie, please?"

"Fine," Eleanor replied, annoyed that Saskia was still going on about it - especially since she'd seemed so interested while she was telling her about the Surface.

"You promise?"

"Yes, I promise," Eleanor answered grudgingly as she got up, letting the door to the Fitness Centre swing shut behind her as she began to make her way to her room.

Slowly walking down the deserted corridor, she thought over their conversation, fuming at how she always seemed to let Saskia run her life. Why does she think she can tell me what I can and can't do? She doesn't control me. Just because she's friends with a Founder doesn't make her any better than me, she thought bitterly to herself.

On reaching her Individual Pod, she scanned her thumbprint on the ID Sensor Plate on the wall and opened the door. She was just about to step through it when an idea suddenly popped into her head.

Why don't I go back? Just to prove Saskia wrong - to show her that I don't always have to do whatever she says.

After hurrying along to the West Side Elevator, she stepped into one, scanned her finger and confidently pressed '0'.

As the elevator gradually rose, her nerves began to intensify. And, as the elevator doors drew open to allow fresh, cool air to flood in, she paused for only a moment before striding down the corridor.

"Really, Ellie?" came Saskia's voice as she stepped from the shadows of a branching corridor. "I wondered if you'd be back - I hoped you wouldn't, but I just wanted to be sure."

"What are you doing here?" Eleanor's voice was shaking slightly.

"Waiting to see if you'd keep your promise," Saskia replied matter-of-factly, although she seemed genuinely hurt that Eleanor hadn't. "I knew you wouldn't be able to, now that you've seen what it's like out there. I saw how much it changed you, so I knew that you'd want to go back."

"But I wasn't going to go through. I just wanted to see the door one last time," Eleanor justified weakly, willing Saskia to believe her.

"Of course you were," Saskia replied sarcastically. "And what next time? What happens when someone follows you up here and then goes through the door after you? It'll happen eventually - it's bound to."

"It won't. I promise it won't!" Eleanor couldn't meet Abbie's gaze.

"But I can't believe any promises you make, from now on. I can't trust you anymore - I wanted to, but I can't."

"What's happened to you?"

"To me? Why would anything be happening to me?" Saskia said defensively.

"Yesterday, you were... well, if I'd asked you to go up there with me I doubt you would have said no. But now you've changed somehow. I don't get it."

"I told you, things have changed since yesterday," Saskia looked away.

"What things?"

"Well, for starters you left," she said. "So yes. I'd say things have definitely changed."

"But you're not the same," Eleanor replied. "Is it about what you wanted to tell me earlier?"

"No. Forget I even mentioned that," Saskia replied quickly, avoiding Eleanor's gaze.

"So what happened?" Eleanor pressed. "Was it... wait, was it that thing you and that Founder were saying about? The thing that you were starting training for today?"

"What thing? What are you talking about?"

"I heard him say something about some training you had to do."

"You shouldn't have been eavesdropping in the first place," Saskia retorted in annoyance.

"What aren't you telling me? We used to tell each other everything."

"Ellie, you don't know the first thing about the real me!" Saskia retorted angrily. "You can't do anything about this - even I can't change it."

"What's going on? What can't you change? Just tell me!"

"I... I can't," Saskia said. "This has got nothing to do with you."

"Fine, then," Eleanor replied, slightly taken aback. "But I-"

"You can't do anything about it," Saskia repeated, more forcefully this time, and turned to head back to the elevators.

"Saskia, I know I lied and I'm sorry," Eleanor said. "I just want the old you back - the real you. Even if everything else has changed."

"I'm afraid I've had to change too," Saskia said, almost regretfully. "I have to go now. Don't follow me."

"Saskia, please don't tell anyone! I swear I'll never go back - I'll never even come up here again," Eleanor pleaded desperately.

"It's not up to me."

"Then who is it up to? Can't you just give me one more chance?" Eleanor pleaded. "I promise I can... I'll be the best citizen this place has ever seen!"

"I trusted you today. This was your last chance, and you shouldn't even have had that. I wanted to give you the benefit of the doubt - I wanted to believe that you'd just forgotten to register this morning or that you'd got lost. But you hadn't," Saskia answered softly. "You've already told me where you were this morning."

And, striding towards the elevator with her back turned to Eleanor, she let the doors close behind her. Utterly defeated, Eleanor went over to the staircase and stumbled her way down the seventeen, long flights of stairs before collapsing onto her bed in a miserable heap.

***

It was just over three hours later when Eleanor was woken abruptly by a sharp rap on the door of her Individual Pod. Leaping up off her bed, she listened anxiously as there was a slight pause before the knock was repeated. Hastily she opened the door, both expecting and praying that it would be Saskia. But instead, two solemn Protectors stood before her. Automatically taking a step back, she moved instinctively to close the door again, until a heavy thud sounded as the larger of the two rammed his foot in front of the door.

"Eleanor Desdemona?" the other demanded formally.

"Yes?" she replied, unsure of what was happening.

"Please come with us. We have been instructed to bring you immediately to GMR Fourteen, on Level Nineteen."

"Level Nineteen? Why?" No one was ever taken to Level Nineteen outside of a drill, unless it was absolutely vital.

The Protectors remained silent and moved back, giving her a chance to leave her Pod of her own accord.

She peered anxiously out of her doorway and grimaced; to her dismay, it seemed that every single one of her neighbours had gathered to watch the display.

News certainly travels fast around here, she thought, bracing herself for whatever was to come. She inwardly cursed Saskia as heat flooded to her cheeks. Stepping from her room, she attempted to keep her head down as the crowd parted to make way for her.

Self-consciously Eleanor moved forwards, wishing the ground would swallow her up. As she stumbled slightly, one of the Protectors nudged her which sent her pitching to the ground. No one offered her a hand, and no one helped her up; it was as though she was already a criminal. She scrambled to her feet as quickly as she could, brushing down her leisure clothes as a bruise began to form just below her knee, and held her head high as she made her way to the elevators.

Once inside, one of the Protectors pushed the button labelled '19' and waited for the doors to close.

Things certainly seemed to have escalated very quickly. She nervously turned her gaze to the Protectors, as they waited for the elevator to reach the depths of the Subterrane.

The elevator stopped in the darkness between levels with a shudder. The Protectors both scanned their thumbprints on the ID sensor plate, before the second tapped on the screen a few times and an automated voice rang through the elevator:

"Eleanor Desdemona, please position yourself in front of the screen for an ID scan."

Anxiously, she obliged and awkwardly stood before the screen, unsure of where she should look. Finally, the voice concluded:

"Identification approved."

The elevator ascended for a few seconds. Then the doors swung open.

Having been absent from the Emergency Pods during the Internal Lockdown that morning, Eleanor had not been down to Level Nineteen since the last Intruder Alarm Drill that had taken place just over two years ago. Moving forwards into the bright and intimidating corridor, Eleanor gazed around at her surroundings. Level Nineteen appeared to be just like any other floor, but had a strange sense of mystery about it nonetheless. Two long corridors stretched across the entire floor, one on each side of the elevators. The Emergency Pods which also doubled as larger meeting rooms were located in-between the two corridors, while the more secure, soundproof Government Meeting Pods lined the perimeter of the level.

As the dull thuds of her footsteps echoed down the corridor, she checked the numbers on each door until she reached the one marked with a small '14' in the centre. Although outwardly resembling the others, it seemed to have an ominous air about it which didn't help her trembling hands as she knocked.

"Enter," came a voice from within.

Eleanor took a deep breath and pushed the door open.

Unlike the Recreational Pods, the Government Meeting Rooms had no panel of glass fitted within their doors; there was no way of stealing a glance into the confidential meetings. Instead, the heavy soundproof doors appeared to be coated in a smooth sheen of white plastic, that was slightly peeling at the hinges to reveal some kind of metal underneath.

Within the rectangular room were three tables forming three sides of a square, with a single upright chair positioned where the fourth side should have been.

"Miss Desdemona." The man at the head of the table looked up as she entered the room. "Thank you for joining us at such short notice. I realise that it probably would have been more convenient to use one of the Recreational Pods upstairs, but we thought this subject matter called for one of our more confidential rooms. We wouldn't want to risk anyone overhearing what this was about. Although, of course, you would never tell anyone, would you?" the man asked slightly smugly, as he exchanged a look with the colleague, an unsmiling man, directly beside him. The speaker was, Eleanor guessed, perhaps in his late forties. His close-cropped hair was fairly dark, making his skin look even more pale and ghostly than it really was. The permanent frown on his face seemed to sum him up perfectly - that and those shrewd, watchful eyes.

"Before we begin, I expect you're curious about who we are, aren't you?" He gave her a rather menacing smile.

She nodded cautiously as she stood in the doorway, caught off guard at his change in tone.

"And please take a seat," he said, waving his arm towards a chair. "We form the central government to the Subterrane. Every decision made comes either from us, or is approved by us. And that's why it was rather strange when we were informed that someone had decided to leave the Subterrane of their own accord," he said, giving her a beady stare before smiling once more. "Forgive me, I'm getting ahead of myself. For now, my name is of no consequence to you. All that you should be concerned with is that I am, I suppose you might say, the spokesperson for the government. But now, let's get back to the real business. Do you know why you're here?" he inquired.

"I-I think so," she replied timidly, her eyes flitting from person to person, interrogator to interrogator.

She was met with a hard, cold silence.

"Would you mind elaborating for us?"

Entirely overcome by nerves, Eleanor sat facing the members of the government. Of course, she had seen Government Members before, but never in a scenario like this. As she surveyed them, what immediately struck her as odd was their clothing. For starters, not one of them was dressed solely in white. Instead, each was wearing some kind of smart suit - from what she could see, the suits consisted of a pale coloured shirt, complete with a fitted jacket and, in most cases, a coloured tie.

Fingers trembling slightly, she began biting down on her lip until the metallic taste of blood filled her mouth. Taking in a shaky breath, she swallowed. "I... I broke the rules, didn't I?"

This time they were not so amused.

"Miss Desdemona, I'm not sure if this is merely a game to you, but let me assure you of one thing. It is not a game to me or anyone else in this room." The spokesman leant back in his chair, never taking his eyes off her as he waited for her answer. "Let me enlighten you on the severity of your situation." He paused, but continued to fix her with a disconcertingly intense gaze.

Why does he keep staring? Eleanor frowned. Does he think it's intimidating or something? If that was the intention, it certainly wasn't working; she stared right back, refusing to look away.

"In leaving the safety of the Subterrane, you not only risked your own life but also the thousands of lives that reside down here with you. What do you have to say for yourself?"

"I'm not going to apologise if that's what you're expecting," she said, gaining her confidence a little. She wasn't quite sure why, but there was something she didn't like about him. They're the ones that lied to everyone, she reminded herself. That puts them more in the wrong than me.

"I wanted to see what was out there for myself," she continued daringly. "Why have you lied to us for so long?"

"Excuse me?" the Founder replied coldly.

"Why have you lied? All this time, we've been told that it's too dangerous to leave, that the people can't be trusted and that there's almost nothing left up there. But none of it's true. Why haven't you told us what's really up there? Why make us believe all these lies?"

Silence.

"In case you are unaware, Miss Desdemona, you are the one being questioned here," the spokesman reminded her, clearly unimpressed at her impertinence as he shifted in his chair. "Now, if you'll permit me to continue, why did you do it? Why did you decide to leave in the first place? It could have been extremely dangerous - especially since you had no idea what would be up there."

"I've already told you why I went. I wanted to see what was up there for myself," she repeated, unwaveringly; she wasn't going to let him win that easily.

"I see. And why would you choose to put every one of the lives down here at risk, so that you could 'see what was up there', as you put it so eloquently?"

"What was going to happen to them? I was only gone for a few hours! Anyway, no one saw me," she told him with a shrug, hoping the lie might make her case a little easier to plead.

"It doesn't matter how long you were gone for. The point is that you left, and in doing so you violated our most sacred law of all," he retorted. "Do you understand?"

"Yes," she replied, nodding slightly.

The spokesman gestured to a woman who strode towards her.

"So no one saw you?" he asked her again.

"No."

"Not one person?" Again that cold smile hovered on his thin lips. But he was just trying to lord his authority over her - she was sure of it.

"No one - like I said," Eleanor replied. Maybe Saskia's already filled him in on what I saw… she thought to herself suddenly, becoming more anxious at the idea, and beginning to regret her answer.

"How remarkable," he fixed her with a knowing look before noting something down on the papers in front of him.

A woman with thick glasses stepped forwards, holding a pen.

"We have an agreement for you to sign," she began. "It confirms that you agree to never again attempt to leave the Subterrane, or endanger its inhabitants in any way. And, that you will not spread the details about what you learnt and saw whilst on the Surface. If you'll just sign here."

Taking the pen from the woman, Eleanor grudgingly printed her name along the dotted line and scrawled her illegible signature next to it. But there was no way she would let a piece of paper dictate what she could or couldn't do.

As soon as she had signed the paper, Eleanor stepped away from the table and waited impatiently until she was dismissed. As soon as she was, she began to make her way to the door, eager to leave, when the Founder's words stopped her in her tracks.

"Make no mistake, Miss Desdemona, we will be… keeping an extra special eye on you," the spokesman told her. "And if we find you guilty of returning to the Surface ever again, there will be consequences. Dire consequences. This is your one and only warning. If I were you, I would refrain from stepping out of line anytime soon. Remember, we have eyes and ears everywhere."

Taking a deep breath, Eleanor attempted to brush away the threat and hurried from the room as fast as she could; there was no way she was taking any advice from that man. Only once she was in the safety of an elevator, did she allow herself to dwell on his cautionary words. A cold chill ran down her spine as she hastily scanned her finger, pressed the button for Level Seventeen and leant her forehead against the cool glass.

Chapter Seventeen

"Ellie? There you are, thank God!" Eleanor was jolted from her thoughts as Saskia came rushing down the corridor towards her. "Are you alright? What happened? Are you okay? Ellie? Hello? Are you even listening?"

"What, to you?" Eleanor answered, outraged at Saskia's sudden change of heart.

"What do you mean?" Saskia asked, as though she truly believed she wasn't in the wrong. "I was so worried when I heard you'd been taken to Level Nineteen. I don't know what I would have done if anything happened to you. Or just imagine if you'd been sent to another zone!"

"Well, perhaps you should have thought of that before reporting me," Eleanor retorted, fuming as she turned away and started down the corridor towards her Pod.

"Ellie, wait, you think this is my fault?" Saskia exclaimed, hurrying after her. "How is this anything to do with me?"

"Because you're the one that reported me!" Eleanor retaliated angrily. "How do you not get that?"

"Ellie, he forced me to tell him," Saskia said, dropping her voice to a whisper.

"Whatever," Eleanor replied, rolling her eyes. She was becoming rather sick of Saskia.

"I didn't have a choice!"

"Saskia, there's always a choice," Eleanor retorted. "You have a say in every single thing you do, and you've made your choice very clear."

"Ellie, I-"

"Don't bother," Eleanor cut her off. "You've always got an excuse up your sleeve."

"But where are you going?" Saskia asked desperately. "Someone said you fell - at least let me take you to the Medical Centre? You should get your knee checked out."

"Don't you dare tell me what to do," Eleanor lowered her voice as someone passed by. "This is your cue to leave me alone, by the way."

"Fine, but where are you going?" Saskia asked miserably.

"I'm going to stay in my room for a while, and then I'm going to go up to the Medical Centre. Alone," Eleanor added for clarity as they reached her Pod.

"So… I'll see you later then?" Saskia asked hopefully.

Eleanor scanned her thumb on her ID Sensor Plate and pushed open her door.

"I doubt it."

***

As the elevator doors opened, Eleanor cast her eyes around Level Seven. Other than for monthly check-ups, citizens of the Subterrane had no reason to come to the Medical Centre unless, of course, if you were ill or partaking in a training course. Consequently, Eleanor hadn't been to the centre since early December.

The Medical Centre consisted of six wards that bordered of the level on all sides: three general wards, one slightly larger one for check-ups, one Maternity Ward that was split into 'Mothers' and 'Newborns', as well as one 'Contagion Ward' - although it was rarely used. The central sector, which lay directly between the two elevator blocks, was divided into three subsections: Research, Development, and Training. All three were entirely off-limits to all citizens except those who worked there, due to the risks of both distracting the medical workers and contaminating their vital research. However, whilst it was discouraged to visit the Centre, all citizens were strongly advised to have any injuries or illnesses checked out immediately, if and when they occurred. This was for two main reasons. The first was that illnesses could easily spread around the Subterrane, due to the close proximity in which they all lived. The second, and more popularly cited reason, was that if it seemed that someone was always there to check any problems or discomforts, no matter how insignificant, then Citizens were much more likely to feel they were a valued member of the society.

Eleanor turned left and made her way down the corridor, pausing to watch through the one-way glass window as the trainees went to and fro, taking samples from various Petri dishes and making them into slides. She continued past the door to the Contagion Ward, noting to herself that the ward must be temporarily closed, as she could see no traces of any light through the small pane of glass in the window.

At the door to the Check-Up Ward, she scanned her thumb on the ID Sensor Plate, then waited for it to recognise her.

"Welcome, Eleanor Desdemona."

The door slid open with a resounding 'click' and closed behind her.

"Hello. What can I help you with…" the receptionist began before pausing and glancing back at the Recognition Plate built into the wall.

"Eleanor," the second receptionist interjected, before returning her gaze to the Receiver Board.

"Ah, Eleanor," the first continued, smiling.

"I fell earlier and I think I must have bruised my knee slightly. It doesn't really hurt anymore, I just thought I should come and get it checked out."

"Yes, you did the right thing," the receptionist reassured her and smiled at her warmly. "Take a seat just there, and a Practitioner will call you in when they're ready."

As the receptionist returned to her paperwork, Eleanor glanced around at the interior of the ward and nodded to the several other citizens waiting, before taking a seat on the white bench that jutted out from the wall. Save for the lobby area, the ward was taken up by rows of several cubicles separated by opaque curtains which were for the use of both practitioners and any more permanent patients who required privacy. Each cubicle was just smaller than an Individual Pod and contained a fold-up bed for patients, with an extra two chairs and a desk for Practitioners, on which was a mesh letter tray containing any relevant information about their scheduled patients.

The system in the Check-Ups Ward was extremely well-devised and orchestrated; each cubicle reserved for a practitioner had a small button fixed into the desk which, when pressed, would cause its corresponding light above the Registration desk to flash red. The next citizen would then be sent to that particular cubicle, and the receptionist at the Receiver Board would in turn press a small switch which would operate a similar light in the Practitioner's cubicle, alerting them that a citizen was on their way. A similar system worked within the cubicles set aside for long-term patients, the only difference being that their light would glow green.

The system was by far one of the most advanced technological inventions that the Subterrane had acquired over the years. Most citizens, including Eleanor, had at some point in their childhood found the idea inconceivable and had consequently presumed it to be some kind of sixth sense on the Receptionist's part.

Eleanor waited as, one by one, the waiting area emptied of people. Finally, a light flashed up and a Receptionist called out her name.

Rising from the bench, she called out: "Yes, that's me," and hobbled over to the desk as the Receptionist relayed the usual instructions to her.

"Cubicle thirty-two, please, to see Practitioner 26. That's the third row, second on the left."

Eleanor hurried to the third row until she reached the second where she awkwardly waited in the doorway as the Practitioner continued to scrawl something on a blank sheet of greyish paper. Giving a polite cough, Eleanor waited until the Practitioner finally looked up.

"My apologies," the practitioner began, placing the paper on the top of her letter tray and rising from her chair. "I hope you haven't been waiting for too long. What did you say your name was?"

"Ellie."

"So what can I help you with?"

"Well it's nothing, really," Eleanor answered. "I fell and bruised my knee earlier - I almost didn't bother coming here but I thought I ought to. Just in case."

"Alright. Let's take a look, then," the Practitioner instructed, motioning for Eleanor to take a seat.

Eleanor settled herself down on one of the chairs and rolled up the leg of her leisure clothes to reveal a slight graze across her knee. The Practitioner took a reusable wipe from a pile on her desk and, taking a large bottle of a clear liquid, poured some onto the cloth before gently dabbing the skin to sterilise it.

"All done," she said. "And let's give you a fresh pair of leisure clothes so they can get the stain out more easily." She opened a drawer full of neatly folded overalls. "What sort of size are you?"

"Um… seventeen small?" Eleanor suggested.

"Let me see. Seventeen small…" she muttered to herself. "I've got sixteen extra small, seventeen medium or eighteen extra small. Eighteen extra small should be about right, shouldn't it?"

"I think so," Eleanor agreed gratefully, as the practitioner stepped outside of the cubicle momentarily to allow her to change.

With her check-up over, Eleanor slowly made her way back to the entrance. She pressed her thumb to the ID Sensor Plate by the door and waited for it to acknowledge that she was leaving.

"Eleanor Desdemona, thank you for coming to the Check-Up Centre today. We hope you are feeling better." The door slid wide open, allowing her to leave.

As soon as she had left the ward she made to turn right, and go back to the East Side Elevators. Then she paused and instead turned left, deciding to have a look around the rest of the level. After passing Ward Four, she continued to the end of the corridor and turned right, passing by the West Side Elevators.

Through a large window Eleanor could look into the Newborn Sector of the Maternity Ward. Thirty-six cots were lined up in front of the window in three rows of twelve, with six of them currently occupied. Of course, they would be taken down to Level Eighteen later on but, for a few hours at least, they always remained in the Newborn Sector. Each cot had a small tag tied to the handle which indicated whether the child was male or female, and each child had a small wristband secured around its wrist which stated its Citizen Number, sex, and date and time of birth. Whilst your Citizen Number remained with you for life, it was only used for identification during the very first months of life.

When a child was exactly one month old, they were carried to the three small boxes positioned in the corner of the Infants' Ward on Level Eighteen. The first box contained male first names, the second female first names, and the third and final box contained surnames for both sexes.

Every week, the three boxes would be brought from Level Twenty, containing names selected and approved by the Founders. Sometimes the names would be repeats of original names that were already in use on the Subterrane, the most common repeats being Lily and Sophia. Or sometimes they were merely regular words that sounded pretty like Iris or Scarlett. Occasionally, the names and surnames would have some kind of reference to something from the Surface, sometimes clear but more often indirect, that would only be remembered by a few, such as Jade or Warren.

Whoever accompanied the child would demonstrate putting their hand in a box and pulling out a single slip of paper, thereby allowing the child to select their own name. The child's arm would then be lowered into either the first or second box, depending on the child's gender. And so, when they were lifted out they would, theoretically, have a name balled up in their tiny fist. However, it often took several unsuccessful attempts before a name was selected. The process was then repeated until the child had selected both a first name and last name from the relevant boxes. The names were then noted down on the child's wristband in the space left blank beside the Citizen Number. And, whilst the process was a little odd, the act of a child essentially choosing their own name would remove any emotional attachment that might be felt by whoever named the child.

Eleanor stood at the window, watching for some time as the tiny bodies rose and fell with each precious breath. A few moments later one child began crying, and in rushed a young nurse who scooped up the child and rocked her back and forth in her arms until the child had quietened. Although the children were supposedly trained from a very early age not to cry, the nurses could never bear to hear a child cry for the first time - it was simply too distressing after they had seen the child safely into the world.

Finally tearing her gaze away from the one-way glass, Eleanor moved along the corridor until she reached the East Side Elevators once more. She pressed the call button but, typically, all of the elevators were already in use. So, she began the long trek back down the stairwell to her Individual Pod, ten levels below.

It was just as Eleanor was walking down the last few stairs, that she heard shouting several floors above her.

"You don't get it. She thinks it was me!" a high-pitched voice yelled.

Eleanor paused to listen as a second voice replied: "And why exactly is that my problem?"

"Because it was all you - I didn't even tell you anything she said. I-" A door was suddenly slammed, cutting off the argument mid-flow.

Eleanor sighed in annoyance as she reached Level Seventeen, then opened the door and emerged from the stairwell. And that was when she caught sight of her; a tall girl with frizzy, darkish coloured hair, who seemed to be trying to keep her head down. Surely it couldn't be...

If only she would turn so I could see her face, Eleanor thought to herself in frustration as she craned her neck to get a better view of the girl who was now fighting her way through the small crowd that had emerged from the elevator. The figure moved from the crowd and began to make her way down the corridor on the far left, turning this way and that, studying the many faces that she passed.

Darting down the corridor after her, Eleanor attempted to keep her eyes fixed on the girl as she dodged people coming the other way. However, she soon became stuck behind a group of girls and, by the time she had managed to pass them, the girl was nowhere to be seen.

Feeling extremely disheartened at the accumulation of her day's misfortunes, Eleanor made her way to the end of the corridor and was about to head towards her Individual Pod, when an arm reached out and grabbed her, pulling her into a Fitness Centre.

Heart racing, she spun around to face her captor.

"Abbie?" she gasped, unable to believe that she was really there.

"Ellie!" Abbie smiled, enveloping her in a warm hug. "I was sure it was you when I spotted you in the corridor - I've been looking everywhere!"

"But what are you doing here?"

"I came to help you escape," Abbie frowned, as though it should have been obvious. "What do you think of my outfit?" she asked proudly, doing a twirl.

"It's... very convincing," Eleanor replied kindly, although the unflattering outfit (complete with an oversized shirt and ill-fitting jeans) was really anything but convincing.

"I got it all together myself - well, mum helped. But still... I think I look like a proper local," she smiled, nudging Eleanor with her elbow.

"Right. Yeah, sure..."

"Hey," Abbie mock-whined, before suddenly becoming more serious. "Ellie, have you noticed how pale everyone here is, compared to up there?"

"Well, obviously. But it's just because of the lack of sunlight."

"No, but I mean... everyone is pale. There's not a single person with a different skin tone. You must have noticed it."

Eleanor frowned.

"You're all the same race," Abbie continued. "It's like your Founders were trying to segregate you, or something. That's why I look so out of place here."

"Are you sure?" Eleanor wasn't entirely convinced by Abbie's theory. She walked over to the panel of glass in the door and peered out at the citizens passing through the corridor.

"See?" Abbie asked.

"But why would they go to all that trouble?" Eleanor turned and walked back over to Abbie.

Abbie shrugged. "No idea."

Eleanor paused for a moment, before frowning again. "Abbie, how did you even get down here in the first place?"

"I came through the Tunnel - like you did," Abbie answered.

"When? And how did you get down here? The elevator requires a thumbprint and the stairs at least need an ID card."

"There was a group of school kids up there or, well, what do you call it down here?"

"A class visit," Eleanor said.

"Right. So there was a class visit and I tagged along behind them as they were leaving. One of the kids accidentally unlocked the door to the stairs before they realised their class was taking the elevator, so I caught the door before it closed and walked down. I wasn't sure where you'd be so I checked a few other levels first, but each time I used the stairs and just followed close behind someone so I never had to open any doors."

"You don't know how lucky you are that you weren't caught," Eleanor said, shaking her head. "But why haven't they sealed the door yet? They found out that I'd been through. And what happens to you if they do seal it?" Eleanor wasn't sure why Abbie seemed so unafraid of losing everything she had ever known. "You could get stuck down here forever."

"I kind of have a plan," Abbie responded vaguely.

"You kind of have a plan?"

"You'll like it," Abbie assured her.

"So what is it?"

"Well, I say you'll like it but you actually might not..."

"Abbie, just tell me what it is," Eleanor burst out in exasperation.

"Okay, alright! So I thought that we could get together all the people that want to leave - I mean, there must be some, right?"

"And then what?"

"Um, well, then we could try and organise a way to leave, and then we could just... go, I guess?"

"How can you even call that a plan? And how would that possibly work?" Eleanor frowned, wishing that it would work, but knowing that it never would. "If the Founders heard about a gathering of people wanting to leave, who knows what they'd do. And as for leaving, I don't think there's any other way out than the way you came in, which is going to be sealed any day now. And there's obviously no easy way to contact the Surface, because if there was then this entire civilisation would come crashing down!"

Abbie was silent for a moment, her eyes downcast. "I'm sorry. Maybe I shouldn't have suggested it."

"There's no way it could work," Eleanor told her.

"Perhaps I shouldn't have come, then." Abbie turned away and walked towards the door.

"No, wait!" Eleanor called just before she reached it. "Look, I'm sorry. I shouldn't have said that. It's not that it's a bad idea, it's just that I've no idea how you'd go about executing it."

"Well, I have a few ideas - if you want to hear them?"

***

That evening, the two of them sat on Eleanor's bed, discussing how they might go about setting the plan in motion, if indeed they could at all.

"We could just leave?" Abbie suggested. "We could try and see if they stop us. They might not - you never know."

"We could, but then we'd be leaving everyone else down here and that's not fair on them. Besides, the door will probably be sealed by to-morrow anyway," Eleanor replied.

"We could..." Abbie paused to think. "I know! We could go and speak to your Government - the Founding whatevers. We could demand that they let everyone know what my world's really like, or else we'll tell them all the truth."

"We can't do that!" Eleanor was alarmed by Abbie's naivety. "There's no way they'd agree to that. Not now - not after they've managed to keep the Subterrane going for so long. Besides, if we threatened them with that, they just wouldn't let us speak to anyone ever again. Or, since you're not from here, they'd probably claim that you were a Revolutionary and that you'd somehow corrupted my mind." Eleanor shook her head decid-edly. "No, that one definitely wouldn't work."

"I don't see you coming up with many ideas. You're the one who's stuck in this horrid place."

"So are you. Remember?"

146

"Then maybe I should leave before it's too late."

"No!" Eleanor called out, just as Abbie was about to rest her hand on the door release button; it seemed to be becoming a rather regular occurrence. "It's just… it's just that this is such a mess and it's all my fault, but I've no idea how to get out of it."

"This isn't your fault, though," Abbie remarked. "It's your Government that did this - not you."

"But everything would still be normal if it wasn't for me. Now everything just feels wrong. And it's not that your ideas are bad, it's just that… I'm too scared to risk everything."

"But you already have," Abbie pointed out.

"No. I haven't even begun to risk anything. Say, if our plan went wrong - what would happen then? I could lose everything I've ever known! My home, my friends, my entire world! I know that this place is bad - it might not seem like it, but I really do. But even then, there's no denying that it's all I've ever known."

Abbie walked back over to the centre of the room and sat down.

"Ellie, we'll work this out," she reassured her. "No matter what happens tomorrow, you'll be alright - I promise. I'll be beside you no matter what. Got it?"

Eleanor nodded gratefully.

"Got it."

Chapter Eighteen

"So what's our plan of action?" Eleanor asked as they made their way down the corridor.

"Don't ask me! You're the one that lives here." Abbie sounded especially irritable after an uncomfortable night sleeping on a hard chair. "How about we just go up to people and ask if they want to leave here or not?"

"Seriously? You think they'll just openly admit that they don't like it here? Great plan. I'm so glad I'm potentially risking my whole life to do this," Eleanor said, glancing down the corridor to check there was no one coming.

"No, just hear me out. You must know of a few people who don't like it here, or who've hinted that they wish they could go back up there."

"I mean, I can think of a few - but nowhere near as many as we'd need."

"A few is a good start. Once we show them proof that we're telling the truth, they'll know of more people, and so on," Abbie explained as if it were the simplest thing in the world.

"Proof? But we don't have any proof."

"That's where I come in," Abbie said proudly. "I am your proof. They don't know me and they've never seen me here before. They can ask me anything they like - including any questions they have. And when they realise that I'm telling the truth, I'm sure they'll agree to come with us."

"I suppose that might work," Eleanor said rather sceptically.

"Come on. Let's put this plan in action," Abbie said, taking charge as they made their way back to the Recreational Pods.

Eleanor grabbed her arm, restraining Abbie from walking any further down the corridor.

"I do the talking. Okay?" she told her.

"Why? It was my idea."

"Yes, but I know these people, Abbie. I've grown up with them."

"You're just saying that so you get to be in charge."

"Don't be daft, I'm not that childish. Look I'll prove it," Eleanor added defiantly. "You see that woman there? She wasn't with her son and daughter on the night that we were evacuated here. She hoped she'd be able to locate them among everyone else, but she never found them. Because of that, she's always wanted to go back. And you see that boy there?" she subtly pointed to a boy who looked just a year or two older than them, emerging from an elevator. "He was just a couple of weeks old when he was brought here by his parents. But the Founders convinced them to give him up and cut their ties with him. Well, they were probably forced to - I'm not sure anyone would give up a child willingly. His parents are down here but he has no idea who they are; he's resented the Founders ever since. See? I know who doesn't want to be here," Eleanor concluded as she strode towards the boy. Abbie followed behind her.

"Hey, Alex. Can I talk to you a sec?" Eleanor began, a little uncertainly.

"Sure Ellie," he replied with a shrug. "What's wrong?"

"Nothing's wrong, really." Eleanor paused, unsure of what to say next. "Oh, have you met Abbie?"

"No," he replied. "I don't believe I h-"

"Hi," Abbie interrupted him. "I'm from the Surface."

He chuckled in response, but was met with unchanging expressions from both Abbie and Eleanor.

"You're not serious... are you?" He stared at her in disbelief.

"Quite serious."

"But... you're not, are you?" he asked. "You don't expect me to believe that she... that they..." He studied their faces for any hint that they might be lying.

"The Founders lied to us," Eleanor answered simply.

"What? But why?" he replied with a deep frown. "Why would they do that?"

"We're not quite sure of that, yet."

"But we're going to find out," Abbie piped in helpfully.

"So you're saying this was all for nothing!" His voice had become much quieter, and he understandably seemed rather saddened at the news. "And there are still people on the Surface?"

"Yes."-

"And they didn't find it a little odd that hundreds of people suddenly went missing?"

"They did," Abbie reassured him. "Months and months were spent looking for each person that had disappeared, but they never found anyone. There were no people, no bodies, yet no answers. What do you do if you find nothing after all that time spent searching? They had no choice but to give up."

"And even if they had never stopped looking, they would never have found us," Eleanor added. "This place was thought out too carefully for anyone to ever find; it's far too well hidden."

"But she found a way in!" Alex pointed at Abbie.

"Only because Ellie had already found a way out."

"You've been out?" the boy looked at Eleanor in amazement. "How?"

"It's... a long story."

"Honestly? You're telling the truth? This isn't some kind of joke?'

"It's no joke, Alex, honestly."

The boy scanned her face for any signs of a smile and found none. "But what was it like? What were the people like? How did it feel?"

"It felt like I'd been trapped my whole life."

He nodded, then paused. "Why are you telling me all of this?"

"We want to start a... a group, I guess," Eleanor warily glanced at the people nearest to them. "People need to know about all these lies we've been fed whilst trapped down here. I know you've always wished you'd never come here, so would you... want to be involved?" Eleanor asked awkwardly.

He thought for a moment, allowing the seconds to drag by excruciatingly slowly. "Absolutely."

"Great," Eleanor smiled. "We thought we'd have a meeting later today. Do you think you'll be able to come?

"I'm sure I can," he replied. "What time?"

"Why don't we say around 1400 hours?"

"Where?"

"Recreational Pod 32," she replied. "But, Alex, you mustn't tell anyone. What we're doing could be dangerous - especially if anyone else finds out."

"I know." He nodded reassuringly. "I'll see you there."

"That was easy," Abbie commented, as they watched him walk away.

"It was," Eleanor nodded, sounding happily surprised.

"So who's our next target?" Abbie gestured in the direction of a boy waiting outside a Recreational Pod. "How about him?'

"Um... I don't think so," Eleanor replied. "I don't think he's the sort of person we're looking for."

"Her?"

"No."

"Her?"

"I suppose she might do," Eleanor said, as they made their way down the corridor towards her.

"Um... hi," she began.

"Do I know you?" the girl replied. She looked like she was in her mid-twenties, and was obviously not too pleased about having two teenagers approach her.

"You're Gemma, right?"

"Yes," she replied. "Can I help you with something?"

"I just wanted to ask you something," Eleanor continued nervously. "Do you... do you like it here?"

"What kind of question is that?"

"Sorry, I'm only asking." Eleanor looked at Abbie for some support.

"Well, do you?"

"No. I don't," Eleanor told her bluntly.

"I'll admit I'm not a huge fan of living underground," the young woman replied. "But so what?"

"Would you ever want to go back to the Surface? If we could?" Eleanor asked.

"I suppose... But why do you want to know? It's not exactly a question you get asked everyday around here."

"I'm just curious. You see, we're trying to get a group together, and-"

"What kind of group?" the young woman interrupted, eyeing Eleanor suspiciously.

Something told Eleanor that the conversation wasn't going to go the way she'd hoped. Could she trust this woman she hardly knew with such dangerous information? Perhaps she'd been wrong.

"It's a... a discussion group," Eleanor changed tack quickly.

"We're discussing what living on the Surface might be like," Abbie added helpfully.

"Look, I've got better things to do with my time." The young woman peered through the window of a Recreational Pod to check the time. "Besides, you could get into trouble for that sort of thing."

***

"So we have five people so far. How about a sixth?" Eleanor suggested a little while later, as they entered the Food Hall.

"What about her? She looks pretty unhappy," Abbie pointed out, gesturing towards Saskia who was sat alone at the end of a bench.

"No. You can't trust her," Eleanor said bitterly, just as Saskia caught sight of them looking at her. After staring at Abbie with a look of confusion, for a moment, Saskia gave a futile wave, matched with a hopeful, weak smile. Eleanor immediately glared at her before turning away. Linking arms with Abbie, she marched her off to the other side of the Food Hall.

"What was that about?" Abbie asked. "Why can't we trust her? Who even is she?"

"That's Saskia," Eleanor answered, as though it explained everything.

"But I thought she was your friend?" Abbie asked as she slid into the space on the bench beside Eleanor.

"She was - until she reported me yesterday." Eleanor surveyed the spread of food lining the table.

"She did what?" Abbie asked, aghast.

"She reported me for going to the Surface. She said that she had no choice or something - I can't remember exactly what she said, but it was some rubbish like that," Eleanor shrugged, fuming inwardly.

"She reported you?"

"Yes, that's what I said."

"But why? You told me you were surprised that she'd never been to the Surface herself!" Abbie frowned. "You told me she was always breaking rules, but that she never got into any trouble."

"Well, it seems that even she's not even breaking the rules anymore."

"But why would she tell on you when you've never told on her? I don't understand why she would do that to you."

"Maybe because I broke a more important rule or, well, I don't know... I think something happened. I overheard a conversation between her and a Founder - I think it must have changed things, somehow. But all I know for sure is that we're definitely not friends anymore."

"Does she know that? She looked pretty upset when you ignored her."

"She should have guessed by now. I bet she's been longing for a chance to snitch on me ever since we met," Eleanor retorted.

"I doubt it," Abbie replied. "Don't you think you should at least listen to what she has to say, or just ask her why she did it? It might help."

"I don't care why she did it - that's not the point. The point is that she did do it and I thought she was supposed to be my friend."

"Alright, if you say so," Abbie shrugged hopelessly. It seemed that Eleanor could be very stubborn when she wanted to be.

Chapter Nineteen

"I'd like to begin by thanking all of you for actually coming - I wasn't sure anyone would turn up," Eleanor began, once everyone they had spoken to had sat down in Recreational Pod 32. "I asked each of you to come because it seems that you still, after all these years, think there's something wrong about this place. Well, not wrong exactly, but just not quite right."

At a loss for what to say next, she looked over to Abbie who stepped forward.

"I-I recently became aware of the situation of your Subterrane when I met Ellie," she began. "And when I realised that she wanted to try and explain that there was a world outside of this place - or at least try and tell you all what was happening - I immediately found a way to get down here. I wanted to do what I could to help those of you who were unhappy with the... situation."

"We want to tell you everything we know," Eleanor explained. "And we especially want to raise awareness of what the world is actually like outside of the Subterrane, because it really is nothing like you've been told. Any questions so far?"

"Isn't this going to be dangerous?" a woman asked.

"I would have thought that was obvious."

"So why are we doing it?"

"Don't you want to leave?"

"Of course."

"Well, we'll never get out of here by just doing what they tell us to."

"So you're actually going to get us out of here?" the woman continued, sounding almost surprised. "Because if what you told me earlier is true, then I want to see my family. It's been over eighteen years." She averted her eyes, as though trying to hide a tear.

"Of course. And that's the ultimate goal," Eleanor replied sympathetically. "The only downside is that it's unlikely we'll be allowed to just walk out of here."

"Why not?"

"Well, since there's so much that's been invested into this place, I don't expect the Founders would be happy for us to just up and leave."

"So what's the point of this group?" someone else called.

"If we spread the truth throughout the entire Subterrane so that every single citizen knows that we've been lied to all this time, then the Founders and Protectors wouldn't be able to stop everyone at once. We should be able to overpower them."

"We should be able to? That's not very convincing."

"I thought the Protectors were only here in case a Revolutionary breaks in?" a girl asked.

"Yes, you're right," Eleanor replied. "But I doubt the Founders would hesitate to use the Protectors to stop us from trying to leave."

"So what do we do now?" the same girl asked.

"We're going to tell you all we know," Eleanor replied.

"About the Subterrane or the Surface?"

"Both. Abbie's going to start by telling you a bit about the Surface, since she's from there. She'll be able to answer any questions you've got - I'm sure you'll all have lots."

Abbie nodded and, as she studied each curious face, she began to relay everything she could to them about life on the Surface.

A little while later, Alex called Eleanor over.

"There's someone outside. I think they might be listening," he added. "I know we're not really doing anything majorly wrong yet, but you might want to check who it is."

The room suddenly went silent, as Eleanor anxiously made her way over to the door and peered through the small panel of glass in the centre. Sure enough, a solitary figure was lurking close to the door. Close enough to listen.

"Who is it, Ellie?" Abbie whispered.

"I'm not sure - I can't quite see," Eleanor replied as she craned her neck to catch a glimpse of the figure's face.

As she did so, the door opened - very narrowly avoiding hitting Eleanor in the face - and in came Saskia.

"What're you all doing in here?" Saskia asked, looking around the room.

"Nothing really," Abbie replied coolly.

"What're you doing in here? I don't recall inviting you," Eleanor said.

"You think I don't know what you're trying to do? You think I didn't hear everything you've said?" Saskia glared at Eleanor.

"And what are you going to do about it?"

"Just you wait," Saskia turned to walk from the room.

Then, as she caught sight of Abbie who was stood at the side of the room, she glared at her and stormed from the room, slamming the door behind her.

"Well, that was… a bit extreme," Abbie commented.

"What was she even doing here?" Eleanor said. "Has she really got nothing better to do than spy on us?"

"You don't think she'll report us?" Abbie seemed a little worried by the encounter.

"She wouldn't dare - not a second time."

Abbie left the subject, not wanting to become too involved in their rift.

"So what was Abbie saying before that rude intrusion?" Eleanor asked.

"You were saying about how people on the Surface reacted after the evacuation," Alex reminded Abbie helpfully.

"Yes, that's right." Abbie couldn't help but notice how everyone suddenly seemed afraid to meet her gaze. "So after the evacuation, no one knew where these few hundreds of people had gone. There were no witnesses because anyone who had seen it would probably have gone with them, although a few people claimed to have heard gunshots. But the main problem was that they couldn't find any trace of where they could have disappeared to."

"So are they still looking? I'm sure my family wouldn't give up without some kind of closure," a boy said, flinching as a silhouette passed the room.

"Unfortunately, the case was put aside several years ago. It was decided that there must have been some kind of riot, after which all those in question must have gone into hiding or have fled to somewhere remote beyond the reach of the police."

"But there were gunshots," a woman called out adamantly. "I heard them - I know I did. If this really was planned from the start, as you say it was, then who fired them?"

"I'm not entirely sure what they were. My guess is that it was a pre-planned thing to scare everyone into hiding - or at least into the Subterrane."

"That can't be right." She shook her head and looked away. "The Founders have done nothing but try to protect us all these years."

"But from what?" Abbie inquired.

"From… from the Revolutionaries."

"They don't exist, remember?"

"But… are you sure?" She seemed almost desperate to know it hadn't all been for nothing. "All this time?"

"I'm afraid there's no such thing as a Revolutionary - and there never has been. There was no war, no attack, and nothing that posed any threat to life on the Surface."

"Why would they do that? What's the point?"

"I don't know. Fame? Control, maybe?"

Abbie was suddenly interrupted by an authoritative knock on the door. Everyone seemed to hold their breath simultaneously as the door swung open slowly and in came two armed Protectors, each equipped with a weapon.

"We need you two to come with us," one ordered, looking first at Eleanor then at Abbie.

"What for?" Eleanor asked a little nervously. The men gave no response, remaining completely silent as they waited for the girls to follow them. As they stepped into the elevator, Eleanor warily watched to see which level they were being escorted to. The first, taller man reached out and placed the flat of his hand on the sensor panel. That's not normal, she thought warily. None of the levels require whole handprints. Then, the man pushed the button labelled '1'. Of course, she thought, her heart sinking as the elevator began to rise. Just my luck.

"What's on Level One?" Abbie whispered nervously.

"I don't know," Eleanor whispered back, her voice slightly cracking as she tried to keep her hands from trembling. "No one knows. No one's ever been."

Chapter Twenty

They stepped from the elevator into a darkened corridor, at the end of which a small lamp was attached to the wall, casting a pale glow over a large door. They slowly approached the door, one Protector walked ahead of them and the other following behind.

The first Protector reached forwards and opened the door before standing back to allow them through. Remaining outside the room, he shut the door firmly behind them. And, with no way out, their only choice was to continue into the large room.

The room was lit by a dim light, not dissimilar to that of the corridor. A wooden desk was tucked away in the corner and a long mahogany table was positioned in the centre, a few papers strewn haphazardly across it. Most of the walls were blank, apart from a few framed newspaper articles and photos that looked rather out of place, except for one wall which was covered almost completely by a large spread of blue paper decorated with various scribbles.

As soon as they entered the room, a photo positioned in pride of place above the desk immediately caught Eleanor's eye. It showed several people standing, smiling, by the front door of a cream coloured house.

"Abbie?" Eleanor said, calling her over. "I recognise that place. Do you know where it is?"

Abbie hurried over and studied the picture. "I've seen it before, but I've no idea where."

"Do you think it's somewhere near the station? It must be, mustn't it? Or else I wouldn't recognise it."

"It might be," she nodded. "Wait, isn't it the house next door to the station? Aren't the red tiles part of the station front?"

"Yes, of course! We walked past the house, didn't we?"

"We must have done," Abbie nodded.

Wandering over to the next picture frame, Eleanor peered closer and began to read the faded, yet striking headline of the newspaper article clipping:

INTERNATIONAL SOCIETY FIND WAY TO ENSURE CONTINUATION OF HUMAN RACE

She stared at it curiously, before turning her attention to the article.

Sebastian Phulax who, we have been informed, recently hosted this year's meeting for the organisation of which he is an extremely influential member, agreed to partake in a short interview with us on the evening of the 23rd November.

Next to nothing is known about this society, other than its name. We do not know who any of the other members are, we do not know where or when they meet - only that it takes place once a year and is always hosted by a different member in his or her country.

During our interview, Mr. Phulax informed us that this Society has, under his leadership, devised a plan that has the potential to preserve the entire human race indefinitely, if or when such drastic actions might be necessary. He later released a public statement which confirmed this, saying: "I would like to reassure the whole of England that, come earthquake, tsunami, war, or any other threat to life as we know it, we have found a way to successfully shield the population. At this moment in time we are not ready to disclose details to the public, but be assured that in the case of any such event ever occurring, the whole population will be safe."

Although she wasn't completely certain who this Sebastian Phulax was, she supposed that what he had said wasn't all a lie. He hadn't given enough facts for it to mean anything - all he had said was that everyone would be safe, which they technically were. Some above ground, some below, and each community as ignorant of each other. He hadn't even mentioned how their safety would be assured, which Eleanor presumed was the point: If you don't give any specific facts, then the facts can never be wrong.

"Ellie, look at this," Abbie called from the opposite side of the room.

"What is it?" Eleanor asked, walking over to the huge sheet of blue paper that was hung across the wall.

"I think it's the plan of the Subterrane - the original plan," Abbie told her excitedly. "It's even got the annotations on it!"

"This is where it must have all started," Eleanor said, eagerly studying the markings.

"That's where your room is, isn't it?"

"Yes. And that's Level Zero-"

"-and those are the lecture halls you said about."

"It's all here."

"Well, it would be, wouldn't it," Abbie said. "It's pretty impressive, though."

"It is," Eleanor agreed, giving it a final glance before wandering over to another framed news article hung on the wall. This one was dated 2nd January 2047 - the day after the evacuation.

WHERE DID THEY GO?

Since the early hours of yesterday morning, the police have been bombarded with calls and demands for the whereabouts of suspected missing persons.

It has now come to light that several hundreds of people have gone missing between the hours of midnight and 5 a.m., which is when the first calls began flooding in. However, what is slightly more worrying is that no one seems to have any information on where they might be. Was it some scandalous government conspiracy? Was it methodically planned between all these missing persons? Only one thing is known: they seem to have disappeared off the face of the Earth.

We have been informed that several notable figures are also reported to be among those missing: Julia Smith (a prominent politician who is in the running for Chancellor of England in the upcoming May elections), David Adams (Vice Chief of Defence Staff in the English Army), Sebastian Phulax (who was working on a project to prevent the extinction of the human race), Esther Morgan (a TV presenter), Liz Brown (an internationally renowned economist) and James Stevens (one of the senior ministers to the current Chancellor).

Currently, police, armed forces and thousands of volunteers, as well as friends and relatives of those missing, are out searching. However, we have been informed by a spokesperson for the group that, without any leads so far, it is "not looking hopeful". Another family has told us that they will "never give up", and a father searching for his twenty-four-year-old daughter told us that he swears to "never stop looking".

For now, at least, these few hundred people seem to have disappeared without a trace. If you have any information about their whereabouts, or if you have seen or heard anything that may be of assistance, please do not hesitate to contact the police. For more information on how to tell us your experience with this event, see page 4...

Eleanor wondered what it must have felt like for all those people that helped search. Did any still hope or had they all given up many years ago, just like the police had? After all, eighteen years was an extremely long time.

Beneath the article was a series of individual portrait photos. The first depicted a tall woman sitting very upright with her hair scraped back and pinned neatly in place; the label beneath read: "Politician Julia Smith". Beside it was a picture of a man in uniform, with a label reading "David Adams, Vice Chief of Defence Staff". She skimmed over the last few photos and was about to turn away to look for other articles, when she noticed the man in the fifth photo. She almost didn't recognise him, for he was much older now - although that was to be expected, of course. But there was no mistaking it: Sebastian Phulax was the Founder that knew Saskia, the same one that had threatened Eleanor only the day before.

Turning away from the photo, Eleanor jumped suddenly and took a step back as she saw him standing silently in the doorway, watching them closely.

Chapter Twenty-One

"Miss Desdemona," the Founder began as he took a step towards her. "I don't believe that I properly introduced myself when we last met, did I?"

Her breathing sped up and, as she began inching back towards the wall, his piercing eyes followed her every step. She couldn't quite shake away the feeling that he knew all too much about her.

"Sebastian Phulax." He extended his hand towards her, then seemed to think better of it and turned to face Abbie. "And you must be..."

"Abbie," she answered unwaveringly.

"Of course," he said dismissively. "I see you've both been reading our publicity articles. The Subterrane was my proposed project."

"And what does that mean?"

He paused. "Well, I suppose it won't do any harm to tell you. Being a member of the IPS meant that you were given the chance-"

"What does IPS stand for?"

"The International Preservation Society," he answered.

"And what's that?"

"Well," he began, surprisingly cooperatively. "The society plans and carries out various projects that benefit the general public, not just in England, but throughout the world. Each member of the society has the opportunity to propose various ideas each year, and the best of them are selected."

"What does it have to do with the Subterrane?" Eleanor asked. "Other than the fact that you were a member ages ago."

"Because the Subterrane was my proposition," he answered smugly. "And it was accepted."

"Why would anyone agree to something like that?" Abbie asked, glaring at him.

"But I thought it was a group idea," Eleanor frowned in confusion. "I thought it was collectively thought up by the Founders - that's what you said in the lecture. I remember you saying it!"

"Someone had to come up with the original idea - thirteen people can't think of the same thing all at once, can they?"

"I suppose not," Eleanor admitted reluctantly.

"The original idea was entirely mine although, naturally, the end result was very different to the original proposition. But I never really expected it to actually happen at all, so it was still a great achievement," he said, trailing off; for a moment he seemed to have forgotten they were even there. Looking up suddenly, he cleared his throat. "Let me explain. You see, for a long time our society had been searching for a new, more… innovative project that we could be known for. It would be a sort of 'saving act' - something to put us on the map."

"Why would you need something like that?"

"It was a society dedicated to preserving and to helping mankind, but we'd hardly managed to achieve anything remarkable. Of course, we also wanted to preserve the society itself, and ourselves along with it."

"Then why make the Subterrane?" Eleanor asked. "No one even knows you exist anymore."

"Well, it was inevitable that a place of safety would be needed someday. Climate protests had been going on for over fifty years, the world's politics were getting messier by the day, we'd lost our royal family - the world was gradually destroying itself! We knew that we couldn't save the whole world, so we changed our focus. But we would be celebrated and admired because, at least to everyone in the Subterrane, we would have saved the whole world."

"The royal family wasn't abolished until some time after 2050," Abbie said quietly, stepping towards them from the wall she had been leaning on. "Don't even try using it as an excuse. And, since you know that, you must know what the world up there is really like."

"Excuse me?" He turned towards Abbie as if he was noticing her for the first time.

"Don't even try telling me I'm wrong," Abbie met his eyes with a steady hostility. "You seem to forget that I'm not from here. Unlike almost everyone down here, I actually know what it's like out there."

"So, your world's perfect, is it?" He smirked, as Abbie faltered momentarily.

"It was never perfect in the first place."

"No, but it was much better than it is now."

"Maybe it was, but would you say your world is perfect?" Abbie shot back.

"I'd say it almost is," he replied adamantly.

"Really?" she raised her eyebrows at him. "This world that you've built entirely on lies, is almost perfect? If you think that, then you're a fool."

"People down here have learned to flourish - much more than they could have ever done on the Surface!"

"Look, it still doesn't change anything," Eleanor interrupted, but Abbie hadn't finished.

"Why only one race?" Abbie continued. "Why not all sorts of people, so that every race was preserved?"

"Because if we'd done that, then there wouldn't be a single race left - they would all morph into one. It was the only way we could think of maintaining one single race."

"But I still don't understand why anyone would agree to something like that. People lost everything - their families, their homes…"

"I was the first to admit that some sacrifice would be inevitable for this to work," he gestured to the blueprint hanging on the wall.

"How noble of you," Abbie muttered.

"But the focus of the plan was the greater good."

"Could it not have been done in a more organised way? Couldn't families have been housed together, instead of in the zone they were closest to?"

"Ah. Now we come to it," he said.

"Come to what?"

"Answer this honestly," he began. "Do you really believe that simultaneous evacuations took place across the globe that night? Even after you've been up there yourself?"

"That's what you told us," Eleanor said, before pausing and looking away. "Well, I did, but I suppose that would have been impossible, wouldn't it?"

"See, that's the one thing no one ever thinks of," he replied. "They worry about where our water supply comes from, or how our ventilation system works, but never question how it would be physically possible to manage millions of simultaneous operations all across the globe. And even if we claimed that the timings were staggered, how do you evacuate billions of people from the surface of the earth? The answer's simple: You can't. Let alone the fact that it would cost billions of pounds - imagine how much it cost just to build this one."

"Then it was a lie? This is the only Subterrane?"

"Precisely."

"But why? And why lie in the first place?"

"Originally I did want to explore the possibility of having several Subterranes, first within England and then potentially in various locations across the world. We had intended to have enough underground settlements for everyone everywhere, but then we realised that achieving something like that was too far out of reach. It also became clear that the funds we had would only stretch to build one underground civilisation. So, we focused on this Subterrane; we thought that perhaps it could be a dry-run - a test, I suppose, to see if it really worked. If it did, we planned to try and raise more funds, but if not we would terminate it."

"So why didn't you terminate it, since you didn't need it in the end?"

"Well, for starters it worked, didn't it? But we also saw the devastation it caused for both those on the Surface and down here, and how desperate they became to find the people that had disappeared. So we planned to apologise, explain why we had done it and back away from the no doubt angry public. But then we saw how this world we had created was thriving - imagine just seeing your idea come to life like that..."

"But this place is filled with nothing but lies - not a single citizen knows the truth! Or they didn't until recently. How can you possibly be proud of that?"

"Lies? The Subterrane was built entirely on the truth," he laughed at her naivety.

"How is this the truth? Everything you've just told us proves that it's the exact opposite! The only reason that there are still people down here is that you fabricated some story that there's a war on the Surface," Abbie burst out, gesturing towards the ceiling.

"Alright, I'll explain," he conceded. "In 2047, there was a slight chance that a war could start at any given moment. So, we decided that the safest precaution we could take was to go ahead with our plan and remove as many people as we could from the Surface. Any potential threats to our civilisation would either stay above ground and partake in the war or would enter the Subterrane, where they would be forced to abide by our rules. So, when the evacuation of '47 occurred, it wasn't a lie. When people were told that there were Revolutionaries on the Surface, it still wasn't technically a lie; we genuinely thought that there was still a threat and that a war would begin within the next few days. But, after nine months or so, we were beginning to grow doubtful of our plan which had seemed flawless at the time. After all, how could we sustain a civilisation of this magnitude forever? We didn't even know if it would be possible.

"We were preparing ourselves to admit defeat, but then we noticed how the people were thriving within the Subterrane. Children were excelling, work sectors were flourishing - the citizens were beginning to come together and form a real community.

"The truth is that wherever you are, whatever country you are from, whatever enemies you make and whatever allies you have, there is always a threat of war - whether it puts humanity at risk or not. Being able to pin it on an infinite 'what if' is a rather easy answer, I'm afraid. It's just that no one ever considers it.

"The only part of the project that was a complete lie is the gunshots: No one fired anything - no one even had any guns."

"I knew it!" Abbie exclaimed suddenly.

"Wait, what was the noise?" Eleanor wasn't sure whether to trust what he was saying. After all, why would he want to tell them of all people. Especially after he'd managed to keep it a secret for so long?

"It was pre-recorded using blanks and played through loudspeakers in the targeted London area. It was executed so well that it seemed to be near enough to people to make them panic, but not so close that they thought they wouldn't have sufficient time to reach the Tunnel safely. Other than that, there are no lies," he concluded proudly. Then his tone changed: "But that's not why you're here, is it? You're here because you, Ellie - it is alright if I call you Ellie, isn't it?" he looked over to her but didn't bother waiting for a response. "You're here because you were explicitly warned - by me, no less - to be very careful what you did and said to people. But then you blatantly ignored my advice."

Abbie rolled her eyes. "Can we just cut to the exciting part?"

"And what would the exciting part be?" he replied, rounding on her

"You telling us what's going to happen now," she answered unwaveringly.

"Very well," he answered. "You are going to leave here and never come back."

"You forget: I'm not from here anyway so that doesn't change anything for me," Abbie reminded him.

"True," he said. "But she is." He gestured towards Eleanor who was now looking a little apprehensive.

"People would notice if I was gone," Eleanor burst out. "I have friends - remember?"

"Friends like Saskia?" he teased cruelly.

"She's not my friend anymore," she replied angrily, not meeting his eye.

"But she was your friend, wasn't she?" He raised an eyebrow, taunting her.

"Yes. She was."

"Do you even know anything about her?"

"Of course I do," Eleanor answered, outraged. "I've known her almost my whole life!"

"Alright. Tell me something about her."

"I know almost everything about her," she replied nervously. Yet something told her he was bound to catch her out.

"Then may I ask you something?"

"Fine." She crossed her arms, thoroughly irritated now.

"What's her last name?"

Eleanor thought for a moment, then looked away.

"Ellie - didn't you hear?" Abbie broke through the silence. "He asked what her last name is."

"I... I don't know," she finally admitted.

"How can you not know what her surname is?" Abbie said.

"I just don't know - she never told me."

"How about I tell you?"

"Go on then." Abbie gave him a dirty look.

"It's Phulax," he stated smugly. "Saskia Phulax. You think you know her, but really you don't. Do you know her room number? Do you know how she was able to report you so quickly both times? Do you know what her real connection to me is?"

No response.

"She's my daughter. She moved here when she was six and has no Individual Pod because she has always lived on Level Twenty - near me."

Both Eleanor and Abbie stared at him as he spoke, gaping in disbelief.

"Would you like to know why she reported you? It was because, from the day after the anniversary, she began her training to be a Protector. I knew you were absent from the Emergency Pods, so I specifically tasked her with finding out where you'd been. She was planning on warning you before you told her, but then you started blabbing about how amazing everything had been on the Surface and she knew she would never be able to make up a good enough excuse for you. That was the one task she had to accomplish in order to be sworn in. Oh, and before you start thinking that you're special, you were only her friend because we randomly selected you to be," he added cruelly. "She knows things about the Subterrane that you would never even dream of asking. For example," he continued, gesturing to the room around them, "people always wonder what's on Level One. And that's because it is closed to everyone - even the Founders. But Level One doesn't contain equipment or meeting rooms or classrooms or lecture halls or Pods; Level One contains the truth."

"How can a room contain the truth?" Abbie asked sceptically.

"Well, one thing not everyone remembers is that a lot of people had phones and other devices with them after the evacuation. And obviously they were very concerned when they found that there were no charging sockets anywhere. We told them that there hadn't been enough time for us to incorporate electrical mains and sockets in the Subterrane, but that we would keep hold of them until it was safe to go back to the Surface. All that we required them to do was put their devices inside a small sealable bag that we provided and write their name on it."

"So, what, did you sell them or something?" Abbie asked, since Eleanor didn't seem to understand what a phone was.

"When the devices were collected, the data from them was downloaded. We used that to find the names of any family members and friends, so that we could reassure them that everyone they knew had been registered in another Subterrane, meaning that they were safe."

"But why didn't you just ask what their names were?" Eleanor suggested.

"Yes, we could have done, but we thought we would be more likely to gain the trust of everyone, if we could say to each of them that, for example, their brother had made it to Zone Seven and was asking if they were safe. That way, they could give us a message for the relative and friend, and then they would be assured that this wasn't just a one-off thing."

"But it was," Abbie said.

"Well yes, but they didn't need to know that," he replied. "We needed them to trust us."

"So why didn't you tell them what was on Level One?" Eleanor asked. "The fact that it's off-limits to everyone suggests that you're hiding something."

"Because of the door over there," he pointed to the far side of the room. "It leads to a set of stairs, which come out in the basement of a house. The house that's next to the tube station that we're beneath - the same one in that photograph," he pointed to the picture they had noticed earlier. "People believe that there is only one way out of here, and that it's through the Tunnel. But that's because people believe anything you tell them. I couldn't risk anyone knowing about the door - it would mean that there was no way I could get out unnoticed. That basement beneath it is where I came up with the entire plan for this underground world; this later became the original meeting room for the IPS' involvement in the project. These papers are even the original plans - the ones I wrote from the very beginning," Phulax said, motioning towards various papers strewn across the table. "Level One is where my life's work came into being. And I wanted it to stay that way."

"But why here?" Eleanor asked. "What's so special about this station and that particular house?"

"The house upstairs is where I grew up. This room was where an entirely new world was created from scratch. No one realised that this was the Subterrane until it was too late - they simply presumed that it was just a very deep basement underneath the house. But that house... well, to me, it's almost sacred," he said, reminiscently.

"That's a very moving story and everything, but what about us?" Abbie interrupted once more.

"You're going to leave, like I told you," he stated.

"But people will notice!" Eleanor burst out, now realising just how serious he was about it. "You can't! I'll... I'll tell people everything - who the government are and who you are and-"

"You don't get it, do you?" He looked almost amused. "I am the government. Yes, there are other members, but I'm the only one who makes any of the decisions around here. This is and always has been my world - my vision. And it's run whatever way I want it to be run," he concluded as he strode over to the small and almost unnoticeable door in the wall. Pulling a key from his pocket, he unlocked it and placed his thumb on a keypad before a faint 'click' sounded and the door creaked open rather eerily. "And as to you telling anyone," he said, turning to face them once more. "Good luck getting them to believe you - especially since the other door is being sealed as we speak, and this one will be sealed as soon as you're gone. An underground world? They'll just think you're mad!"

Eleanor frowned as he looked at them expectantly, then tilted his head towards the door.

"You don't seriously think we're going to walk out of here as easy as that, do you?" she said.

"I know for a fact that you're going to leave through that door today, but whether it's easy or if you walk out is entirely up to you." He walked over to the door they had entered the room from, then opened it and called in the Protectors that had brought them there. "These girls were just leaving. I trust you'll be able to help... encourage them," he said, with a stony expression that clearly told the Protectors that they had no choice in the matter.

"I..." The first Protector stared blankly at the Founder.

"Of course, sir." The other hurried over to where Eleanor and Abbie were standing and began guiding them towards the darkened doorway. It soon became clear, however, that he couldn't manage both girls at once.

"Where... where does that go, sir?" the other Protector finally managed, glancing at the Founder with wide eyes.

"Where do you think?" Abbie shot back, still struggling against the other Protector.

There was a brief pause, before Phulax took a step towards the Protector. "Are you going to help, or should I arrange for you to revisit your training?"

"No, sir. I... no, sir. Absolutely not," he replied, hurrying over to restrain Eleanor.

And, within minutes, they had forced them through the doorway. But just as the Protectors began wrestling to close the door, a sudden thought occurred to Eleanor.

"Wait! Just... let me ask one thing." Eleanor paused, unsure whether she wanted to know the answer. Would it help? No. Would it change anything? Perhaps. But either way, she had to know. "Did Saskia even like me? Did she want to be friends with me? Or was it all just a lie?"

"I suppose you'd have to ask her," Phulax replied as the Protectors finally forced the door shut and a key clicked in the lock.

Chapter Twenty-Two

Eleanor placed her palms on the wall to maintain her balance, her eyes adjusting to the darkness of the staircase.

"Are you alright, Ellie?" Abbie whispered.

"I'm fine," she answered abruptly, although it was obvious that she wasn't.

They waited in absolute silence until they were finally able to make out their surroundings. They were standing between the closed door - which would doubtless remain closed for some time, now - and the foot of an endless upward spiral of stairs. Fumbling her way towards the bottom step, Eleanor sat down and began to think over the bombshell of information that had just been dropped on her.

"How could I have been so stupid!" she burst out angrily. "There was so much I didn't know about her - how could I not see that it didn't add up?"

Abbie sat down beside Eleanor and wrapped an arm around her shoulders.

"It won't help to blame yourself - none of this is your fault," she comforted.

"But it is!" Eleanor shot back, moving away from Abbie. "If I hadn't told her that I'd left in the first place, she would never have had a reason to report me and we wouldn't be in this mess."

The seconds dragged on as they sat in silence; neither knew what to say.

"What happens now?" Abbie said, finally breaking through the stillness.

No response.

"Ellie, we can fix this - we'll sort it all out," she continued. "You'll get through this, you'll..." Abbie paused as a subtle sniff sounded from her left. "Ellie, you really will be okay. "

"I know. I'm fine," Eleanor answered sharply, wiping her eyes hastily.

"Are you sure? Because you don't seem fine and it's understandable if you're-"

"-Abbie, I'm fine," Eleanor assured her brusquely.

"Okay." Abbie paused as she peered into the darkness. "So what happens now? What do we do? Where do we go?"

"I don't know, alright? Can you just let me think in peace! Just for a minute?" Eleanor snapped back.

"I-"

"If you hadn't come down there trying to save the day and everything, then this wouldn't have happened in the first place! You just had to come and interfere and mess everything up, didn't you?" Eleanor exclaimed harshly.

Abbie said nothing for a moment, taken aback by Eleanor's outburst.

"I'm sorry if this really is my fault - I was only trying to help," she mumbled quietly, moving so that she was sat with her back to Eleanor.

The awkward tension began to fill the expanse of unknown territory.

"No, I know you didn't mean for this to happen," Eleanor replied. "I'm sorry - I shouldn't have said that. It's not your fault. You've done nothing but help me, and I shouldn't have taken it out on you. I really am grateful to you for your help with all of this, you know. I don't know how I would have managed otherwise."

"It's okay," Abbie smiled, forgiving her easily. "But just remember that I'm on your side."

"I know. And I'm sorry for snapping. So... what now?" Eleanor echoed Abbie's previous question that still hung clumsily in the air.

"Well, I guess there's only one way we can go," Abbie answered, gazing into the blackness at the top of the stairs.

After a little deliberation, they agreed that the climb was wholly una-voidable. In single file, they each clutched the ancient wooden bannister tightly to stop themselves from slipping on the worn steps.

"Ellie, why do you think he told us all of that?" Abbie asked quietly.

"That's just what I've been asking myself."

Abbie squealed suddenly as she lost her footing and gripped onto the bannister tightly to regain her balance. "But I just don't get it. Surely it's a huge risk for him to tell anyone - let alone us."

"Why are we more of a risk than anyone else?"

"Because we're going up to the Surface. We can tell hundreds - thou-sands of people."

Eleanor gasped. "That must be why."

"So we can tell people? What do you mean?"

"No." Eleanor couldn't help shaking her head, although she knew Ab-bie couldn't see her through the darkness. "It's because he doesn't think anyone will believe us."

"What?"

"Think about it. Who in their right mind would?"

"Well, I did, remember," Abbie pointed out.

"Somehow I don't think many other people will though," Eleanor re-plied, pausing as they reached the top of the staircase.

"Where now?" she whispered to Abbie who was mere steps behind her.

"I can see a light coming from over there - is it a door?" Abbie asked, passing Eleanor and feeling along the brick walls in an attempt to reach the source of the dim light. She brushed her hand across the doorframe before locating a handle which, when she applied pressure, allowed the door to slowly swing open.

Abbie emerged into a dark and dingy basement room, lit by only a dimly flickering strip light. At the opposite end of the small room was a short set of steps, leading upwards to a trapdoor. A few cardboard boxes were stacked neatly in the corner, their contents spilling over onto the cold stone floor. Eleanor gazed around at the papers scattered around

177

them haphazardly. Gathering a few from the ground, she began to skim through the various crumpled documents.

"Where do you think it goes?" Abbie whispered, gesturing towards the trapdoor up ahead.

"I've no clue," Eleanor answered, shrugging her shoulders.

"My guess is we're still very near the tube station," Abbie declared confidently. "Didn't he say that the staircase led to the basement of that house?

"Yes, but we might have gone the wrong way at some point."

"At least it was a spiral staircase, so we know that we're still directly above the door from Level One."

"I suppose so," Eleanor agreed half-heartedly. "But we still don't know where that leads to." She pointed dismally at the trapdoor.

"Well, we're not going to find out where it goes by staying down here, are we?"

Eleanor sighed and put down the handful of papers, before slowly making her way over to the stone steps.

"Are you sure about this?" she asked Abbie.

"Either it opens or it doesn't," Abbie replied sensibly. "But if it doesn't, then we'll be trapped, because there's no way that your founder person would have forced us out just to let us back in again."

Eleanor nodded and slowly made her way up the steps until her fingers could reach the trapdoor above her head.

"So do I open it?" she asked.

"If you can."

Placing her fingertips on the underside of it, gently she pushed upwards. The trapdoor opened a fraction, allowing in a meagre splinter of natural light.

"Can you see anyone?" Abbie whispered excitedly.

"Not yet." Eleanor continued to struggle with the door.

"Okay, so open the hatch completely," Abbie began in a business-like manner. "Then we can see where we are and get out of this place."

"Can you give me a hand?" Eleanor's hands were shaking as she attempted to raise the heavy door.

Abbie hurried up the steps behind her and pushed upwards until the hatch was almost at ninety degrees.

"I'll hold it while you get out, then you can hold it while I get out. Good plan?" Abbie proposed.

"Why do I have to get out first?" Eleanor's hands were still trembling.

"I can if you want," Abbie reassured her.

Abbie slowly clambered up the few remaining stairs but then tripped as she stepped out into the corridor.

"Sebastian?" called a voice from a room towards the front of the house. "Is that you?"

"Ellie, quick!" Abbie whispered frantically, taking hold of the trapdoor to allow Eleanor to exit the basement room. "There's someone coming - we need to hide!"

Eleanor hurried out and helped Abbie close the trapdoor as quietly as they could.

"Which way?" Eleanor whispered.

Abbie glanced each way down the corridor: "That way," she pointed to the left.

"Quick - in here," Eleanor said on reaching the first door. She wrenched it open and hurried inside the room, allowing Abbie to shut it behind them. "Where can we hide?" she whispered, seeing that there was no furniture large enough to conceal both of them.

"Behind there?" Abbie motioned to a large pair of cream curtains that framed a wide window. From there, they could see into a small space with a short set of stairs leading upwards to what was probably the street level.

Hastening towards the curtains, they each hid behind one; Eleanor behind the left, Abbie behind the right. They waited, listening, as the footsteps drew nearer and nearer, then finally passed the room. Nevertheless, they remained motionless behind the curtains for a few more minutes before edging into the room.

"Let's get out of here," Abbie said, heading to the door. But, just before reaching it, she stopped. "Ellie, this isn't me being funny or anything, but I could have sworn that looks exactly like-"

"-Saskia," Eleanor finished, nodding.

A framed photo stood on a small round table beside the door. It depicted a child of three or four with white-blonde curls and big blue eyes, squirming in the arms of a mother who was looking down at her with a tender, loving smile.

"You don't think..." Abbie halted mid-sentence.

"What?" Eleanor frowned.

"You don't think that she, well..." Abbie wasn't quite sure how to word her idea. "I know you said you've known Saskia since she was six or something, but what about before that?"

"What do you mean?"

"Phulax said she moved there, but he didn't say where she moved from. What if she didn't grow up in another zone at all? What if she grew up here with her mum, and then moved down to the Subterrane a bit later?"

"But why would she have done that?"

"No one would have known that her dad was a Founder, because no one would ever have seen him with her mum if she lived up here. He had easy access to her house from the Subterrane, so could come and go as he pleased. But I don't know why Saskia wouldn't have stayed with her mum."

"Actually, I think I might know," Eleanor realised suddenly. "I completely forgot about it until now, but after the Anniversary Meal the Founder - her dad, I suppose - he asked to have a word with her. I wanted to know what it was about so I listened in from the stairwell, and I remember her asking why she couldn't have just stayed with 'her'."

"What do you mean?"

"I don't know. Saskia just said 'her'."

"And then what did he say?"

"I don't remember his exact response, but it was something like they decided it would be better for her to grow up in a society like the Subterrane."

"They didn't happen to mention anything about why her mum lives up here, did they?" Abbie asked.

"Actually," Eleanor began in surprise, "I think they might have. I'm pretty sure he said she chose to."

"She chose not to live in a world that her husband created?" Abbie reiterated.

"I guess it's kind of understandable, though," Eleanor said. "Would you choose to spend the rest of your life trapped underground, forever being told what you can and can't do?"

"Maybe not, but her husband created it from nothing!"

"I know what you mean," Eleanor replied, peering into the corridor to check that the coast was clear. "But it's not like she would never see him again - he's got exclusive access from his private floor. It just meant that she could continue to live a normal life at the same time."

"I guess," Abbie conceded as she turned away from the photo and followed Eleanor into the corridor.

"I can't believe Saskia never told me," Eleanor added, still not able to believe it.

"I know," Abbie said, before changing her tone dramatically. "Come on - let's get out of here."

They hurried back along the long hallway then, after taking two left turns, finally found themselves standing before the front door. Opening it as quietly as she could, Abbie stepped out into the golden glow of the afternoon sunshine and turned to Eleanor with a smile. "Welcome back."

As they emerged from the house, Eleanor noticed that the street was entirely deserted, except for a black car parked just outside the house.

"Was that here before?" She approached it apprehensively and peered through the darkened windows.

"I don't remember."

"I'm sure I've seen it before." Eleanor frowned as she tried to remember.

"There's probably a lot of cars like that in London," Abbie pointed out.

"Yes, but I... I'm sure it was this exact one."

"If you say so. But it's kind of unlikely. Maybe it belongs to whoever lives there?" Abbie motioned to the house they had just come from. "We might have walked past it when you showed me the Subterrane."

"Maybe."

"Come on, let's go. I don't like this place."

Slowly Eleanor turned away from the car to follow Abbie, and as she did so, glanced up at the house beside the station. Just in time to see a curtain on the first floor twitch. It was almost unnoticeable - almost insignificant. But to Eleanor, it proved the very thing she had dreaded.

We're being watched, she realised. Maybe there are spies on the Surface after all.

Chapter Twenty-Three

It was late afternoon as they crossed the bridge to the market, the sun casting a faint golden glow across the sky as a church bell tolled in the distance.

"Where do we go now?" Eleanor asked, turning to face Abbie. "What should we do?"

"Well, we can't go back there, so we'll have to come up with something from up here."

"How do we do that?" Eleanor asked apprehensively. "Phulax doesn't seem the type of person to go down without a fight - he could create an entire army down there if he wanted. We've got no chance against him."

"But Ellie, we've got the whole world to help us up here," Abbie answered swiftly. "Think about it. There are far more people up here. If we managed to convince a few people from the Subterrane about the Surface, then imagine how many we can convince from up here. Once they realise that we're telling the truth and that actual people are being held against their will, we can easily expose Phulax. And, he won't be expecting us to come back, which also works to our advantage."

"You think people would really believe us?" Eleanor asked.

"They might," Abbie replied, sounding slightly unsure. "I mean, people have believed far worse before - I'd say we stand a pretty good chance."

"Can't we just ask your parents what we should do?" Eleanor asked, still slightly dubious about Abbie's plan.

Abbie nodded. "My mum's visiting my grandparents, so she won't be back for a few hours, but I can call my dad." She reached into her right back pocket, then her left. "Dammit, I must have dropped my phone somewhere," she sighed as she checked again in each pocket. "When did I last have it..."

"What should we do now?"

"I'm not sure."

"Isn't there anyone else we could ask?"

"I suppose we could ask... well, we've got a few family friends who work here?"

"Will they believe us?" Eleanor followed Abbie as they wound their way through the market.

"I'm not sure. The only reason I believed you was because I got to know you first."

"We could just..." Eleanor paused to think.

"We could start with the facts and go from there?" Abbie suggested

"We can try that, I guess."

"We might as well give it a go," Abbie said, making her way over to a stall.

"Abbie!" a girl sat alone behind a stall exclaimed. "What a nice surprise! How are you?" The blonde girl looked a few years older than Abbie and seemed pleased to see them.

"Um, I'm alright."

"Who's this?"

"This is Ellie. Ellie this is Natasha."

"Hi Ellie. So, what are you two up to?"

"We've, well, mum's away for the day and dad's at work but I don't have my phone so I can't call him. We... we were wondering if you could help us with something. We're not sure what to do."

"Of course. What is it?"

"It's about Ellie - and where she's from."

"Okay. What about it?"

"We... she... there's people trapped there, and we don't know how to get them out."

"Where?"

"Well, Ellie's from an underground world, but there's an entrance near here."

"An underground world? Nice try Abbie." The girl began to tidy things around the stall.

"You don't understand - people's lives could be at stake!"

"Well in that case, it's probably best if you either wait for your dad to finish work, or go to the police yourself." She turned away from them.

"Natasha, please. You've got to listen to-"

"Abbie, no," she replied abruptly. "I don't mind you being here, but if you're just going to muck around then I don't have time for it."

"Everything alright here?" Abbie spun around to see who the voice belonged to.

"Everything's fine, thank you." Natasha smiled politely at the police officer.

"Well it's not. You just don't believe us," Abbie mumbled, almost inaudibly.

"What was that?" The officer turned to Abbie.

"I just... I was saying that everything's not really alright."

"And why's that?" The officer frowned.

"Well, you see, Ellie's from this underground world, and there's people trapped there but we don't know how...."

"An underground world? Sure there is. Good one." He began to walk away.

"We're not joking!"

He turned back for a moment. "And why would I believe that?"

"Because it's true."

The policeman shook his head slowly. "Haven't you heard you're not supposed to drink before five?"

"Won't you just listen to us for a minute? Please?"

"Go on, then," he sighed. "Let's hear it."

"Okay. Well, in the early hours of the 1st of January 2047, loads of people disappeared," Eleanor jumped in. "But, what we're saying is that

185

they were all rehoused in a secret underground bunker, where they've been trapped ever since."

"Right." The policeman looked as though he was ready to walk away again.

"We're being serious."

"That's where I'm from," Eleanor interjected. "I've lived there my whole life."

"Of course," the policeman replied. "And I'm from Mars."

"You don't understand! We need your help. Won't you at least let us tell you what we know?"

He sighed again and glanced at his watch. "I suppose there's no harm in it."

Eleanor looked over at Abbie triumphantly; at least someone was going to listen to what they had to say. They hurried after the policeman as he made his way through the crowd of shoppers, until they reached a police car.

He motioned for them to get in the back, and taking out a walkie-talkie, he spoke into it for a moment. "I've got a couple of girls who say they've got evidence on some disappearance, so I'm taking them to the station. Over."

"So, girls, how exactly do you expect me to be able to help?" He asked as he began driving towards the station.

"Well, we can tell you what we know, and then... maybe you'll be able to come up with something."

"Okay."

"Who are you?"

"Officer Wilde."

Eleanor remained silent for a moment, then, becoming too impatient, she asked: "So what happens now?"

"We'll get to the station, then you can tell me all about this disappearance, and then you can probably go."

"How long will it take?"

"Well it depends how long you talk for. But I'd say around two hours."

"So where are we going?" Abbie edged a little closer to Eleanor, to try and look out of her window.

"The police station."

"Well I know that!" Abbie retorted. "I meant which one."

"Metropolitan."

"Oh." It seemed Abbie had been hoping it might have been where her dad worked.

"Right," he said, pulling up in front of the station. "Here we are."

Chapter Twenty-Four

"We've been over this twice already," Abbie muttered in irritation, as she began to pick at her nails. "Do we really need to go through it all again?"

"Yes, we do," the officer retorted, ignoring the obvious eye-roll of his despairing colleague. Turning back to face Eleanor, he continued. "Once again, could you tell us where you've been living for the past seventeen years of your life?"

"How many times are you going to ask her that same question?" Abbie asked, bored out of her mind. "Maybe it's time for us to go."

"If you want our help, then answer the question," the officer snapped back.

"You really are bad at this," Abbie muttered. "I think I could have done a better job."

"I said, answer the question." The officer shook his head a little and glanced down at his watch.

"Alright, then. She's been living on the moon," Abbie answered back. "She's from outer space and she's an alien - that's why she's so pale. There. Does that answer work for you? It would make this a whole lot more interesting, let me tell you."

The officer's gaze lingered on her as he attempted to determine whether her reply was genuine. Quite frankly, at this point he wouldn't have put anything past the argumentative girl.

"I'm kidding, obviously," she burst out at his inability to take a joke.

"I've been living in an underground world, known as the Subterrane," Eleanor cut in, willing their interview to hurry up. "The same one that I told you I lived in ten minutes ago…"

"I see," he replied, as he noted down her response. "And who is in control of this world?"

"It's run by a government, which is run by an exclusive group of thirteen members - the Founders."

"And the members of this group, what are their professions?"

"Well, in the Subterrane they run the government and oversee… well, everything, I suppose. But before that, I think they were things like scientists, politicians and other things like that."

"And who are they led by?"

"Finally a new question!" Abbie commented.

"Who are they led by?" the officer repeated, looking directly at Eleanor as he tried to ignore Abbie.

"One of the members, called Sebastian Phulax."

The officer turned to his colleague: "Right, can we get a full report on Sebastian Phulax, please."

"What should I check him for?" his colleague replied.

"Criminal record, family, occupation, where he lived or still lives - anything you can find about his general past," the officer instructed, before turning back to face Abbie. "So, your friend claims she's from an underground world, but what about you? If she's not supposed to know that anyone even exists up here, then how does she know you?"

"Because she found a way out and then happened to meet me," Abbie explained simply. "She explained her situation to me, but wanted to go back because she didn't feel it was right to leave everyone else behind. She showed me where the entrance was but wouldn't allow me in, and then she went back and we didn't really expect to see each other again. But then I decided I couldn't just leave her down there without anyone else who knew the truth about her world, so I went down to help her get out."

"Right," the officer said doubtfully. "And remind me of who you are, exactly?"

189

"Abigail Heim," she said, resisting the urge to remind him, yet again, that it hadn't changed in the time since they had arrived there.

"And where are you from?"

"London. I grew up near Covent Garden and then we moved near the Southbank Centre for convenience - my mum has a stall at the Southbank Market."

"Okay, well, it might help us if you stay here for a bit longer, to give us time to ensure your stories check out."

"I definitely should have let my dad sort this out," Abbie murmured to herself.

"Your dad? Then what would be the point of the Police Service?"

"For the sixth time this afternoon, my dad's part of the London River Police. He's literally at work right now. Look, I think we're done here - I'm going to go and call him."

"You can if you want, but we are right in the middle of an interview. I can call him to inform him of your whereabouts, but it really would be best if you let us finish this interview first."

Abbie crossed her arms and slumped in the seat. "What exactly are you hoping to get out of this, anyway?"

"It's so that we can help you. And I'm asking the questions here, re-member?"

"Fine. Then why don't you ask some?"

"What were you doing when we saw you?"

"I couldn't reach my parents, so I was trying to tell someone about where Ellie comes from."

"Who were you trying to tell?"

"Just a family friend."

"And why did you feel that you needed to tell someone?"

"Because we need to go back to where she's from, so we can get eve-ryone else out," Eleanor explained. "We can't go back on our own be-cause we kind of got kicked out... But it means that we're going to need some help getting back in there."

"And what makes you think anyone will believe you?"

Abbie shrugged. "Nothing, really. They've got no reason to."

"I think that's why he told us everything," Eleanor added. "Because he knew that no one would listen to us."

"Right," the officer replied.

"Sir, I've got that report on Sebastian Phulax," his colleague announced as he re-entered the room.

"Great," the officer said, taking it and skimming through it.

"Can I just ask you one thing?" Abbie sat forwards in her chair and tilted her head to the side. "And then I promise I'll answer whatever stupid questions you ask me."

"Fine," he conceded, without needing much persuasion. "Go ahead."

"What happened that night?"

"What night?"

"You know - the one we've been talking about," Abbie replied. "New Year's Eve, 2047."

"Oh, that. Well, hundreds of people disappeared - everyone knows that," the officer answered matter-of-factly. "It might have been more, but it was quite hard to make a list of all those who were unaccounted for, since we had no leads and very few security cameras in that area."

"So where did they disappear to?"

"I'll give you that. You're right, we're not entirely sure. Some people say they heard gunshots that night - it could be that there was an attempted coup or uprising. But that doesn't mean that your extraordinary story is true. And if you're making all of this up, I should remind you that you're wasting valuable police time, which is a very serious matter."

"But you haven't answered my question. Where did they disappear to?" Eleanor butted in.

"Well, they must be dead," the policeman said with a slight shrug of his shoulder.

"Oh, I see. So I presume you found their bodies?" Abbie continued.

"Well, not exactly, but-"

"So you didn't find the bodies?"

"Well I-"

"Yes or no?"

He paused and exchanged a look with his colleague, before turning back face to her. "No."

"So you have no clue what happened to them? No evidence as to where they might have ended up?" Abbie clarified.

"Apparently not."

"And you presume these hundreds of people to just be dead?" Eleanor added. "Purely because you can't find them?"

"Yes, that's what I said, isn't it?" the officer answered, not quite meeting her gaze.

"Yet, you don't think it's a little odd that not one of the bodies has ever been found?"

"Not really. They could be virtually anywhere in the world."

"Wow, okay. Don't tell me you actually believe that crazy theory!" Abbie exclaimed.-

"I only know as much as you do about this," he said.

"Well, that's not true because we've just spent the last thirty minutes explaining to you that we know a lot more than you do about it. You have a choice here, and it's very simple and it's entirely up to you. Either, you don't believe us and do nothing, which may or may not mean that you're endangering hundreds of innocent people. Or, you can believe us and phone my dad, which will potentially help to save hundreds because he'll believe us and he can help us, too. Or, you can not believe us and still phone him. And let's face it, if you phone him, you can at least get rid of us. But, as I said, it's entirely up to you," Abbie finished, giving him a hopeful smile.

"Well, I'm sick of you two and I've no idea whether to believe you or not," the officer announced. "I'll let your dad deal with this."

Abbie sat back in her seat, thrilled at her victory.

"So which station did you say he was at?"

"River."

"Can you go and get the River department on the phone," the officer asked his colleague. "Get her dad to come and get them. I don't trust them enough to just let them loose in London again."

"Who should I ask for?"

"What's your dad's name?" the officer asked Abbie.

"Inspector Heim," Abbie replied.

"Right, ask Inspector Heim to come and pick up his daughter and her friend."

His colleague nodded and hurried off.

"You know, in a few days' time you'll probably regret not believing us," Abbie said. "My dad will help us whether he trusts us or not, but you could have helped."

"Or I could have made a complete fool of myself," he replied, closing the book in which he'd been taking notes. "Why didn't you go to your dad straight away, if you're so sure he'll believe you?"

"I lost my phone, and I didn't know where he'd be today," Abbie replied with a shrug. "So I tried telling a friend, but then we thought you might be able to help. Looks like we were wrong, though."

Just then, his colleague came back into the room. "He's just on his way. He said he'll be here in about twenty minutes."

"Thank you," the officer said.

"You might as well go and wait by the front desk, if you're done here," his colleague suggested.

"Good luck with... whatever you're trying to do - if what you told me really was the truth," the officer said.

"It was," Eleanor answered, following Abbie from the stuffy room.

They sat in the entrance hall in silence, until someone came rushing through the doors, looking around the room in a panic.

"Can I help y-" the officer behind the desk began.

"Abbie?" he called, before spotting them sitting at the side. "There you are! What mess have you got yourself into now?"

"I'm fine, dad," Abbie said, walking over to join him. "They were just asking us a few questions and then we finally convinced them to phone you."

"We?"

"Yes, this is Ellie," Abbie said, beckoning Eleanor over to join them.

"Your friend that came over for lunch yesterday?"

"Yes, this is her."

"Right, of course," he said. "Your mum mentioned her. Hi Ellie, nice to meet you."

"You too Mr Heim," Eleanor replied. Like Abbie, he was fairly tall. But, in contrast to her dark, frizzy hair, his was short, tidy, and light brown.

"Call me Matt," he said, then rounded on Abbie again. "But I still want to know what you were doing to get yourself brought here. Don't think you can get out of it that easily."

"Nice parking, dad," Abbie teased, changing the subject as they made their way towards a car that was parked very crookedly between two spaces.

"Well, I was a bit preoccupied thinking that my daughter had been arrested," he replied.

"I'll forgive you, then."

Eleanor smiled at Abbie as she rather apprehensively followed her into the car, before gazing out of the window. Then she froze.

A black car was parked on the other side of the street. Narrowing her eyes, she could just make out a driver dressed entirely in black. And, as they began to drive off, Eleanor noticed that it seemed to be following them, careful to keep a little distance between the two cars. But this time there was no mistaking the black car; it had been following them since they left the house.

"So," Abbie's dad began, looking at Abbie sternly in the rear-view mirror. "Tell me what happened."

"Alright," Abbie surrendered. "Basically Ellie needs some help getting back to… where she lives, and so I asked Natasha to see if she would help. Then the police just happened to be there, so we spoke to them to see if they could help," she blurted out. "We were only doing it because mum's not at home, and I'm not sure where my phone is, so I couldn't call you."

"Right, and what do you need help with, exactly?" he asked.

"It's, well, it's a rather long story," Abbie began reluctantly.

"I've got time."

Abbie looked over to Eleanor.

"Should we tell him?" she mouthed discreetly.

"I don't see why not," Eleanor shrugged.

"Okay, dad," Abbie began. "I need you to drive us somewhere. Do you mind?"

"Depends where it is."

"Aldwych Station - just off the strand. That okay?"

"Alright," he replied. "Any reason why?"

"Well, basically that's where Ellie's from."

"Aldwych station?" he repeated doubtfully.

"Yes," Abbie confirmed.

"Whereabouts around there?" he continued.

"Underneath it," Eleanor said.

"Underneath it? Very funny."

"She's not kidding, dad," Abbie added.

"Course she's not," he replied, rolling his eyes. "No wonder they didn't believe you at the station."

"I've been there and it's real."

"What's real?"

"The place I'm from, it's… it's an underground world," Eleanor explained clumsily. "It was established in January 2047."

"That's when all those people went missing after New Year," Abbie added.

"I'm sure it was," her dad replied sarcastically.

"Dad, you have to hear us out."

"The people where I'm from are brought up being told that nothing exists up here and I believed it until a few days ago, when I found a way out. But then I went back and tried to tell people that it was all a lie and then we kind of got kicked out," Eleanor told him.

"We?" he said, frowning at Abbie.

"I just kind of… went to see what it was like down there," she replied meekly. "I thought she might need some help getting out."

"So you risked going down to some underground world, just because you thought she might need some help?" He turned around to face her as they stopped at the traffic lights for a moment. "It's a very entertaining story," he said.

"It's not entertaining, it's real." Abbie frowned, becoming rather vexed at him.

"Yes, of course it is."

"Call from Rosalind," a robotic voice interrupted suddenly, as a faint beeping noise came from an illuminated screen at the front of the car.

"Accept call," Abbie's dad said, glad for a distraction from Abbie's strange story. A small button flashed green, indicating that the call had been connected.

"Are you at work, honey?" Eleanor looked around as a voice filled the car.

"Who's Rosalind?" she whispered to Abbie.

"My mum," she replied.

"Oh, right. I remember her telling me."

"No, I've just left," her dad replied. "Why?"

"I thought your shift didn't finish until six?"

"It doesn't, but..." he paused, trying to come up with a reason. "There wasn't much going on, so there was no point in me staying."

"That was nice of them!"

"It was."

"So will you be home soon?"

"No, I'm just on my way to pick up Abbie."

"Where from?"

"She was staying with Ellie, remember?"

"Oh, of course! She seemed like such a sweet girl - it's a shame you didn't get to meet her yesterday."

"Yes, but I'll probably see her when I'm collecting Abbie," he pointed out.

"Yes, you probably will. It would be nice if she came over again."

"Maybe," he said, nodding hesitantly. "Do you... do you know anything about her?"

"Not much really. Why?"

"I'm just not convinced she's a great influence on Abbie."

"We are still here dad," Abbie hissed.

"But you haven't even met her!" Abbie's mum replied.

"I know, I just… I've had some funny texts, that's all."

"Really? That's not like Abbie."

"Yes, she seems to be making things up," he added quietly, almost as though he didn't want Abbie and Eleanor to hear.

"Look, I've got to go now because I've just got to Ellie's," he said, catching sight of a very annoyed-looking Abbie in the rear-view mirror.

"Alright," she said. "I just wanted to let you know that my parents send their love, and I'm just on the train home."

"Did you have a nice day?" He asked, as they pulled up in front of Aldwych Station.

"Yes, I did," she replied. "Anyway, go get Abbie and drive safely."

"Will do. See you soon."

The call ended with a definitive 'click'.

"What's wrong with you?" Abbie said, sounding exasperated as she got out of the car. "Why won't you believe us?"

"Have you heard what you're asking me to believe?"

"Look, I know it's not the most believable thing ever, but you have to trust me!"

"Really, Abbie? I'm not in the mood today."

"Please, just… if you don't believe me, at least let us show you," she pleaded, walking up to the front of the station.

Her dad sighed. "If this is all some elaborate story you've made up, you're just going to make it worse for yourself."

"I'm not making it up though!"

"Alright, but maybe Ellie made it up."

"She didn't," Abbie retorted, "because it's true. Every word of it."

"Fine, you can show me it." He shook his head in disbelief as he walked over to where she was standing. "But I'm warning you, Abbie. If you're lying…"

"I'm not!"

Chapter Twenty-Five

"It's in there?" Abbie's dad asked sceptically, looking thoroughly unconvinced as he stepped from the car and took in the ageing facade of the abandoned tube station.

"Yes. The door's down on one of the old platforms," Abbie replied, as Eleanor followed her out of the car.

Walking up to the station, Eleanor wrenched the doors open with a clang and looked back at Abbie who was studying her dad's expression, anxious of what he might be thinking.

"Now come on, Abbie," he began. "If this is a joke, then it needs to end right now."

"Dad, I'm not kidding," Abbie insisted. "There's a whole world down there - I've seen it."

"Yes, you said that," he said. "But still, it's just... it's very hard to believe."

"Well I can't force you to believe us, but I'm telling you that there are people trapped down there," Abbie told him. "And we're going to help them with or without you."

"Yes, I got that impression."

"You've got nothing to lose," Abbie said, glancing over to where Eleanor stood, patiently waiting by the door.

"I know, Abbie, but still I-"

"Look, are you coming or not?" Abbie asked, turning back to face him.

"I... Alright. Fine," he answered, shaking his head in disbelief. Sighing, he clapped his hand on Abbie's shoulder as he followed her towards the metal door. "Your mother's going to kill me if she ever finds out about this."

Eleanor waited until Abbie and her dad had both passed through the door, then looked up and down the road to check if the car had followed them. But there was still no sign of it.

She was so sure they were being watched, but perhaps she had just imagined it.

"Come on, Ellie." Abbie was looking at her expectantly.

Once she was certain that the car wasn't there, Eleanor ducked through the small gap that had been concealed by the door and emerged into the ghostly corridor where Abbie and her dad stood waiting.

Door after door, corridor after corridor, they followed the trail of footsteps imprinted in the thick layer of dust that indicated the way to the platform.

"This is the northbound platform, I think," Abbie told her dad as they reached the foot of the final staircase and walked underneath the 'EXIT' sign.

"So where's this Subterrane, then?" Abbie's dad asked sceptically.

"Don't be like that," Abbie retorted, giving him a disapproving look.

"Alright. But where is it, then?"

"This way," Eleanor called as she continued ahead of them, eagerly advancing down the platform to the far end. She yanked open the door at the end of the platform and hurried down the short spiral staircase until they faced a final door.

"Abbie," Eleanor began nervously, as a sudden thought hit her. "Why's there no light coming through?"

"I... I don't know. Maybe whoever went through last shut the door a bit harder than usual?" Abbie attempted to reassure her. She moved towards the door and, feeling for the doorframe, scratched around the wall as she tried to pry it open as she had done the last time.

"Ellie," she said, her voice trembling. "It won't open."

"What?" Eleanor answered, rushing forward. "It has to - let me have a go."

Pushing Abbie to the side, she scrabbled around the edge of the door as she attempted to wrench it open. When the door still refused to budge, she began frantically kicking and pounding it in frustration.

"Surely there's another way in?" Abbie's dad suggested, trying to give them the benefit of the doubt. "Maybe there's another door?"

"There isn't. At least, not one that we can use," Abbie replied. "They must have sealed the door already - he said they were doing it while he was with us. I just didn't think he seemed like he meant it," she thought aloud.

"No," Eleanor answered quietly, her breath growing more ragged and panicked. She began pummelling the door harder until she became more desperate and finally burst out: "No - they can't have done! I have to get back there. People will realise I'm gone; Saskia will notice. They can't do this - they can't!"

"It'll be okay," Abbie said, running to Eleanor's side and wrapping her in a safe hug. "We can work this all out."

"But it won't be okay - that's my home," Eleanor sobbed as she pulled away from Abbie, who could now make out the tears streaming down her friend's cheeks.

"But I thought you wanted to leave?"

"Not while everyone else is still in there!" Eleanor exclaimed. "Let me in!" she screamed at the door, giving it a final kick. She was the most vulnerable Abbie had ever seen her; her eyes red with tears, her voice cracking through her sobs as she sank to the ground. Abbie said nothing as she put an arm around her again.

"So it's not here?" Abbie's dad asked, breaking through the few precious moments of silence as Eleanor wiped her eyes and sat up.

"Dad!" Abbie whispered, willing him to be a little more tactful.

"It's a simple yes or no question. Is it here or not?" He eyed them both quizzically.

"It's through there," Abbie replied, waving her hand in the general direction of the door.

"Wouldn't there be a keyhole if it had been locked?" He still didn't sound convinced.

"No," Abbie answered. "It'll just be sealed with some kind of adhesive."

"So that's it, now? She can't get back?"

"No," Abbie replied, wishing he'd try and be more sympathetic.

"Well, there's no point giving up just yet," he said, striding towards the door.-

First, he attempted to wrench the door towards himself, which proved rather a challenge as the door handle was missing. Then, he tried ramming his shoulder up against the door, which only resulted in several splinters and a small gash across his hand. As a final resort, he took a knife from the casing within his belt and pushed it between the door and the frame. Wiggling it around all sides of the door, he proceeded to use it as a lever, whilst trying not to cut himself as the knife began to bend under the strain.

He suddenly lurched backwards and the door gave way, flinging him to the ground and sending the knife flying through the brightly lit hallway.

Eleanor looked nervously towards the corridor as they all remained completely still, watching for any signs of citizens who might have witnessed their break-in. The eternal seconds ticked by until, finally, she breathed through the darkness: "You did it!"

Abbie's dad smiled at her. "If there's a door, then there's a way through it."

"But you really did it!" she beamed.

Approaching the door, Eleanor slipped off her shoe and placed it between the door and the wall, before closing the door a little, to cut off the light that was now flooding the stairwell with a blindingly bright glow.

"So what do we do now?" Abbie asked through the darkness, as she stepped closer to Eleanor. "Should we go in?"

"I'm not sure…" Eleanor answered, anxiously glancing towards Abbie's dad to see what he thought.

"You two wait here," he said as he moved up to the door, pulling it open and striding out into the light on the other side.

Anxiously, Abbie and Eleanor stood in the doorway, watching his every move.

"What are you doing?" Eleanor whispered as he began making his way further down the corridor.

"Dad! What if someone sees you?" Abbie hissed.

He ignored them and continued until he reached the far end of the corridor, where he paused to peer through the small glass panel in the outer set of elevator doors. Just as he did so, a faint alarm sounded several floors below, and a distant whirring noise came from somewhere deep within the Subterrane. Suddenly, Eleanor drew in a sharp breath as the thin outline of a green circle lit up beside the elevator.

"What is it?" Abbie asked, looking worriedly at Eleanor.

"The elevator..."

"What?"

"Quick!" Eleanor yelled. "You need to get out of there."

"What do you mean?" Abbie's dad turned back towards the door. "What's wrong?"

"Someone's coming up in the elevator - we need to go, now!" Eleanor shouted.

"How can you tell?" Abbie asked.

"I could hear it and there's a light, see?" She motioned desperately for him to come back. "It's coming to this level."

"What?" Abbie's dad shouted as he turned back towards them.

"It's coming here?" Abbie gasped.

"Yes - that's what I've been saying!"-

"Dad, hurry up," Abbie ordered. "Quick!"

Her dad sprinted back through the doorway, letting Eleanor and Abbie quickly push the door closed, leaving a tiny gap for them to watch through. And, mere moments later, the elevator arrived and the doors slid apart to reveal a single figure.

They watched cautiously as Sebastian Phulax emerged from the elevator, peering suspiciously towards them. Almost as if he knew they would be there.

"Should we go, now?" Abbie whispered nervously.

"Let's wait here for a bit," her dad replied. "I want to see how this plays out."

"Dad, this doesn't feel right," Abbie whispered, shaking her head a little. "I really don't think we should be here."

"I'm with Abbie on this one," Eleanor whispered back. "I think we should go while we still can."

"Just a minute - I want to see what he's doing up here," Abbie's dad replied.

Abbie gave Eleanor a despairing look.

"I don't think we should," Eleanor said, anxious of the fact that Phulax was continuing to inch his way towards them.

"There's only one of him, and there's three of us," Abbie's dad replied. "What's the worst that could happen?"

"You have no idea how much you're underestimating him," Eleanor muttered back.

Once Phulax had reached halfway down the corridor, a second elevator arrived and out stepped a formation of Protectors.

"You don't think he suspects we're here, do you?" Abbie asked anxiously. "There's no way they could know, right?"

"I... I don't know," Eleanor replied uneasily, as they began to back away from the doorway.

"Is there an alarm up here or something?"

"There might be," Eleanor shrugged. "And maybe a camera, too. Come on - I don't like this. We need to get out of here."

"There's not enough time," Abbie's dad replied logically as they hurried up the stairs to the platform.

"What do we do?" Abbie sounded scared now. "Couldn't we outrun them?"

"We'd never make it," Eleanor looked around frantically. "There's probably a million different shortcuts that we don't know about!"

As they stood on the platform, the sound of heavily booted feet began thudding along the corridor. A squad of Protectors had emerged from the elevator and were getting closer and closer.

"We need to hide, now!"

"Under the bit that juts out there." Abbie's dad pointed to the centre of the platform.

The three of them clambered down from the platform edge to the tracks below.

"Don't touch the live wires!" Abbie's dad whispered fiercely, just in time to stop Eleanor stepping on one.

Hidden with their backs to the wall, and the lip of the platform edge protruding just above their heads, they caught their breath and waited.

"Don't worry. We'll be okay," Abbie's dad told her soothingly, giving her hand a reassuring squeeze. "They'll go as soon as they see we're not on the platform."

Abbie nodded vigorously as she tried to calm down, desperately attempting to convince herself that he was right.

None of them could help but flinch as they heard the Subterrane door swing open through the eerie silence. But, at first, they heard only one pair of footsteps ascend the stairs and begin to crunch across the dirt-strewn platform. Perhaps the Protectors had been sent to another area of Level One. And maybe Phulax's arrival had nothing to do with them and was just a strange coincidence. Perhaps he had been planning to go somewhere else anyway. The clatter of multiple pairs of boots approaching across the platform dispelled Eleanor's optimism.

He would never have used this door, she realised. They sealed it - properly, this time. So if he saw it was open then he would know it was us; no one else in the Subterrane would be brave enough to open it."

From their hideout, they could see occasional flashes of light as the Protectors swept their torches over every inch of the platform.

"What if they check down here?" Abbie whispered almost inaudibly.

"I'm sure they won't," her dad pulled her closer to him.

"But they could," she whispered back.

"She's right," Eleanor replied. "They could do. They'll want to find us at all costs - especially if they saw that you were with us. Trust me; no one will leave that platform until we've been found. Or at least until they're sure we've already left."

"What do we do?"

Eleanor said nothing.

"Ellie?" she whispered, shuffling a little closer to her in case she hadn't heard.

"I…" Eleanor seemed to have run out of ideas.

"What should we do, Ellie?" Abbie repeated desperately.

"I'm thinking."

"Could you maybe think a little faster?" Abbie whispered urgently.

"Alright," Eleanor began decidedly. "We can crawl along the tracks until we reach the Tunnel up there. Once we get there, they won't be able to see us so we can carry on until we find an alcove or some other place where we can hide. Okay?"

They nodded their heads, although Eleanor had no idea why they would trust her of all people. After all, she was the one that had got them into the mess in the first place.

"This way," she pointed. "Don't make a sound."

As quickly as they could, they began to crawl along the tracks whilst remaining under the cover of the platform edge. Every so often, they paused to listen to what Sebastian Phulax was telling the Protectors or to dust the grit from their palms.

It was only when they were about fifteen metres from the Tunnel when they heard a strange noise in the distance.

"Did you hear that?" Eleanor whispered, looking back at Abbie as the Tunnel fell quiet again. "What was it?"

"What's what?" Abbie frowned.

"That noise - didn't you hear it?"

"Yes, but I've no idea what it is," Abbie shrugged.

Suddenly her dad gasped and looked towards them. "It's a train."

"What?" Eleanor whispered sharply.

"A train. The station's derelict, but that doesn't mean the tracks are," he explained urgently. "And in a few minutes or so, it's going to come through that Tunnel."

"What do we do?"

"Get to the Tunnel quickly," Eleanor said urgently.

"The Tunnel?" Abbie repeated.

"They won't find us if we make it into the Tunnel."

Abbie set off after Eleanor as fast as she possibly could without standing up and running, hoping her dad was following.

"Sir," a Protector shouted to Phulax. "There's a train coming."

"And?" Phulax replied, seeming irritated.

"What should we do, sir?" the Protector asked warily.

"I suggest that you carry on looking - unless you have a particular desire to board the train at the next stop, in which case you would need to run extremely fast along the tracks until you reach a station."

"Of course, sir," the Protector replied.

"Sir," came another voice.

"Yes?" Phulax replied, sounding thoroughly vexed this time.

"I was just wondering if..."

"If what?"

"If there's a chance we might be seen by people on the train?"

"Only if they look."

"But sir," he pressed on. "Don't you think they will look? After all, surely they'll see us in the lights from the train?"

"Well, we'll obviously vacate the area momentarily as the train goes by," Phulax said casually.

"Of course, sir," the Protector agreed. "My apologies for interfering."

A momentary silence fell across the Protectors, in which everything seemed to be completely still, save for the whooshing of the wind that was sent along the tracks by the oncoming train.

"What was that?" Phulax hissed. It was a low clunking sound, followed by an almost dull thud. Like a small pebble hitting the tracks and then falling to the floor. Eleanor looked back along the tracks to see a panic-stricken Abbie frozen in place.

"What was what, sir?" one Protector asked.

"I heard a noise."

"Are you sure, sir?" another Protector shouted. "It's hard to hear much over the noise of the train."

"No, I'm certain," Phulax stated before a sudden realisation hit him: "They must be on the tracks!"

By the time the Protectors had begun to move closer to the tracks, the train was roaring nearer to the station.

"RUN!" Eleanor yelled, standing up and sprinting towards the Tunnel entrance. "Either they see us now, or we'll all be crushed by the train."

"There they are!" Phulax shouted. "Get them back here!"

A glow appeared up ahead. The train was mere seconds away, just around the bend.

"Sir, there's no time," a Protector called. "If they're in the Tunnel they won't make it."

"Back to the Subterrane," Phulax ordered, hurrying back down the staircase with the Protectors following close behind.-

"Ellie?" Abbie yelled, as the footfalls of the Protectors faded.

"Don't stop running!" Eleanor shouted back from up ahead. "We can make it!"

The front of the train was almost in sight, the reflection of its lights on the wall more blinding with every footfall.

"Ellie, it's not going to work!" Abbie's dad shouted frantically. "We need to get off the tracks now!"

"No - trust me," she yelled. "Just a little further!"

The train suddenly rounded the bend and began speeding towards Eleanor as she dashed into the Tunnel, Abbie struggling to keep up.

"Ellie!" came Abbie's desperate shout. "We need to turn back!"

"Keep going! There's a gap in the wall," Eleanor shouted. "We can still make it!"

She continued running straight at the train, determined she could reach the alcove in time. Glancing behind her, she saw Abbie and her dad sprint to reach the gap. Just before joining them in the small space, she turned to look down the Tunnel to ensure that none of the Protectors were following. And, as she did so, she felt heat on the back of her neck and spun round to see the train mere metres from her and closing in fast. Just as she opened her mouth to cry out, she felt someone suddenly whirl her away from the blinding light, and into the darkness.

Chapter Twenty-Six

"Ellie? Ellie! Can you hear me?"

A blurred figure swam across Eleanor's hazy vision, as she moved her head ever so slightly and groaned. The ache was terrible.

"Ellie? Can you hear me?" the same voice repeated, as a bright beam of torch light was shone across her face.

Shakily, Eleanor held up her hand to shield her eyes from the light, and squinting hard, she was just about able to make out Abbie leaning over her.

"Ellie, are you alright?" the worried voice asked. "Can you-"

"Yes, I can hear you," Eleanor finished. Placing a hand on Abbie's shoulder, she began attempting to slowly sit up.

"Careful," Abbie instructed, putting an arm around her shoulders to help raise her to a sitting position.

"What happened?"

"You... well, you turned to look at something and you were facing away from the direction the train was coming," Abbie explained. "I suppose you didn't realise quite how close it was to you, so you didn't have a chance to move out of the way."

"So what happened?" Eleanor said. "Did I get hit?"

Abbie chuckled. "If you had, I doubt you'd still be here to tell the tale."

"I didn't?" she repeated in confusion.

"No."

"But then how did I end up on the floor? Why did I black out?" she asked, trying to replay what she had seen inside her head. "There was...

there were bright lights and then... someone pulled me into here, didn't they?"

"Yes, you spun around just before it got to you," Abbie told her, nodding. "You were just in time to see it coming right at you. But then I saw that you didn't look as if you were going to make it into the alcove in time - you were like a rabbit caught in the headlights. I managed to pull you into the gap just before it would have hit you, but I think you must have banged your head or something, after that."

"Good thing you were here, then." Eleanor looked up at Abbie gratefully.

"So now d'you believe what I said about your name?" Abbie said with a teasing smile, attempting to change the subject.

"What did you say about it?" Eleanor asked, struggling to remember.

"I said it's a bit of an unlucky name."

"But you... you don't really think that, do you?" Eleanor replied.

"Of course not - I was only joking!" Abbie sounded amused, but a look of concern was still etched on her face.

"I guess you do have to admit that over this past week or so I've been nothing but unlucky."

"You're probably only noticing the bad things happening because you're looking for them," Abbie added. "There's no way it could actually be true," she assured her.

"Really?"

"Really."

Abbie turned to look down the Tunnel towards the platform as a tall figure walked towards them, growing larger by the second.

"Have they gone?" Abbie asked, as her dad reached them.

"No sign of them. They must have presumed we didn't make it," he answered. "How're you feeling Ellie?"

"I'm alright," she said.

"We should probably get going - only if you feel up to it, of course, Ellie," he added after a disapproving look from Abbie. "It'll probably do you good to get some rest. But I think we should get out of here first. Who- ever those people were, they've gone for now. But we don't know that they won't come back."

"I suppose so," Abbie agreed. "You up to it Ellie?"

"Sure," she said with a slight shrug. "Can you help me up?" she added, holding out her arm for Abbie to tug on.

Abbie heaved her up from the ground then helped to steady her. "Do you need an arm to lean on or anything?"

"I'm alright for now, I think," she smiled gratefully. "But thanks."

The three of them trekked back along the tracks until they reached the deserted platform once more. Abbie's dad clambered up first closely fol- lowed by Abbie, who helped pull a weakened Eleanor up.

"It's that way, right?" Abbie's dad asked.

"Yes," Abbie replied.

"Ok. I'll go first - just in case any more of those soldiers are there."

"They're called Protectors," Ellie said firmly.

"I thought they'd already gone?" Abbie remarked.

"They have, I think. But it won't hurt to be careful," he replied. "You two stay behind me."

They quickly wound their way through the darkened passageways, ea- ger to reach the safety of the Surface. The abandoned station no longer seemed safe - even to Eleanor; now it was simply a bridge between the two worlds.

"It's that corridor over there," Eleanor called as Abbie's dad walked out into the booking hall and waited for them to catch up.

Abbie's dad looked at Eleanor closely. "Are you alright Ellie? How much further is it?"

"I'm fine. It's not far," Eleanor said. "Just keep going down there."

Once again, they proceeded through the arched corridor and passed by the metal doors that led to the old lift. Finally, they reached the pad- locked gate and slipped through the opening where it had been bent back.

"Thank God that's over," Abbie's dad said as he wrenched the final set of doors apart and stepped out into the daylight.

"Won't they follow us out here?" Abbie asked.

"Well if they came out here then they'd see what it's really like up here. They'll already be suspicious enough after knowing that both of you were down there."

"So what do we do now, then?" Abbie asked, unsure who to direct the question to.

"I think we should get home," her dad replied as he wrestled to close the station door.

"Home?" Eleanor followed Abbie into the empty street.

"Our home," Abbie smiled at her apologetically. "We won't be sending you home any time soon."

"Just as well," she replied, relieved.

"We will have to go back in there at some point," Abbie's dad reminded her. "You do know that, don't you?"

"Yeah but not for a while, right?"

"You'll have a bit of time to recover," he said, as he took a small rectangular object from his pocket. "And I'll make sure we've got some backup with us next time, too."

"That's probably a good idea," Eleanor nodded. As she did so, she subtly glanced up at the house next door to the station, searching for any indication that they were being watched. But the house showed no telltale signs of life. "So how do we get back to yours from here?"

"I'll drive, but I've got a few missed calls from your mum, first," he said, looking down at the shiny object. "You get in and I'd better make sure Becca hasn't set the house on fire," he joked, walking a little way away from them.

"Look! I told you the car must belong to that house," Abbie pointed to the black car that was once again parked in front of the house.

"Right. Yes. Yes, you did," Eleanor tried to act as though nothing was wrong.

"You okay?" Abbie asked, as she saw Eleanor eye the house again.

"I'm fine." Eleanor didn't meet Abbie's gaze as she quickly changed the subject. "What's that?" She pointed to the small object that Abbie's dad was now speaking into. "I saw you using one, but what actually is it?"

"It's called a phone," Abbie explained as they climbed into the backseat of the car. "It's like... well, do you know what a computer is?"

"No."

"Okay, well it's a device that you can interact with and contact other people through."

"Right," Eleanor said, still not really sure what it was.

"You can get it to do other things, too," Abbie added. "It's an interactive screen, which means you just tap on it and it does what you want."

"What kind of things?"

"All sorts," Abbie assured her. "What my dad's doing now is phoning my mum. So his phone will connect with her phone, and he'll be able to have a conversation with her."

"Seriously?"

"Yeah," Abbie nodded.

"And everyone has one?"

"Not anymore," Abbie said. "Twenty or maybe twenty-five years ago, almost everyone would have done from when they were ten or twelve. But there was this huge communications collapse about seventeen or eight-een years ago. They tried to introduce this thing called 8G and then every-thing crashed. They've only just begun re-introducing phones and stuff quite recently. Ronni and Becca don't have them because my parents said they aren't old enough yet, but they said I could have one if I wanted since I'm the oldest."

"So what was it that crashed?" Eleanor asked as Abbie's dad got into the car.

"The 8G?" Abbie's dad asked, tuning into their conversation.

"Yeah," Abbie said. "I'm explaining about phones and everything."

"Right."

"The 8G was... how do you explain it?" Abbie turned to her dad for help.

"Well I suppose it's like - have you ever looked anything up in a book?" her dad asked Eleanor as he began driving away from the station.

"Only in a textbook and we didn't have many of them anyway."

"That's fine. A textbook works," he said, turning onto the main road. "So on a phone - or any other kind of device - you can find out any information from any book, but just by searching a question. And 8G is what allows you to do that, among other things."

"Any book?"

"Yes," Abbie's dad replied. "And bear in mind that there are absolutely millions of books out there."

"And you can find it all on that?" Eleanor asked in amazement.

"Yes," he said. "But it's not just books. Anything you wanted to know, it could tell you."

"Can I ask it something?" she said excitedly.

"'Course you can," Abbie said. "Dad, can I borrow yours?"

"Sure." He passed his back to her, and after unlocking it, she handed it over to Eleanor.

"Um... What time is it?" Eleanor said loudly, holding the phone close to her mouth. Abbie's dad looked back at them, smiling at how loudly she was speaking.

"That's not how you do it," Abbie said laughing. "Here, let me show you."

Abbie took the phone from Eleanor, tapped on something and leant over to show her.

"Look just there," she said. "It shows the time at the top, so you don't need to ask it that. Ask it something that you'd genuinely like to know about... well, about anything."

"Okay," Eleanor nodded, concentrating hard. "But how did I do it wrong? How are you supposed to do it?"

"You type it in there," Abbie pointed to a small bar that was illuminated at the top of the object. Tapping on it gently, a keyboard popped up. "What are you going to ask it?"

"What my name means," Eleanor answered decidedly.

"Okay," Abbie said with a smile. "You just have to press each letter - like you're writing it by hand, except it'll write it up there."

Eleanor fumbled around trying to find each letter, until she had finally typed: 'Wgat dors the nsme desdemoba meab'.

"I'm not sure it'll know what you mean by that. Should I have a go?" Abbie said.

But, strangely enough, the screen popped up saying: 'Showing results for What does the name desdemona mean'.

"Looks like I don't need to," Abbie corrected herself.

"What do I do now?"

"Just tap any of the things underneath your question."

"Okay," Eleanor said and prodded the first one.

"What does it say?"

"'Desdemona is a girl's name of Greek origin. The name means un-lucky, ill-starred or ill-fated'," Eleanor read.

"You know, no one believes those things," Abbie's dad chipped in as they drove across the river.

"Exactly," Abbie replied, unsure why Eleanor kept dwelling on it. "I only told you it meant unlucky as a joke, really. And because it's such an unusual name."

"Then what does Abbie mean?" Eleanor asked, hoping Abbie's name would mean something ridiculous.

"I can't really remember," Abbie shrugged honestly. "You can have a look if you want."

"'The name Abigail comes from the Hebrew, meaning 'my father's joy''," Eleanor read, after tapping around on the screen for a while.

Abbie said nothing.

"Yours is right, isn't it?" Eleanor remarked slowly.

"Probably only a third right," Abbie laughed. "Just ignore it."

"But it's close?"

"I'd say it's very close," Abbie's dad admitted, winking at Abbie in the rear-view mirror.

"But yours is a surname, not a first name, anyway," Abbie said quickly.

"I suppose."

"Seriously," Abbie began reassuringly. "It really doesn't mean any-thing."

Eleanor nodded, although she couldn't help but wonder if Abbie was just saying that.

"Right, we're here," Abbie's dad said suddenly, as the car slowed to a stop halfway down a row of brick houses.

"Do you need us to help with anything?" Abbie asked, handing his phone back.

"You go and do whatever for a while," he replied. "I'm going to make some calls. We're going to need some help getting all those people out of there."

"Why don't we just get the police to come?"

"Because I doubt that they'll believe us. They didn't when you tried earlier, did they?" he said. "It's a very unbelievable story - even I didn't really believe you until I'd seen it. I'll call in some favours with a few people from work, but other than that I think it's best to keep the police out of it. At least until the worst is over."

"So when are we going to get everyone out?" Eleanor asked.

"Let's aim for tomorrow afternoon. We'll need to brief everyone on what to expect once they're down there."

"What about clothing?" Abbie asked suddenly.

"What about it?"

"They'll need to be wearing white, won't they?"

"Even police?" her dad said.

"People from the Subterrane won't know what the police are - or at least it won't give you any influence," Abbie explained.

"They're more likely to trust you if you're wearing white, because you won't seem like such an outsider," Eleanor added.

"And no logos, either," Abbie added, as they pulled up in front of a large house.

"Alright, I'll tell everyone," Abbie's dad promised, switching off the car engine. "But what about those guards that were there earlier? Are they dangerous? Should we be worried?"

"The Protectors? They... well, they do whatever they're told to do." Eleanor shrugged as she glanced up at the house. "Their job is to protect the citizens - or at least protect the Subterrane from any outside interference."

"So are they armed?"

"Well, they are, but I've never actually seen any of them use a weapon."

"That doesn't mean they won't."

"No, of course it doesn't," Eleanor said. "I just wonder if they might be reluctant to use them on anyone. Especially if us being there proves that they've been lied to about everything."

Abbie's dad nodded. "Let's hope you're right. Come on, let's go inside."

Chapter Twenty-Seven

"Abbie, you're back!" A very over-excited Becca darted towards Abbie and enveloped her in a hug the very moment they stepped through the front door.

"I thought you were staying with Ellie for another couple of days, Abigail," came her mum's voice from a room off to the left.

"No, sorry mum," she called back. "I've got her with me, though. Is that alright?"

"Of course it is!" her mum said, stepping into the hallway to greet them. "Lovely to see you again, Ellie."

"You too - thank you for having me."

"It's a pleasure, dear," Abbie's mum said, smiling fondly. "Truth be told, I think we all rather enjoyed having a new face around when you came to the market."

"Well, I had a really nice time," Eleanor replied.

"Is it okay if she stays the night, mum?"

"Of course," her mum replied. "Dinner'll be about fifteen minutes - why don't you get Ellie settled upstairs, Abigail?"

"Alright," Abbie said, making for the stairs. "This way Ellie."

Eleanor walked over to the foot of the stairs and looked up from where she stood. Instead of the white, uniform endless flights of stairs that she was used to in the Subterrane, she was pleasantly surprised to see only one turn in the staircase and, above that, a flat pale blue ceiling.

"You coming, Ellie?" Abbie called from the landing at the top of the stairs.

"Yes, sorry," she replied, hastily running up to join her.

The large carpeted landing was furnished with an ornate bannister that overlooked the stairs. A few photographs hung beside the doors at each end, and between them stood a jumbled row of wooden cupboards.

"That's my parents' room down there," Abbie said as she pointed to the door on the left, before opening it and allowing Eleanor to peer down the dimly lit corridor. Then, leading Eleanor back onto the landing, she continued with the tour. "Becca and Ronni's rooms are through here," she said, pointing towards a door on the right.

"Where's yours?"

"You'll see," Abbie smiled mischievously as she opened the door and walked out into a short corridor. "This used to be my bedroom," Abbie continued, stepping into a room immediately on the right of the door.

"Why isn't it anymore?"

"Ronni and Becca used to share a room until quite recently but, well, you can imagine..." Abbie trailed off. "After the endless squabbling began, I said one of them could have my room and Becca rather liked the sound of that, so it's hers now. And this one's Ronni's," she added, opening the door directly on the left of it so Eleanor could look inside.

Abbie was about to usher her out of Ronni's room when Eleanor suddenly noticed something through the window. From the window, she looked down on the street below. And, sure enough, she could just make out the side of a black car parked next door. Of course, it was partially obscured from view, so she was unable to see if it was the same car that she had seen earlier. But she was fairly certain.

"You okay?" Abbie walked over and peered through the window, as though trying to spot what had caught Eleanor's eye.

"Yes, sorry. I was just... having a look."

Eleanor quickly made her way back into the corridor and pointed to the next door. "So is that your room?"

"No," Abbie said, walking towards the last two doors. "This is the bathroom and this is the guest room."

Eleanor stayed silent, trying desperately to work out what she might have missed.

"I don't get it," she said finally. "Where's your room?"

"Upstairs."

"But I thought this was upstairs?"

Abbie didn't reply.

"What are you doing?" Eleanor asked as Abbie started walking to a much smaller, inconspicuous door. And, after opening it, Abbie stepped inside.

"This is the way to my room," Abbie answered. "You coming?"

Eleanor dubiously walked into the small space and found Abbie already halfway up a ladder.

"Your family really like ladders, don't they?"

"Who wouldn't?" Abbie laughed as she opened the trapdoor and flicked on a light switch at the top of the ladder. "There actually are stairs up here, too, but where's the fun in that?" Clambering through the trapdoor, she reached down to give Eleanor a hand up.

"So, what do you think?" Abbie asked, as Eleanor popped up through the floor and gazed around the room in amazement.

"Is this all just your room?"

"We thought I might as well have it all for my room - no one else was going to use it."

The vast room stretched the entire width and length of the house. One end of the room was covered from the floor to the ceiling entirely in shelves that bent under the weight of the masses of books piled on top of them. At the other end, a large double bed was positioned against the wall, surrounded by a huge pile of coloured cushions and beanbags. Wardrobes were built into the sloping roof on one side, and on the other, a wooden desk was positioned in front of a large window overlooking the rear of the house. And, beyond that, the breathtaking London skyline.

"I've never seen anything like this," Eleanor marvelled, first wandering over to the window and then to the bookshelves. "There must be hundreds and hundreds of books here - have you read them all?"

"Of course not," Abbie laughed. "Perhaps one day. Any that you've read?"

"No books in the Subterrane, remember?" Eleanor reminded her regretfully.

"Right. I forgot. You're welcome to borrow some if you like," Abbie said. "In fact, you can keep any you want. I'm sure I've got enough to last me a very long time."

Eleanor smiled back gratefully.

"Where does that go?" she asked, pointing to a staircase at the side of the room that she seemed to have missed.

"It goes to the landing downstairs," Abbie said. "It's just so much more fun coming up the ladder."

"But I didn't see a door," Eleanor said.

"Yeah, it's pretty well hidden," Abbie explained. "It comes out behind one of the cupboards down there. They look as if they're positioned against the wall, but there's actually a bit of a gap. We took the back panel off one of them so I just go through it to get to the stairs. Obviously, we move it if I need to get stuff up the stairs, but dad seems to think it's hilarious."

"I didn't notice it at all."

"You wouldn't unless you knew it was there, really," Abbie said. "By the way, where do you want to sleep tonight?"

"Whatever's easiest. I really don't mind."

"Well, you've got a choice of the guest room or a camp bed in here - but bear in mind that the guest room is next door to Ronni's room. And, there's a fully-functioning sliding door between Ronni and Becca's rooms that my dad keeps meaning to lock, but always forgets to."

"Sounds like up here's the better option."

"Good choice," Abbie said, heading over to one of the cupboards built into the slanted roof. Opening the door at one end of the cupboard, she pulled out a fold-up bed and a self-inflatable mattress. She first spread the mattress out on the floor so that it could inflate, and then set about assembling the camp bed.

"You can have a look at any of my stuff while I do this - or any of the books," she added as she plonked the mattress on top of the bed and grabbed some sheets from another cupboard.

"Any you'd recommend?" Eleanor asked.

Abbie stood and walked over to the bookshelves, before reaching up and taking a worn book from a shelf.

"Have a look at this one," she suggested, passing it to Eleanor who began curiously flicking through it.

And, just as Abbie finished making up the camp bed, her mum called them downstairs for dinner.

***

"So what d'you want to do now?" Abbie began, flopping down on her bed beside Eleanor after dinner.

"I don't mind, really," Eleanor replied. "I suppose we could-"

"Abbie? Ellie? Can I come in?" came the voice of Abbie's dad from just below the trapdoor.

"Come on up, dad," Abbie shouted back.

He came up the ladder and then stopped to glance around the room.

"Those shelves, Ellie," he began, pointing towards the bookshelves lining the far wall. "They took me absolutely ages to build - they were unimaginably fiddly."

"You loved it really," Abbie laughed.

"That's not quite how I remember it," he replied doubtfully. "Anyway, I came up here to say that - oh, are you reading that?" he asked Eleanor, pointing to the book she had left open on the bed.

"Yes, I just started it," she replied.

"It's a great book. I must have read it when I was, what, fourteen I think? I read it over and over again," he added. "I thought it was-"

"Dad," Abbie interrupted. "Any particular reason why you came up here?"

"Oh, right," he nodded. "I've been making some calls, and I've arranged for a few people from my work to come tomorrow, as well as some other people I know. I briefly explained the situation to one of them, and she's agreed to get her husband to come along with a couple of men from his work - he's in the army, so that could come in handy."

"That's great dad," Abbie said, then paused for a moment. "You haven't told everyone at your work about it, have you? You haven't reported it, right?"

"Like they'd believe me if I tried to," her dad replied. "But just you wait until we've got everyone out. They'll be all over it, saying that they planned the rescue right from the start - the papers too, I expect. "

"Well, at least everyone will be out by then," Eleanor said.

"What time are we meeting them all?" Abbie asked.

"Around one, I think. We'll need to fill them in on everything first, but after that, we should be ready by about two or two-thirty."

"And did you tell them about clothing?" Eleanor asked.

"Yes, they all know."

"Great."

"Are you going to tell mum?" Abbie asked suddenly.

"I, um... not until after, I think," her dad said decidedly, leaning against her bookcase. "If she knows, she'll just worry unnecessarily, so if I were you I wouldn't mention it. After all, I could pretend it was something for work and Ellie could pretend she was going home, but you'd be stuck here with mum all day."

"I know, I know," Abbie rolled her eyes. "I won't tell her."

"I'm just saying that it's in your best interest not to."

"But since when have I ever told tales about something like this?"

"Well, I can think of a couple of times..."

"Like what?" Abbie sat up and crossed her arms.

"How about that time Ronni was planning to sneak out to camp with her friend for a night?"

"That was only once and it was for her own good. She was planning to climb out of the window!"

"Okay, if you say so," he replied. "And that time when-"

"I've got it, okay?" she interrupted. "Note to self, don't tell mum."

"Good," her dad laughed. "So can you two be ready to leave by twelve-thirty tomorrow? I've just got a couple of calls left to make, but other than that I'd say we're fully prepared."

"Alright," Abbie said.

223

Her dad made for the ladder but as he got half-way down, he popped his head back up. "And don't stay up too late," he said, looking at Abbie expectantly. "You don't want to be too tired for tomorrow."

"Okay, we won't," she replied with a sigh.

"See, I already know you're lying,"

Her dad replied with a quick wink as he turned, descended the final few steps.

"I was only joking," she whispered to Eleanor. "There's no way we're going to bed early tonight."

"I heard that!" her dad shouted from the floor below.

Chapter Twenty-Eight

Several hours later, Eleanor stood by the bookcase, still unsure of what she should do. Should she tell them about the black car she had seen? She couldn't decide. They already had enough on their plates with organising the whole rescue attempt, and Eleanor really was no expert on cars. After all, it could be just a coincidence that she'd seen the black car again - she didn't know how to tell one from another. But on the other hand, if it wasn't a coincidence...

"Come and see this," Abbie's voice jolted Eleanor from her thoughts.

Shifting her desk a little to the side, Abbie headed over to the window. Fiddling with the latch, she jostled it about until it finally opened, sending a gush of cool evening air into the room.

"I'm not really supposed to do this," she told Eleanor, "but it's just too good a night not to. Besides, you'll love it."

She climbed up onto the window sill, before hopping down onto the roof of the lower floor's extension.

"You coming?" she asked, looking back at Eleanor, who carefully clambered onto the window ledge and followed Abbie out.

"Look up there," Abbie instructed as they sat down.

"What are they?" Eleanor gasped, as she took in the star-studded night sky above her.

"They're stars," Abbie told her, raising her eyebrows. "I need to just go and check something downstairs quickly - you can stay here if you want. I'll be back in a minute."

"Okay," Eleanor said, nodding as she soaked up the captivating scene above her.

She sat alone on the roof, gazing at the distant lights that littered the stars, listening as an array of voices floated up to her from the open kitchen window two floors below.

"What's going on?"

"I just wanted to come and say thank you, dad," Abbie said.

"What for?"

"For today. I know it's really weird and unbelievable and everything, but thank you for trusting us."

"I'll always trust you - you know that."

"Thanks, dad."

"Now, go have fun with your friend."

"And a very early night, obviously," she joked.

Emerging through the window a few minutes later, Abbie came and sat back down beside Eleanor. "You know, the stars literally never look like this, normally."

"Why not?"

"The sky's just never normally this clear."

"What's that?" Eleanor asked, pointing to a larger shape that hung from the sky.

"It's called the moon. Fun fact," Abbie began. "The moon doesn't actually give off any light at all. It just reflects it from the sun."

"Really?" Eleanor asked in disbelief. "That's incredible," she added, as she continued to stare.

"Yeah," Abbie agreed, smiling at how everything seemed to amaze Eleanor. "It must be weird for you - being here and seeing all of this. Since I met you, I guess I haven't really stopped to think about what it must be like in your shoes."

"You have no idea," Eleanor replied. "But it's nice, seeing all of this."

"What's the best bit you've seen? What was your favourite part?"

"I'd say..." she paused to think. "I'd say tonight comes pretty close."

"Seeing the stars?"

"Definitely." Eleanor lay back on the roof with her arms behind her head. "You know, a week ago I didn't even know what the sky looked like. I didn't know that any of this would still exist."

"Well I'm glad you got to see it," Abbie said, lying back beside her.

They lay staring up at the stars for a while, until they had both begun shivering.

As she scanned their surroundings, she caught sight of a figure standing at the window of a building overlooking Abbie's house. Though the figure was too far away to see clearly in the darkness, Eleanor couldn't help but wonder if it was watching her.

She peered closer, desperate to know she was right, but it was no use. The figure had gone.

"What are you looking at?" Abbie sat up and looked at the house next door.

"I... nothing. Come on, let's go in," Eleanor stood and walked back over to the window. "It's freezing out here."

They headed back over to the window and awkwardly scrambled back in.

"Anything else you want to do now?" Abbie asked as they scrambled back in through the window.

"Not really." Eleanor slid the window shut and pulled the curtains across. Just in case they're still watching.

"Okay, well I'd say we have three options; you can either read a book, or we can watch a film, or... well, actually there isn't an option three. What do you feel like doing?"

"What's a film?" Eleanor asked.

Abbie turned to her, wide-eyed with surprise. "You've never seen a film before?"

"No?" Eleanor replied, unsure whether it was a good thing or not.

"Okay, we're definitely watching one," Abbie decided, heading over to her desk and taking something from it. She perched on the edge of her bed and, after opening the strange rectangular object, tapped on a few black keys until a list finally popped up. "So the genre options are action, mystery, thriller, romance, comedy. Which one do you fancy?"

"Well, I don't really know what most of them are."

"Right. Sorry, I forgot," Abbie said. "I'll pick the film. Can you put some of those cushions on my bed?" she added pointing to the heap beside her desk.

"Sure," Eleanor replied. "All of them?"

"Might as well," Abbie shrugged, as she set the device down at the end of the bed and helped puff up the pillows.

"So what are we watching?" Eleanor asked, as they settled back on the cushions.

"It's a romantic comedy. It's my absolute favourite!" Abbie burst out excitedly, as music began to play in the background and the screen faded into a shot of somewhere in Paris.

"What's a romantic comedy?"

"It's... well, you'll see," she said, a mischievous smile playing upon her lips. "But trust me, you'll love it."

"Great," Eleanor said distractedly as she glanced at the closed curtains, still wondering whether she should confide her fears in her new friend.

Chapter Twenty-Nine

Eleanor woke early the next morning to find the sun streaming in through a gap in the curtains. She was lying at the edge of a large double bed that was piled sky-high with cushions, pillows and blankets. On the other side of the bed, she could just about see Abbie lying face down in the covers and sleeping soundly.

She wandered over to the large window behind Abbie's desk and drew the curtains open. Standing there, she watched as the sun gradually began to climb its way higher and higher into the sky. After studying the city skyline for a while and seeing nothing suspicious, she quietly wandered back over to the bed, grabbed a blanket and wrapped it around herself. Heading back to the window, she watched the building next door for any kind of movement; still nothing.

"Ellie? You up?" A drowsy voice interrupted her thoughts.

"Yes, I'm just over here," she called back.

"Have you been up long?" Abbie asked as she rolled over to see where Eleanor was sitting.

"Not really."

"Oh," she replied, rubbing her eyes groggily as she stumbled over to the window seat and sat down beside Eleanor. "I guess we'd better start getting ready - big day today!"

"I almost forgot that was today," Eleanor said. "How long do we have until we leave?"

"Don't worry. We've got ages," Abbie replied.

Around an hour later, Eleanor and Abbie headed downstairs for breakfast.

"Just help yourself to whatever you want," Abbie said as she began to fill a bowl with cereal. "What do you normally have?" she prompted.

"Just fruit, usually."

"That's all?" Abbie asked.

"Basically."

"Well, the fruit's just over there, but help yourself to whatever else you want."

"Okay, thanks."

Just as they went to sit at the table, Becca came thundering down the stairs and skipped into the kitchen. After grabbing some breakfast, she bounded over to the table and sat beside Abbie. And a few minutes later, after hearing them all talking, Ronni came running down to join them.

"You look pretty today, Ronni," Becca said as Ronnie headed over to the counter behind her and tried to refrain from giggling.

"Shut up, Becca," Ronni shot back.

"But what d'you mean? I only said that you looked pretty!" Becca retorted.

Ronni walked past her and whacked her on the head.

"Ow!" Becca whined. "I'm telling mum!" she added as she got up and ran from the kitchen.

"What's wrong with saying that?" Eleanor whispered to Abbie.

"Well, when Becca says she thinks something's pretty, she usually adds 'pretty awful' afterwards, so now she doesn't even have to say the 'awful' part, because it's kind of added silently by each of us," Abbie explained, smiling. "But, if you'd said it, she would've accepted it as a compliment, because it wouldn't mean the same coming from you."

"Right, and do you realise how confusing that is?" Eleanor said, frowning as she tried to understand.

"I know. Becca's a bit like that," Abbie said. "But I'm not sure if she realises that we all know it's just her trying to get at Ronni, so it doesn't work when she tries to complain to any of us about Ronni hitting her. And Ronni always hits her when she says it," she added as they heard Becca complaining to her mum:

"But she hit me!"

"Am I supposed to be surprised?"

"Aren't you going to tell her off and make her apologise?"

"Well, are you planning to apologise to her?"

"Of course not - she's the one that hit me!"

"Well, until you decide to apologise to her, I'm not going to make her apologise to you."

They heard a door slam, and shortly after Becca came traipsing down the stairs, looking as though she was feeling very sorry for herself.

"Dad said you're going somewhere with him," Becca began, eager to change the subject. "Can I come? Please?"

"Sorry, not today Becca," Abbie replied.

"You never let me come anywhere with you," Becca complained, sitting down heavily in her chair.

"Well, I'm afraid it's a definite no today."

"What's a definite no?" Abbie's mum asked as she entered the kitchen.

"Abbie said I can't come with them today."

"I'm sure they want to do their own stuff. Maybe they'll let you tag along another day."

"But dad's going with them today!"

"That's only because he's showing us something," Abbie replied quickly.

"What's he showing you?"

"Just this weird derelict building he found - I think it's a bit like our old apartment."

"Right." Her mum nodded as she took a mug from the cupboard and waited for the kettle to boil. "And where is it?"

"Um…" Abbie turned to Eleanor desperate for help. "Where did he say it was?"

"Up near - was it Aldwych station? Somewhere around there, I think," Eleanor answered quickly.

"Yes, that was it. He said it was just along from Covent Garden."

"Alright then," her mum replied, seeming to believe them. "When are you going there?"

"This afternoon I think."

"Any plans for this morning, then?"

"Not really," Abbie said, glancing towards Eleanor. "We had a pretty busy day yesterday, so I'm not sure we'll do much. Anything you fancy doing, Ellie?"

"I don't mind," Eleanor answered.

"Alright, well we'll have a think," Abbie said. "If you're done, should we go back up and decide what to do?"

Eleanor nodded and took her things over to the sink with Abbie.

"We've got a while until we need to get ready to go," Abbie said once they were back in her room. "Anything you've got a burning desire to do before we head into battle?"

"Into battle? I hope that's not what it'll be like." Eleanor frowned and walked over to the window.

"But what do you think will happen?" Abbie asked, no longer joking.

"I have no idea," Eleanor replied honestly. "I wish I could say I did, but nothing like this has ever happened down there before. I don't know how people will trust us or not - I don't know if they'll even believe us."

"Are you scared?"

"No... not scared. I'm just a bit worried about how Phulax might react."

"Do you think he's dangerous?"

"He might be. I'm not really sure."

"Would he hurt us?"

"He... I don't know. Maybe? My guess is that he hurt so many people when he tore them away from their families, that he might not care anymore. But then again, I suppose that he only hurt them emotionally, not physically."

"I suppose so..." Abbie trailed off nervously.

"Are you worried?" Eleanor asked, perching on the window seat.

"No," she replied, shaking her head decisively. "But I'm beginning to wonder if maybe I should be."

***

"Girls, are you nearly ready?" Abbie's dad called from the foot of the ladder. "We're leaving in fifteen minutes."

"Okay, we'll be down in a sec," Abbie called back as she tucked her school shirt into her scruffy white jeans and spun around slowly in the mirror.

"I'm beginning to think it's a mistake going back," Eleanor said, nervously chewing on her thumbnail. "We've got absolutely no idea what will happen, and we're totally unprepared. I bet that most of the people helping won't even believe that the Subterrane's real. Besides, I don't want you or your dad to get hurt."

"We won't! Now that my dad believes you, there's no way he'd back out."

"But what if something goes wrong? It'll be my fault if anything happens to any of your dad's friends."

"It won't be your fault," Abbie replied. "Anyway, they're not just friends - they're professional colleagues, with expertise, who have volunteered to help."

Eleanor looked at her, seeming unconvinced.

"The definition of a volunteer is literally someone who takes part in something of their own free will. And that means it wouldn't be your fault or anyone else's."

"But without me, no one would even know it existed, let alone be in danger," Eleanor reminded her.

"Listen to me, Ellie," Abbie said sternly. "Nothing is going to happen. We're going back so that we can help people get out, and then we're going to leave. Or maybe stay if you want, I suppose. But nothing will happen."

"It's in the nature of my name for something bad to happen," Eleanor said as she looked out of the window. "Remember?"

"Not on my watch," Abbie said with a smile.

"You know, that's just what Saskia said," Eleanor remarked.

233

"Will you say anything to her - while we're down there?" Abbie asked, careful not to seem too nosy.

"Not while we're down there," Eleanor said. "But I will afterwards. I... I think it's time to forgive her."

"That's probably a good idea," Abbie agreed, her eyes flitting to the window as a church clock somewhere chimed twelve. "You'll need someone to face the world with - someone that's experienced what you've been through, I mean."

"Yes, you're probably right," Eleanor nodded.

"I meant to ask you," Abbie began. "Do you think she's ever been to the Surface?"

"I hadn't thought about it until yesterday, actually," Eleanor replied, thinking it over. "She must have come up to see her mum - I think I overheard her saying that she sees her mum every year. I doubt she'd go outside of her mum's house, though."

"Why not? Surely she'd want to?"

"She didn't seem to know much about the Surface when I was telling her about coming up here," Eleanor shrugged, watching as the sun gradually began to inch its way higher in the sky. "Maybe she just didn't see the point in seeing a world she wasn't allowed to be a part of."

"I suppose so," Abbie said.

"I kind of miss her," Eleanor said quietly. "I know she lied to me and everything, but she really is the closest thing I have to family."

Abbie nodded. "Sounds like you'll definitely need each other once this is all over."

"I expect so."

"But I'll still be here for you if you need me at all."

"Thanks," Eleanor smiled nervously.

"Come on," Abbie said, linking her arm through Eleanor's. "We'd better get going."

They made their way downstairs and into the kitchen, where Abbie's dad was sat waiting for them.

"You both ready?" he asked.

"We're ready," Abbie nodded. "Nice outfit, by the way," she added. "You look… interesting. Let's just be glad that I only have to see you like this for one day."

"It's not that bad!" he replied adamantly, before considering how strange he must look. "Is it really that bad?"

"No, it's fine," Abbie laughed. "That's the sort of thing people wear, isn't it Ellie?"

"Yes, you'll blend in very nicely," Eleanor agreed.

"Alright, alright, I get it. It looks bad," Abbie's dad said. "But I'm afraid you'll have to put up with it for today."

"It's fine - I'm sure I look just as bad," Abbie said kindly. "Come on, we'd better get going."

"Drive or walk?" her dad asked.

"I don't particularly fancy walking through London dressed like this. Do you?" Abbie asked.

"Good point. I'll get the car started and why don't you run upstairs and grab a couple of jumpers so we don't look completely weird. No offence, Ellie, but it is kind of odd clothing."

"None taken," Eleanor replied, smiling awkwardly as Abbie ran back into the hallway and raced up the stairs. "After seeing what everyone wears up here, I couldn't agree more."

Abbie's dad led the way outside to the car, which unlocked itself as he pressed the flat of his thumb to the door handle on the driver's side. And, after watching how he had opened the door, Eleanor grabbed hold of the door handle for the backseats and wrenched it towards herself, trying to follow his example.

"You okay with the door?" he asked, seeing her struggling. "Just pull it a little harder."

"Got it," she said, staggering backwards as it suddenly opened. She clambered into the back and slid over to the opposite side.

"Shut the door a sec," Abbie's dad said, starting the car.

"Aren't we waiting for Abbie?" Eleanor asked, shutting the door.

"We are, but just wait until she gets here."

They sat in the car in silence. Eleanor fidgeted in her seat, wondering if it might be a good opportunity to tell Abbie's dad what she'd seen. But, just as she was about to speak, Abbie came running through the front door, letting it slam behind her. And just like that, the moment had passed.

Abbie walked towards the car and, just as she was about to place her hand on the door handle, her dad began to drive away slowly.

"I'm not really in the mood, dad," she yelled as he beeped her and then continued to drive off.

Her dad lowered his window and looked back at her. "Come on, I'm only joking."

"Not today," Abbie replied, seeming rather annoyed with him.

"Looks like the fun's over," he added, glancing back at Eleanor.

Abbie glared at him as she climbed into the car and tossed his jumper at him. "How long till we get there?"

"About ten minutes," he replied. "That okay?"

"Yeah," she answered. "Is everyone meeting us outside the station?"

"Hopefully."

"What do you mean 'hopefully'?" Abbie asked. "I thought you said you'd spoken to them all."

"I did, but you've got to admit it's a very far-fetched story."

"But we can't do it on our own - what if no one shows?"

"Don't worry," he replied. "I'm sure they will."

"But-"

"-Abbie, it'll be fine," he interrupted, looking pointedly at Eleanor who seemed a little nervous.

"Ellie, you okay?" she asked.

Eleanor nodded hesitantly. As far as she could tell, there was no sign of the black car yet.

"I promise it'll all work out," Abbie reassured her.

"I know it will. It has to," Eleanor said.

"Exactly."

"Do you mind if I quickly run through what the plan is when we get there?" Abbie's dad asked.

"Alright," Abbie said as Eleanor nodded.

"So when we get there, I'll park right opposite the station and then I'll probably begin by talking to everyone who's come to help since I know them all," he informed them. "After that, they'll probably have a lot of questions so I think we should probably answer a few since they're doing us a favour by helping. The more they know about your world, the better."

"That's a good idea," Eleanor nodded. "I'll answer some questions - I don't mind."

"Good," he replied. "That'll be a great help."

"What should I do?" Abbie asked.

"Just wait until we go inside, I think," her dad suggested as he changed gear and pulled onto the main road. "Although it might help if you mention that you've been down there, since a lot of them will have met you before."

"Okay," Abbie agreed, a little disappointed not to be more involved.

"We're almost there," her dad said. "Any last-minute things to add?"

"Nope," Abbie replied. "Ellie?"

"No, I'm fine," Eleanor answered anxiously.

They rounded the corner and turned off the Strand onto a smaller road that was dotted with people dressed all in white.

"Are you ready?" Abbie's dad asked, glancing at Eleanor as he pulled over to the side of the road and switched off the ignition.

"I'm ready," Eleanor replied with a firm nod, her hand trembling slightly as she opened the car door and stepped down onto the pavement. She was about to walk towards the gathering, when she suddenly faltered. She'd put it off for long enough, but she couldn't leave it any longer - it wasn't fair on them. Even if it might make her look pathetic or paranoid, she had to tell them.

"Wait, there's something you should know," she blurted out nervously. "I'm not completely sure - and I might be wrong, but I think someone's been following me."

Chapter Thirty

"What?" Abbie's dad hurried over to her. "Following you? Are you sure?"

"No, not entirely. I just... I keep feeling like I'm being watched."

"But you haven't seen anything?" he asked, looking a little relieved.

"I don't know. It might be nothing, but I keep seeing a car - a black car."

"And you think it's following you?"

"Yes." Eleanor glanced down the street to check it wasn't there now. "It was parked over there when me and Abbie left the Subterrane, then it was outside the police station, and it was parked next door to your house."

"Next door to our house?" Abbie's dad seemed shocked. "But how do you know it's the same car? Maybe it's just a coincidence."

"Maybe," Eleanor said. "But I'm not so sure. I just thought you should know."

He nodded, before looking over at the group of volunteers, all wondering what was taking so long.

"So what are we going to do?" Abbie asked.

"I think we should still go ahead with this," her dad replied, turning back to them. "Especially since everyone's already here and willing to help. Besides, there aren't any cars here now, so we should be alright. Are you both ready?"

Taking a deep breath, Eleanor nodded.

The gathering of strangely dressed people watched Eleanor, Abbie and her dad in complete silence as they made their way to the front. Once they had reached the station entrance, they stopped and faced the multitude of people. Standing before them, Abbie couldn't help thinking that anyone who saw them might have wondered if they were forming some kind of party or union to overthrow the Chancellor's government.

"Right. Hello everyone," Abbie's dad began. "I wanted to personally thank you all for getting here at such short notice - I'm extremely grateful to each and every one of you. Now, I know what I told you seems very unbelievable, but at least you're all here. I thought it might be best if we start by answering any questions you might have, and I'm sure you have a lot."

"Is the place real?" someone shouted.

"Yes. It is," Abbie's dad replied. "There's a door just below one of the platforms which leads to the underground world, known as the Subterrane."

"How do you know?"

"I'm glad you asked," he replied, looking towards Eleanor. "This is Ellie. She was born in and has lived in the Subterrane her whole life. The only reason she is here with us today is because she found her way out."

"So what are we here for?"

"You are all here because there are hundreds of people trapped in this underground world. Each person down there believes that there is nothing left up here; they think there was a war that wiped everything out around fifteen or twenty years ago. And there's a lot of people down there that were born in what they call the Subterrane and have never known anything else. After all, twenty years is a very long time, when you think about it."

"Can't they just walk out? You said that she did." The crowd seemed rather restless, shifting about nervously, like before some big event.

"Unfortunately, the government of this... underground world recently became aware that Ellie found a way out and, since they are brought up to believe that nothing exists outside of their Subterrane, she was forced out as soon as she became a threat. Their world is governed by a dictator, although it seems to me that each person believes themselves to be entirely free to do as they like. In my opinion, I would say it's the most dangerous kind of governing."

"So what do we have to do to get people out?"

"Right. So the way that they've been indoctrinated will make it slightly harder, the main reason being that they are told that the only people who live on the Surface, as they call it, are Revolutionaries - people who caused the war that they believe is still going on up here."

"Are they the people that went missing in 2047?" someone yelled from the back. "The one's from New Year?"

"Yes, I believe they are."

The crowd fell silent for a few moments.

"Why should we believe you?" another voice shouted; obviously they hadn't all been quite so willing to face the possible danger. "This could be a complete lie - it could just be a trap! Why should we trust her? We don't even know her."

"But you know me," Abbie interjected, stepping forwards. "Not all of you know me, but there's a lot of faces here that I recognise. I know that you don't know Ellie and you've got absolutely no reason or obligation to believe her at all. When I first met her, I didn't really believe her either. I mean, who in their right mind would believe that someone you've just met - in the centre of London, no less - is from an underground world? But just before you make your minds up about whether you believe her or not, I'd like to tell you what I think." Abbie paused and, although her voice hadn't wavered once, she seemed a little nervous of all the faces staring up at her. "I only believed Ellie when she brought me here to show me this place. And you know what? She was really proud of it. And rightly so, because it was her home. But then she took me inside the station, to let me see the doorway to her world, and that changed everything for me. Sure enough, that very evening I went back and this time I actually went into the Subterrane. To say it was unbelievable wouldn't do it justice. It's an entirely self-sufficient world; they have everything they could ever need down there - they even grow their own crops. I've tried them and, believe me, they're good."

A laugh of derision escaped from somewhere in the crowd.

"None of you know Ellie, but you do know me - or you all know my dad, at least," Abbie continued. "We can hopefully do this with or without your help, but we're telling you that hundreds of missing persons are trapped down there. I'm not going to ask if anyone has family or friends that went missing in 2047, because it's very likely that some of you do and I'm not trying to guilt-trip anyone into doing this. I'm just telling you that there are hundreds of people down there, and all they need is to be shown a way out."

Abbie exhaled deeply and stepped backwards to join Eleanor against the wall as her dad split the crowd into divisions and gave each group their instructions.

"Well done," Eleanor smiled. "You were great."

"Yeah, right," she replied, rolling her eyes. "I didn't exactly say much."

"Are you kidding? Without what you just said, I doubt anyone would still be here."

Abbie couldn't help but smile nervously.

"Abbie," Eleanor whispered suddenly. "Don't look now, but I think there's someone watching us in that white house."

Abbie subtly glanced up at the white house.

"Where?"

"On the first floor," Eleanor told her. "Just behind those big curtains."

"I see them. Do you… do you think it could be Saskia's mum? Wasn't she the one that lived there?"

Eleanor nodded. "I've got a bad feeling that it might be."

"She wouldn't tell him we're coming, would she?"

"Phulax?"

Abbie nodded.

"I've no idea if she even could - I know as much about her as you do."

"But if she tells him, then he might try and stop us."

"He might."

"Do you think he would? Even when we've got all these people with us?"

"I think anyone who's given up as much as he did to create the Subterrane, would do whatever he could to keep it intact."

241

Just then, Abbie's dad turned to them. "Anything either of you want to add?"

Eleanor nodded and stepped forwards.

"Now, remember," Eleanor began. "Keep your heads down and only do what we've told you to do. Our job is to clear the Subterrane of as many people as possible; if some don't want to go and can't be easily convinced, then don't bother - just move onto the next person. Get as many people out as you possibly can, whilst keeping a low profile. Now, I know that none of you are armed, so please avoid any violent confrontation if you possibly can. If it looks like there might be trouble, get out of there." She looked at Abbie's dad. "I understand that some of you are trained police, but please don't endanger yourselves unnecessarily. Our main priority is getting people out - the more people we convince, the more believable it becomes, so it'll be much easier if we need to go back a second time. Don't interfere with anything you're not sure about and don't go into any rooms or else you'll probably get lost. The same goes for staying close to the elevators and stairs. Any questions?"

No one moved.

"Will any of them be armed?" someone shouted.

"Yes, we're anticipating that the guards will be armed. I'm not sure how heavily armed they'll be, but we do expect them to have some kind of weapon, so please keep that in mind."

"Right - listen up," Abbie yelled as a dull murmuring began to ripple through the crowd. "Group One are taking the stairs to Level Ten led by my dad," she continued, motioning towards him. "Meanwhile Group Two will be taking an elevator to Level Eleven, led by Aidan, myself and Eleanor." She gestured towards a man in army uniform. "Group Three stays down by the entrance to reassure those that are ready to leave, and Group Four will be waiting out here to help guide them out. Is everyone okay with that?"

"Who's in charge of groups three and four?" Eleanor whispered to Abbie's dad.

"Everyone, this is Monica, a colleague of mine from the River Police," he announced, stepping forwards and gesturing to someone standing near the front. She's taking charge of groups three and four. She'll organise you all and tell you where you need to be."

"Does everyone know which group they're in?" Abbie asked the volunteers and received another unanimous murmur in response.

Eleanor stepped forwards to continue on from Abbie. "Since we need to talk to as many people as possible, I would suggest that groups one and two split up so that the word spreads quickly to different levels, but no groups smaller than two or three. If you get lost on your own it'll take a while for you to be found again, and there'll be a lot of people down there. If any citizens become suspicious of you or your group, then you need to try and get out of there without making them aware of other groups. And I'd even urge you not to communicate with the other groups unless you really have to. If anyone runs into any Protectors, just... pretend you've got nothing to hide. Avoid them if possible, though. Has everyone got that?"

Abbie stepped forwards again. "Is everyone ready?"

One by one, the sea of heads began to nod in response.

"Ok, then. Let's go," Abbie instructed as she linked arms with Eleanor and they led the way through the labyrinth of passageways towards the Subterrane.

Upon reaching the open door through to the Subterrane, Eleanor stopped abruptly.

"Do you really think this is a good idea?" she said quietly, turning to Abbie as she saw the opening up ahead.

"It's up to you," Abbie replied with assurance. "But just remember that everyone here wants to help. Chances are I expect they'll do it even if you don't, now that they know what's down there."

"But what if something goes wrong? What if no one believes us? What if the Protectors intervene?"

"Then we'll deal with it."

"Everything alright?" Abbie's dad asked as he pushed his way through the queue of people behind them.

"Everything's fine," Eleanor answered, nodding as though she almost meant it.

And, after shoving the grate open, she walked into the darkness of the station, a handheld torch at the ready.

***

"What's going on here? Would someone like to tell me why you're all standing around here, and not dealing with the disturbance that's been detected on Level Zero?" The Founder didn't look at all pleased as he surveyed the gathering of Protectors outside the Level Nine meeting rooms.

"We... sir, we don't feel comfortable doing it."

"And when did I ask for your opinion?"

"Sir, what I mean, is that we're not going to do it."

"Fine. You know you're not the only Protectors around here."

"We know, sir. But I think you'll find that none of the Protectors are going to do it."

"But there are Revolutionaries in the Subterrane as we speak. What am I supposed to do about them myself? Surely you're not going to leave all the citizens to fend for themselves?"

The Protector shrugged. "You see, the thing is, sir, that we're not entirely convinced that they are Revolutionaries."

"What do you mean? They're from the Surface - of course they're Revolutionaries."

"But sir, we've been told what happened on Level One. Those Protectors heard everything you told that girl."

"What girl?"

"The one you sent up to the Surface - the one who didn't have a choice."

"I-"

"Sir, there's a rumour that she's coming back, but this time it's to help get people out."

"What?" The Founder looked furious.

"Sir, if it's true, we don't want to stop her, or anyone who's helping her." The Protector looked at the others standing around him. "We don't believe that the Surface is dangerous."

"Don't you?" The Founder looked at the other Protectors to see if they shared the opinion.

"No, sir," another replied. "We don't."

"But you don't know anything about the Surface. I can't expect you to understand the influence that the Revolutionaries have had on that girl."

"Well, even so, we're not going to stop her. Not today."

"Very well, then," The Founder replied. "But you'll regret this. I'll make sure of that."

He strode away from them and entered the elevator without looking back. His mind was made up: he was going to get rid of that girl once and for all.

***

"Wait," Eleanor called, hurrying back to the Tunnel entrance with Abbie as her dad emerged into the corridor of Level Zero. "Take this - it's an ID card," she said holding it out to him. "We usually use finger ID or sometimes face ID, but you're supposed to carry one with you in case a recognition lens malfunctions or can't identify you. You need it to open some doors and to access the elevators."

They turned to leave, before Abbie paused and swivelled back around to face him. "Be careful, dad, please."

"Of course," he replied. "We'll have everyone out of here in no time."

"If you say so," Eleanor said, a little doubtfully.

"What makes you say it like that?" Abbie asked, surprised she wasn't being more optimistic.

"It's just... don't underestimate this place."

"I didn't think we had," Abbie's dad said, looking concerned for the first time.

"No, but I... all I mean is that it's easy to get caught up in the lies of this place. Next to nothing here is the real truth."

"And we all know that," he replied.

"But... well, what I'm trying to say is that you might forget that when you see what it's like. If you didn't know anything about this place, you might think it was some kind of paradise."

"We'll all be careful," he reassured her.

"And make sure everyone's aware of the Protectors. I'm not sure how heavily armed they'll be, but just watch out for them."

"We will."

Eleanor nodded, although she still seemed on edge.

"Anything else you're worried about?" he prompted her.

"Well, I can't help but wonder why the door was open."

"But what does that prove?" Abbie frowned, looking at the crowd of people around them.

She looked away for a moment. "Do you think they might be expecting us?"

"They can't have been - they didn't know when we'd come back," Abbie pointed out.

"But they knew we managed to open it last time - and they knew I showed you it."

"Ellie, I think you're maybe overthinking this," he replied.

"But what if it's a trap?"

"It won't be," Abbie reassured her.

"Look, I don't want you two getting into any kind of trouble. I'll see if Aidan minds switching," Abbie's dad said, heading over to where Aidan was standing with a group. He returned a few moments later, and led them over to where Group Two was waiting. "I'm not letting either of you out of my sight, okay?"

They both nodded, although Eleanor still seemed uneasy, then she added: "Thank you for believing me. Other than Abbie, you were the only person that did. Without you, we wouldn't have had a chance of getting anyone out - we wouldn't even have managed to open the door."

"Well, it's just as well I trusted you both in the end," he replied.

"It was a very far-fetched story, though, so I don't blame you for not believing us when we told you."

"Although it might have helped to know about the car a little sooner, Ellie."

"Yes, I realise that now. Sorry."

"It's alright," he replied, glancing over to check that their group was still waiting. "Abbie, promise me you won't wander off?"

"Course," she said.

"Right, let's go."

Group One immediately began to make its way down the long flight of stairs with Aidan; Group Three remained on the platform ready to escort any citizens out of the Subterrane, once they had decided they were ready to leave. Group Four was positioned on the road by the station exit - ready to take charge of any citizens when they left the station - and a pair of lookouts were positioned just out of sight behind the door to the stair-well, where they would be able to see if anyone was coming. Finally, Elea-nor, Abbie and her dad were left alone with Group Two. They led the way towards the West Side Elevators where Eleanor stepped forwards and pressed the call button with trembling fingers.

Herding the eight members of their group inside, Eleanor pressed the button labelled '11' and pressed the flat of her thumb against the ID sen-sor plate. After a slight shudder, the elevator began to descend into the depths of the Subterrane. Abbie flinched a little as the doors slid open with a slight 'ping', exposing them to a group of citizens milling around outside the Recreational Pods.

"Okay," Abbie's dad said calmly. "Remember we follow Eleanor and Abbie's lead."

"Ready?" Abbie said in a low whisper, glancing around the elevator at the nervous-looking volunteers, who were probably regretting offering their services in the first place. At the very least, they certainly did not look ready. "Remember, don't take risks and stay in pairs."

"Right," Her dad signalled them to move forward. "Let's go."

As soon as he had given the instructions, the group scattered them-selves among the citizens lining the corridor. The idea was that each pair would start by targeting one small group of people. They would begin by laying down the facts about the fateful night, before touching on other details of the Subterrane, which would in turn force those within the group to question everything that they had previously been told.

Eleanor and Abbie approached a couple who both looked several years older than them, and appeared to be having a rather intense argument over something.

"Excuse me," Abbie began, butting into their squabble.

"Can't you see we're busy here?" the man shot back in irritation.

'I'm sorry - it's quite important," Abbie persisted, taking another step towards them.

"What is?" the man asked.

"Well, I just wanted to ask you why you live down here?" Eleanor asked blatantly. "Do you not have friends or family that live up on the Surface?"

"What a preposterous question!" he answered, almost offended by the audacity of it.

"I'm only asking you what happened to cause you to live down here," she persevered.

"There's a war going on - everyone knows that," he replied, dumbfounded at her need to ask such a simple question.

"A war? Really?" she questioned. "Who told you that?"

"I-I- well..." he trailed off, seeming to be at a loss for words.

"The Founders told us that," the woman prompted, joining the conversation. "The Thirteen Founders."

"And what would you say if I told you that was a lie?" Eleanor asked. "What if I told you that there hasn't been a war since before you moved down here? That all the time you've been here, there has still been a whole world above ground - on the Surface."

"Well... I-I-" he stuttered in disbelief.

"It's the truth," Abbie replied unfalteringly.

"And you honestly expect us to believe that rubbish?" he threw his head back and laughed. "I might not be the smartest person here, but I'm no idiot."

"Just hear her out," the woman cut in as she began to consider the possibility. "We should hear what she has to say - it could be true."

"You mean you think that we've been living a lie here, this whole time?" The man glanced down the corridor behind him, seeming eager for some kind of distraction to draw him away from the conversation.

"I... I don't know," the woman admitted, although she seemed pleasantly surprised at the possibility, nevertheless. "At least it would account for a lot of things - like how we've never met anyone from another zone. I'm not sure I've ever heard them mentioned outside of those speeches. We've no proof that there even are other zones."

The woman turned her attention back to Eleanor and studied her expression carefully for any telltale signs of deception.

"But I heard those gunshots. I was only young, but I know I heard them," the man remarked, returning his attention to them.

"Those were specifically designed, pre-recorded sounds used to create a general sense of panic and chaos that would force everyone underground in a short space of time," Eleanor informed him.

"I suppose... well, that might make sense," he concluded, before returning his attention to the woman.

"But what now?" the woman asked. "Even if it is true, what can we do about it?"

"Why not see it for yourself? The entrance to the Tunnel is open, so go and take a look - even if you don't believe us," Eleanor said.

"Take anyone else with you who will go," Abbie added as the couple headed over to the elevators. "It might not be open for much longer, but you'll never know if you never look."

They made their way over to Abbie's dad, who seemed to be having trouble convincing one particular citizen.

"So you're trying to tell me that the people who spent millions of pounds building this place, who feed me and every other person here, who gave us jobs and who keep us all safe, are the 'bad guys'?"

"Well, originally no," he began, as Eleanor and Abbie joined him. "But over time they have become-"

"So they are, but they weren't? You should make up your mind before trying to convince us of any of this rubbish," a large man argued angrily.

"We're just trying to help," Abbie said. "We can't force you to believe us, but-"

"-You most certainly can't," the man interrupted.

"Of course," Eleanor nodded. "We're just trying to tell you the facts so that you're properly informed. It's only fair if everyone knows what's going on."

"Well, I'm afraid I couldn't care less about whatever nonsense you're going to try and tell me about."

"Okay, but-"

"That means I don't want to hear it."

"Yes, but-"

"So that's your cue to leave me alone and stop pestering me!" the man declared in frustration.

"Fine," Abbie shrugged, as the three of them turned and headed towards a large cluster of friends who appeared utterly astonished at the news they had just been informed of by another pair.

"Is this true?" one gasped, recognising Eleanor as she joined them.

"Every word," she confirmed.

"You can see for yourself," Abbie chimed in. "The Tunnel's currently open. Take a look at the Surface - nothing you've ever been told about it is true."

"How do we know we can trust you?" One of the friends was still looking rather sceptical.

"You don't," Abbie replied with a shrug. "But if you don't look, then you'll probably spend your whole life wishing you had."

"I suppose," another muttered, turning to look at the rest of the group. "Should we?"

"Why not," one replied.

"It can't do any harm," another echoed as they hastily began to traipse towards the elevator, their excitement obvious.

Eleanor and Abbie immediately moved away and made a beeline for those they had previously spoken to about leaving, while Abbie's dad headed over to another small group.

"Alex!" Abbie greeted with a friendly smile.

"Abbie? Ellie? What are you doing here? How are you here?" he asked in confusion. "What happened yesterday? Where did they take you?"

"We don't have time to explain now, but we'll tell you later. Go up to the Tunnel now - you'll be able to get out," Abbie told him, gesturing in the direction of the elevator.

"We've got people waiting on the other side of the door, but you need to leave now. Take as many people with you as will go," Eleanor urged, egging him towards the elevator.

"We'll see you up there," Abbie promised, as her dad glanced over to check they were alright.

Hastily they moved onto another group of citizens, eager to rescue as many as they could before someone informed the Founders of their intentions.

They had almost succeeded in emptying the corridor, when the door to a very large Recreational Pod opened, and at least another hundred people flooded out into the corridor, Saskia among them. Eleanor sighed, trying to force her pent up anger away and quickly turned to corner her next target, as the elevator doors pinged open.

Eleanor almost didn't see Sebastian Phulax stepping from the elevator and into the crowds with a man dressed entirely in black. She almost didn't see him grab the gun from the man's belt and aim it right at her. And she almost didn't see the bullet as it flew straight towards her.

Chapter Thirty-One

It was then that everything seemed to slow down. There was a sudden movement in the crowd just as Eleanor attempted to fling herself from the bullet's path, but she already knew that it would be too late.

A scream ripped through the hallway as the sudden gunshot echoed off the walls. The corridor became shrouded in an eerie silence, as hundreds of pairs of eyes scanned the crowd to locate the source of the scream. Then, as suddenly as it had stopped, the talking and whispering began again, only this time it was more frantic as people backed away from a small clearing that had opened up in the centre.

"Abbie? Eleanor? Are you both alright?" Abbie's dad rushed over to them, pushing his way through the crowd.

Eleanor frowned as it slowly dawned on her that she hadn't been hit. Looking around slowly, a sudden movement caught her eye as she saw a Protector and a couple of volunteers run through the crowd and dart into the elevator after Phulax, just as the doors were preparing to close. At least he's taken care of, she thought. But then another thought entered her mind: Where was the bullet? And if she had been its intended target, then who had it hit?

She began to push her way through the crowds until she finally spotted Saskia sprawled across the floor, coughing as she spluttered for air. The colour was slowly draining from her cheeks as a crimson stain began to seep across her chest.

"Saskia!" she shrieked as she rushed to her side.

"Someone get help!" Eleanor yelled into the crowd as a fresh blood stain spread across the jumper. "Stay with me," she coaxed, as Saskia's head began to recline and her eyelids began to flutter closed. "Come on, stay with me. You can get through this," she said as she slid her hand behind Saskia's head to keep her upright.

"Run and call an ambulance!" Eleanor heard Abbie instruct one of the volunteers.

Saskia weakly laid a hand on her arm. "It's okay," she said, smiling up at Eleanor. "I just couldn't let him get you."

"Listen to me. There's help on the way and you're going to be absolutely fine. Worst-case scenario you'll have an impressive battle scar, but other than that you're going to be fine," Eleanor said, holding back her tears. "And I'm right here, okay?"

"Ellie, I'm scared," Saskia whispered shakily.

"Don't be," Eleanor replied, giving her hand a tight squeeze. "I'm right here with you."

"Where's that ambulance?" Abbie shouted, as an elevator full of Protectors arrived and the crowd dissolved into chaos.

"Ellie, I'm so cold."

"Quick, someone give me a jumper or something," Eleanor called out, looking around at the crowd desperately.

"Here." Abbie quickly shrugged off her jacket and handed it over.

"Thanks. There you go," Eleanor continued as she shuffled Saskia closer to her so that her head was resting on Eleanor's lap, before laying the jacket over her and tucking it up to her chin.

"What's going on?" she heard a Protector asked Abbie.

"She's been shot."

"Can we help? What do you need?"

"An ambulance, medics, doctors - anyone who can help," Abbie instructed.

"I'm so sorry for... for everything," Saskia breathed, barely audibly, as a group of Protectors disappeared into the elevator. "And I'm sorry I didn't tell you who I was."

"Shh. It doesn't matter now," Eleanor replied, blinking as her eyes began to well up. "Your name doesn't change who you are. Just because you didn't tell me it, doesn't mean that I don't know the real you."

"I'm so tired."

"I know you are," Eleanor replied, her voice quivering. She knew that she had to let her go. "Just shut your eyes for a moment."

Finally allowing her already drooping eyelids to close, Saskia relaxed her pained breathing as Eleanor gently began to stroke her hair.

"Tell me a story?" Saskia whispered pleadingly and, of course, Eleanor obliged.

"Alright," Eleanor agreed, although she wasn't really in the mood to make up a story.

She thought for a moment, before finally remembering the story Abbie had been trying to tell her on the first day they met. "Once upon a time, long ago in a city named Venice, there lived a man named Othello."

Eleanor paused for a moment, watching the Protectors direct the mass of citizens towards the stairs.

"Carry on."

"Othello had travelled the world. He'd crossed jungles and deserts, he'd been captured and sold before eventually joining the army of Venice where he was later promoted to a general. But then, one day, he fell in love with the young daughter of a nobleman. And she was called Desdemona."

"Like you," Saskia mumbled, surprisingly attentively.

"Yes, sort of," Eleanor replied softly, glancing up at the now almost-empty hallway, where Abbie was standing with her dad and a Protector. "The two of them were married in secret, for they couldn't risk her father knowing because he would never approve of the match."

A group of Protectors suddenly emerged from the elevator with two Practitioners, who hurried over to where she was sat with Saskia.

"Then, when her father found out about it, he was very angry, but because they were already married he could do nothing to separate them. Instead, the army gave him a job to do on an island called Cyprus and he took Desdemona with him. They believed that they would be able to start a new life together."

The Practitioners quickly examined the wound, before applying pressure and attempting to blot up the blood.

"Has this got a happy ending?" Saskia muttered drowsily. "I like happy endings."

"Of course," Eleanor said decidedly, racking her brains to think of a suitable ending for the story since she hadn't been paying attention when Abbie had told her it.

"Carry on, I'm listening," came Saskia's faint yet still bossy voice.

"Alright," Eleanor said quickly, as the Practitioners exchanged a grim, knowing look. "When they arrived on the island, it was like paradise. The sun was warm, the sand was golden and the rustling trees were a heavenly green. Othello and Desdemona made a home on the peaceful island." Eleanor had understood what that look meant, and she knew all too well that the story needed to come to a close. "They spent every minute they could surrounded by friends, and cherished every moment until the end of their days. The end."

Eleanor gave the Practitioners a grateful nod as they moved back to give them some space.

"Thank you," Saskia breathed.

"That's alright."

"For everything."

Eleanor froze in shock before finally letting out a muffled cry as Saskia's hand became limp in her own, her face having lost its usual radiant glow. Abbie immediately rushed to Eleanor's side and wrapped a comforting arm around her shoulders as she sobbed, her tears now falling freely.

***

When Eleanor had finally regained some of her strength, she carefully shifted Saskia so she was laid on the floor and gently placed Abbie's jacket over her, making sure her face was hidden from sight to prevent staring from the inquisitive Protectors behind her.

Standing, she looked around the corridor and took in the remaining faces that were studying her for some kind of reaction.

"Where is he?" She turned to Abbie in a frantic state. "I swear to God I'll kill him!" She threatened desperately, tears fuelling her sudden rage.

"They'll have got him," Abbie said. "I sent someone from our group to tell Aidan, and get him to find Phulax, but apparently the Protectors got there first. Long story short, they disarmed him and they've taken him to the Surface, so he'll have been arrested by now."

"What about the spy? The one who was with him?"

"What spy? I didn't see anyone with him."

"He was dressed in black - kind of hard to miss."

"I… I didn't see anyone like that." Abbie frowned. "But don't worry, I'm sure they'll see him on the way out."

They were silent for a moment.

"It should have been me - the bullet was meant for me."

"Well, I guess you got lucky."

"Lucky?"

"No, that's not what I meant," Abbie apologised hastily. "I shouldn't have said it like that. I only meant that, well, you're lucky to have such a great friend."

"Yes," Eleanor said quietly.

"Ellie, I think we should probably go."

"Ok," she replied before turning back suddenly. "What about Saskia? I can't leave her here."

"I'll sort it all out. Don't worry - let's just get you outside first."

Eleanor nodded and followed Abbie into the elevator in a strange sort of trance. The last half-hour hadn't all sunk in quite yet.

"Come here," Abbie comforted her, drawing Eleanor into a long embrace as the elevator doors slowly slid shut.

"What do I do now?"

"You'll be alright," Abbie said. "I promise."

"But she's gone," Eleanor said, as tears began to run down her cheeks once more.

"I know she has."

"I've never been without her before - not for more than a couple of days," Eleanor said. "I was going to apologise and then I wanted us to leave together. I can't do this without her!"

"I'm so sorry," Abbie said, trying desperately to keep herself strong for Eleanor. "You'll get through this, and I'm always going to be here for you. We'll get through this together."

The elevator doors opened onto Level Zero to reveal a bustling crowd of citizens, all jostling one another in an attempt to enter the Tunnel faster. It was as though nothing had happened.

Almost immediately, the woman in charge of Groups Three and Four rushed over to them.

"I just heard - I can't tell you how sorry I am."

"Thanks," she said quietly.

"Why don't we get you outside?" Abbie suggested.

"I never want to see this place again," she answered, nodding as her eyes began to well up again.

"Let's go," Abbie said and led her towards the Tunnel entrance, weaving between people until they reached the door.

"Wait," Eleanor said and suddenly stopped.

"What's wrong?"

"Nothing, I just, well... this is where it all began."

"I know," Abbie said gently, as her dad rejoined them.

"If I'd never come up here that day, then she'd probably still be here."

"Ellie, you mustn't think like that. This isn't your fault."

"But it is! It's because I interfered with everything."

"No, it really wasn't your fault. You didn't know what he'd do, and you couldn't have done anything to stop it. You mustn't blame yourself for it - it won't help."

Eleanor sighed and looked around at the blank corridor.

"Come on," Abbie coaxed. "Let's go."

They walked in silence as they made their way through the once derelict station that was now buzzing with people. Once they had finally reached the exit, Abbie led Eleanor out into the afternoon glow. Hundreds of citizens stood crowding the road watching, transfixed, as the sun slowly began to dip towards the horizon.

"Is that... Saskia's mum?" Eleanor said suddenly, pointing towards a tearful woman who was being led to a police car from the cream coloured house next to the station. "What are they going to do with her?"

"She knew about the Subterrane and never came forwards about it," Abbie's dad explained.

"So will she be charged?" Abbie asked.

"Phulax has admitted to blackmailing her - he told us that he'd said if she ever told anyone, she'd never see her daughter again," he explained. "We're taking her into custody, but it's more for her own safety."

"So she's going to prison?" Abbie asked in surprise.

"No," he answered. "She'll be held in a safe house until this has all blown over. We don't want her to be targeted or bombarded by the press or anything."

"That makes sense," Eleanor nodded. "It's probably what Saskia would have wanted."

"Exactly."

"And the rest of the Founders?" Abbie asked.

"They've all been taken for questioning," her dad replied.

"What about the Protectors?"

"Turns out they refused to go against us - they thought what we were doing was right. That's why they helped when... well, you know."

"Did Phulax try to run?" Eleanor asked quietly.

"No, he gave up as soon as he saw the Protectors. He was just in shock - she was his daughter, after all."

Eleanor nodded.

"What about the spy?"

"Who?"

"He was dressed in black. Surely somebody caught him?"

"I'm sure they have," Abbie's dad reassured her.

"If they haven't, I-"

"Ellie, we've got this all under control. You don't need to worry," he told her kindly.

Abbie took Eleanors arm and led her to a concrete barrier by the side of the road.

"How are you feeling?"

"I'm okay," Eleanor answered, sitting down on the barrier.

"How are you really?"

"I just... I keep thinking she's going to suddenly walk through that door."

Abbie nodded.

"And I keep imagining what she might say in a situation like this," Eleanor smiled weakly.

"What would she say?"

"She'd walk up to me and - actually, she'd probably come up behind me and try to scare me first," Eleanor paused. "And then she'd say 'I don't think the building's going to fly away anytime soon, so you don't need to watch it all night'. Or something equally as stupid."

"Ellie," Abbie began carefully. "I think maybe we should go, now."

"Where?"

"Anywhere you like, really," she replied softly. "Or we can just go back home - to my house, I mean."

"Okay," Eleanor said. "Let's go to yours."

"Alright."

Just as they stood up to leave, a group of four doctors dressed in white hospital overalls emerged from the entrance. Between them, they carried a stretcher that was covered with a white sheet, and a white jacket. The jacket she'd covered Saskia with. Eleanor's breathing became a little more laboured as she desperately fought back the thick tears that were threatening to spill.

"Come on, let's go," Abbie whispered, as kindly as she could manage. And, one step at a time, they began making their way down the street that was now flooded with citizens gazing around at their new world in awe.

Epilogue

Eleanor Desdemona looked out over the daunting mass of spectators, and took a deep breath as she stepped up onto the tall podium and placed her shaky hands on the lectern. Glancing down at her speech which had been printed and laminated just half an hour ago, she recalled the opening sentence which she had committed to memory along with the rest of the speech. Then, she returned her gaze to the blank faces staring up at her and began.

"I would first like to thank every one of you for being here today - it means so much that each of you bothered to come and hear me speak. And I'd also like to acknowledge those few familiar faces I can see dotted amongst the crowd because, although I'm the one speaking today, I am by no means the only one who was affected by this rare event."

She paused and took another deep breath before continuing: "The building behind me is where it all began. But even excluding recent events, this station has a spectacular past. Over the past year, I've learnt that it was home to artwork and historical artefacts during both World Wars. And, after being discontinued for use in 1994, it became a popular filming location until the Tunnel was used for a faster route to Waterloo station.

"Since then, there have been several notable additions to the station's history. It was key to the calculated disappearance of hundreds of unsuspecting members of the public. It then housed them for almost twenty years and, as of today, it will be the official home to many of the people that lived within the Subterrane.

"The International Preservation Society was a society that worked to improve the ways of living for the greater good - or the majority of people - and was usually successful in improving lifestyles. However, when they received the proposition for what would be their most ambitious project yet, they failed to see several things. Not only would it be unfair on those affected by it, but the project also violated several of the rights protected by the 1998 Human Rights Act.

"I've tried to think of so many different ways to explain the Subterrane, but it really is impossible to do it justice. I'm not denying that it was awful to ensnare a small percentage of England's population like that. And worse than that was how each citizen was forced to live in an environment of such strict supervision, whilst indoctrinated into believing that it was, in fact, a good thing. However, to each of us down there, the Subterrane was also a home.

"I was born in the Subterrane eighteen years ago - just after the Subterrane's new way of life had been established. As a result of the rules set in place down there, I grew up not with doting parents, but instead surrounded by other children, friends, nurses and teachers. And, whilst I do believe that every child needs a parental figure in their life, all those around me in the Subterrane were as much a part of my life and my family as any parents could ever have been. And they all remain so, to this day.

"When I was told that I would be making a speech today, my first thought was what could I possibly talk about that would interest anyone? Everyone already knows my side of the story, and how I helped put an end to all the lies we had been fed whilst kept in the Subterrane. But today I'm not going to talk about my story, because it wasn't just because of me. There are so many people who it wouldn't have worked without. Most importantly, Abbie and her family for believing and trusting me enough to go along with it, as well as helping with absolutely everything. Then, of course, the volunteers who chose to go into the Subterrane, not really knowing what to expect. The Protectors, because if they'd come to fight us off, we wouldn't have stood a chance. And so many other people, too.

"But today - one year since the liberation of the Subterrane - I'm dedicating this speech to someone else entirely. Because without Saskia, I would not be standing here today." She paused for a moment and blinked to fight back her tears.

"My first memory of Saskia is of meeting her when we were about six. She was being led into our classroom by a tall and rather scary looking man, who I now know to have been her father. He explained to our class teacher that he had found her wandering around the corridor and that the next door's class teacher had said that she was supposed to be switching classes. She hadn't known anyone and I suppose it must have been intimidating for her to be surrounded by wide-eyed faces staring up at her, because she immediately turned back to the man and wrapped her short, six-year-old arms around his legs and refused to let go.

"He quickly prised her arms from him and moved away, not wanting anyone to notice the slight emotional attachment between them. But as soon as he'd left the room, Saskia's bottom lip began to quiver and she started crying. I specifically remember her saying that she wanted her mum, because we had no idea that, unlike us, she had grown up with her mum, outside of the Subterrane. Our teacher had no idea what to do, as we'd all grown up knowing that crying gets you nowhere, so I was the only one that went to hug her and the only one that told her - in my squeaky six-year-old voice - that I'd be her best friend. From that moment on, we were completely inseparable.

"Now, I'm not a stupid person, but I also know that I'm definitely not even close to being the smartest at anything. Saskia, however, was one of the brightest for our age. But, unlike the other smarter kids, she didn't flaunt it. Instead, she'd often cheat in tests and try to help me by flicking bits of paper that contained the answers to various questions at me. And, when we sat our placement exams about a year and a half ago, Saskia went as far as convincing me to switch our papers.

"For those of you who don't know, Placement Exams were a set of tests that were taken by all children in the Subterrane at the age of sixteen. They were then used to determine future careers and responsibilities and other things like that. Saskia, of course, scored something phenomenal - one of the highest marks in our year group - whereas I scored something far more average. But, since she had written my name on her paper and I'd agreed to write her's on mine, the high mark was attributed to me, as she had intended. She would always just tell me that she didn't want to be predictable or that she didn't need top marks.

"I'm sure it was because her family's status protected her, which probably meant that she was guaranteed to receive a highly influential position within the Government anyway. But even then, she still chose to help me. She didn't need to and had no obligation whatsoever to, but she still did it. She never strove to be the best, although she could easily have been. She never tried to stand out, although she easily could have done. She was content with being the lovable, often rebellious, yet incredible person who I knew and trusted until the very end." She paused for a moment, letting the words sink into the crowd.

"People have asked me if I knew she was up to something with her father or if I knew that she was from such a ruthless family. The answer is that of course I didn't know - now it seems like I almost didn't know anything about her. She never told me who she really was, but then again there were so many things that I never asked. Surely any of us would want to hide a secret like that - why would you want to stand out or have people to treat you differently when you could live a completely normal life?

"Many people have said that, since she knew what was actually happening on the Surface, she was just as responsible. But I don't think that's true. In fact, I think that's utterly false and disrespectful to her memory. Yes, she knew what was going on, but she didn't understand the severity. It's true that Saskia had occasional contact with her mother on the Surface - her mother has testified to that, in fact - but that's not to say she understood what it was like to be on the Surface."

Eleanor pointed to the house beside the station: "That house just there is where her mother lived, and it's connected to the Subterrane by an extremely long spiral staircase. But once a year, when Saskia visited her mother, she never crossed the threshold of the house; it was almost as if she never left the Subterrane in the first place. I think it would have been impossible for her to understand the severity of the situation she was in, without actually hearing the public's views about the disappearance and seeing the devastation it had caused.

"Saskia and I fell out around the time I discovered the truth about the Subterrane. But even during that period of time, I would never have blamed her for anything that happened as a result. And contrary to popular belief, she wasn't even close with her father - it would have been very difficult to maintain any kind of relationship with him without their connection being noticed. So, in my eyes at least, she was just the same as any of us that were down there. She might have been more aware of the outside world, but she was completely powerless to do anything about it."

Eleanor looked out at the multitude of faces staring up at her, and then looked back at the wall behind her. For just a moment, she allowed her gaze to linger on Saskia's silver memorial plaque that was fixed to the front of the red, tiled facade of the old station. She gave it a faint smile as though it was really Saskia that she could see, and then looked over at Abbie who was watching from the side of the stage. As she finally turned back to glance at her notes, she almost couldn't believe that it was really a year since it had all happened. The time had flown by so quickly, it still felt like yesterday.

With a reminiscent smile, she looked back at the attentive crowd. "One year ago today, my people were liberated from the Subterrane, and families and friends were reunited after nearly twenty years of being apart. And…"

For a moment, Eleanor's eyes fell on a face in the crowd and a pair of eyes staring right back at her. There was something vaguely familiar about the face, but Eleanor couldn't quite place it. Brushing away the thought, she continued: "Saskia Phulax saved my life. And for that single act, I will be forever in her debt."

Printed in Great Britain
by Amazon

85083495R00151